Taking the Night

Book One of the Nightshade Series

By J. F. Posthumus

Three Ravens Publishing
Chickamauga, GA USA

Chapter One

As the sun slipped below the horizon, flames of orange and yellow filled the sky, shading into pink then purple. The skyscrapers of New Campania were silhouettes against the fading light. Not as well-known as New York, or Chicago, at least to the rest of the world, but Selia never tired of the view, despite the years she'd lived in the city. Every day the sunrises and sunsets were different in some way, and every day, she enjoyed seeing them.

The walk to the office building where she was to pick up a package for Soren Lascari, though short, allowed her to watch the sun as it fell from view and admire the vibrant colors of sunset. Most people would have preferred driving, but she enjoyed the exercise.

Having spent her first sixteen years of life on a tropical island where modern technology didn't exist, walking three blocks from where she worked as Soren's assistant was nothing. Though she had spent the last decade in New Campania, she had not lived a slovenly life.

She took a last look at the sunset and smiled. Though she didn't 'celebrate' her arrival in the city, or the day she became Soren's daughter, she did mark it on her calendar. It would be eleven years to the day in two weeks. Eleven years since she had been forced to flee her homeland and became Soren's daughter. Being banished hadn't been easy, but it was better than being dead.

Shaking her thoughts away, she opened the door to the office building and found the stairs. The email she'd received stated the package would be in the mail room on the third floor. There had even been detailed directions on how to find said mailroom, since she hadn't been to this particular building before.

Not seeing anyone, though she heard muted voices, she guessed most people had left for the day. If it hadn't been for the fact she frequently did quick errands for Soren, she would have already been on her way home herself.

Years of living in the city hadn't diminished the instincts she'd developed during her youth and teen years. Survival of the fittest wasn't just a saying in her homeland, and Selia had learned her lessons early. She took notice of the fire escape outside the windows of the offices, as well as the empty offices and their open doors. None of those doors, however, held name plaques.

The mailroom was the standard kind found in most businesses. Large, multifunctional printers were against one wall, a long counter over cabinets filled the opposite wall. Above the counters were pigeonholes. It took only a couple minutes for her to find the correct hole with S Lascari on the tag. As stated in the email, a simple manila envelope awaited her.

It wasn't difficult to figure out the envelope contained a flash drive. The shape, size, and weight of the contents gave it away.

Shrugging, Selia folded the envelope until it fit into her jacket pocket. There was no reason for her to open it, and she respected Soren's privacy. She may have been his personal assistant, but that didn't mean she needed to know everything. If he had wanted her to know what was on the flash drive, he would have told her.

Her task complete, she headed back to the stairs, and pulled her cell phone from her jacket pocket. She tapped the icon on her screen to open her email. As she descended the stairs, she began scrolling through her inbox, deleting the junk mail. She paused in composing a message to her father as she exited the stairwell. The hairs on the back of her neck stood on end. She looked up.

Two men in the foyer moved towards her. She doubted they were there to escort her to Soren's office. They reminded her of enforcers for one of the Families. Both were around six feet and resembled professional guards. Each of them wore dark blazers over black dress shirts and moved with military precision. They even had the usual short, military-style haircuts. The only difference between them was that one wore matching pants, while the other wore khakis.

Her suspicions were confirmed when the taller one spoke.

"We'll take the package."

Selia drew a breath and stared at them. They stared back. No one moved. It allowed her a few moments to get her thoughts together.

"No, I don't believe so," she replied, keeping her tone polite. "Soren requested the package be delivered to him. I plan on doing just that, gentlemen." She paused, reached for her side, and sighed. "Drats. I must have left my purse in the ladies' room upstairs. If you'll excuse me, I'll go get it."

"We'll escort you," the taller goon said. He unbuttoned his blazer as he spoke. The grip of the automatic pistol, kept in his waistband, was intentionally visible.

"If you wish," Selia replied.

Turning, she opened the door and began ascending the staircase. The pair followed behind her. Chewing her lower lip, Selia knew she had to do something. She could either attempt to run up the stairs and find another way out or do something a little more dangerous and daring. Considering how close the pair were to her, she doubted there would be enough time, or space, for her to escape by running up the stairs.

Ten years. Ten years she'd been good. She'd kept her secrets close to heart, letting no one else aside from Soren know everything. Now, look at her. Being followed by two goons in a building she didn't work at and having to break a promise to never use magic in front of anyone.

Admittedly, it wasn't the first time she'd used magic since her banishment from her homeland. It was simply the first time she'd be using it where someone might realize exactly what she'd done.

Too late to worry about that, though. Not if she wanted to escape.

Feigning tripping on a step, she flung her hands backward, sending the goons down the stairs without revealing she used conjured energy to push them. Her fingers brushed against the legs of one of her pursuers, so hopefully they would believe she managed to shove them. Maybe they wouldn't understand that she had used magic.

Racing up the steps, she darted through a doorway and ran for one of the offices with the fire escape outside the window. Locking the door behind her, she opened the window just far enough for her to slip through.

The door to the office rattled with a sudden impact. The goons had caught up and were no doubt slamming their shoulders against the door. The door buckled beneath their combined weight.

No time to waste, she thought, slipping out the window and racing down the fire escape.

Five steps from the first landing, she heard the gunmen reach the metal landing outside the window. She ducked her head as she heard a popping noise, followed by a bullet hitting the bricks. Chips of stone flew as the bullet imbedded itself into the stone

She glanced up at the darkened shadows of her pursuers on the fire escape but saw only their feet and well-dressed legs. They were one measly set of stairs above her, and she was thankful they hadn't attempted to shoot down through the grated stairs.

Too much chance of a ricochet or of someone hearing them, she decided as her feet hit the next landing. One more set of stairs, then she'd have to either climb down the last metal ladder or jump the last four or so feet to the ground. Once there, she would be a sitting duck.

Caught in the middle of her thoughts, it took Selia a few moments to realize the single streetlight had gone out. Two heavy thuds followed, and it took her a few heartbeats to realize no more steps reverberated down the fire escape behind her. She paused, pressing up against the inside of the fire escape's ladder, holding her breath in an attempt to hear the sounds around her.

She heard… nothing. No steps on the fire escape's metal stairs, no soft pops from the silenced guns, no soft scrape of a window being raised or lowered. Her hand shook as she debated between a fireball and the flashlight app on her phone. Making a decision, she unlocked her phone and held it up.

Looking up, she saw only a pair of shadowy forms lying flat against the grated stairwell. At least she knew why they were silent. Turning, she peeked around the corner of the stairwell. Caution screamed at her and the same nagging feeling that had saved her life many times already, including just now, told her something wasn't quite right.

A scream caught in her throat as a male figure strode down the stairs with an eerie cat-like grace and silent steps. His long black trench coat billowed out around him, reminding her vaguely of a certain caped crusader named after bats. The image was shattered, though, by the black fedora pulled down low over his brow. That would have effectively hidden his eyes, but the high-grade sunglasses he wore completed the task quite well. She could barely make out the fabric of an expensive ski-mask, or possibly a military-grade balaclava, ruining any chance she had of figuring out her savior's identity.

"Neat trick. Wish I could do that," the masked man said.

He stopped a few steps above Selia, causing her heart to jump higher in her throat. She followed his black-gloved finger to her left hand to find a baseball-sized orb of orange flames. Oops. She hadn't even realized she'd conjured up a fireball. Some instincts never faded.

"What do you want?" Selia asked, keeping her voice low. She desperately wanted to glance over the railing, to see if more thugs waited below, but she didn't dare turn her eyes away from the stranger.

"To know what you were doing here so late and why those two-" he nodded towards the unconscious forms above him, "-were chasing you." She opened her mouth to reply, only to have him add, "And don't lie to me. I don't like people who lie."

Selia swallowed hard. "Who are you?"

A sudden stretching of the balaclava near the mouth made her think of a concealed smile, and she could imagine his eyes narrowing behind the odd sunglasses. It would fit with the tone and occasion.

It did nothing to slow her racing pulse as he said, "The Sandman."

Her hand twitched, but she didn't throw the fireball. Everyone in New Campania knew of the Sandman. He stalked the night, helping citizens. Although they disliked admitting it, the police benefited from his actions. He prevented attacks, muggings, and burglaries, and wasn't against taking out a few of the syndicates' more notorious rackets. In a city founded by the Italian mafia, crime did pay, and the two ruling families were typically in the midst of it all.

"Oh, gods," Selia breathed. "I was sent to retrieve an envelope from here. I don't know anything other than that." The Sandman just stared at her. Selia guessed he was trying to figure out if she was telling the truth or not. She sighed and clenched her fingers into a fist, dispelling the fireball. "I practically sold myself to Soren to keep from being killed in my homeland. I owe him."

She neglected to mention she owed Soren many times over. Not that she would dare say she owed him her life, even if it was true. He could figure that out for himself.

That didn't mean she didn't like Soren. Quite the contrary. He had saved her, and she had grown to love her adopted father over the years. Even now, she wondered if Soren had been who sent the message to carry out this deed. He had tried to keep her out of the 'family' business since she stepped foot on his ship. For the most part, he had succeeded.

The fact she knew several of the enforcers, who the head accountants were, and had figured out pretty much which businesses belonged to the Lascari Family was due to her undying curiosity. Albeit it was the same curiosity that had compelled her to open that damned tome and learn the spells that had become her downfall in her homeland. This was different, though.

Knowing names, faces, and places had kept her out of many dealings. Until now, that is. Until tonight, her job had been more subtle and low-key. She'd managed to convince everyone, including her adopted uncle – the don of the Lascari Family – she was a meek and mild-mannered assistant to her father.

"You don't owe them your life," the Sandman said, tucking his hands into his coat pockets. The move made Selia nervous. Unseen hands could do gods knew what out of a person's sight. He continued, as though they were discussing the weather. "The way I see it, you have a choice."

Selia narrowed her eyes as she glanced up at the pair above her, still lying silently on the cold metal. She asked, "What choice might that be?"

"You can hand over the drive and I make it seem like I strong-armed you, complete with bruises. That way you can tell your boss I took it from you by force, leaving you free and clear. Or you go on your way and hand that drive over to your boss."

"Just like that, you'd let me go?" Selia asked. His offer sounded too good to be true, which meant it was probably a trick.

The mask twitched and then he gave a single, slight nod in the darkness. "You'll owe me, but yeah. I'll let you go."

Selia glanced up at the pair above her, still unconscious. She gave a rueful smile to the man standing above her. "They aren't going to stay unconscious forever." He gave a slight shrug, obviously not concerned. "I think I'll keep the drive. Whatever Soren is doing, it's the least of the evils."

That got her a chuckle. Deep, with a dark edge to it, Selia realized this man had taken lives and the deaths didn't prey on his conscience. He would do it again, in a heartbeat, if he had to, but she doubted he would take pleasure in it.

He shook his head a little and Selia lifted a brow. The Sandman shrugged again as he said, "It's your choice. I'll see you around."

"I look forward to it," Selia replied, surprising herself with the words. "Thanks for the help."

The Sandman didn't reply. Instead, he nodded, turned, and vanished back up the fire escape. She watched as he disappeared into the darkness of the night. Shaking her head, she ran down the last few stairs before leaping down to the alley below, landing in a crouch. She might not have trained her entire life as a warrior, like most in her homeland, but she wasn't a novice, either.

Ignoring the office above her, she ran the three blocks to her car, slid into the driver's seat. Reaching into the glove box, she fished out a spare flash drive. She had stashed it there a few weeks ago when she'd bought a pack to back up her laptop. Taking the envelope from her pocket, she removed the flash drive. That one went into her right pocket and her spare went into her left.

J. F. Posthumus

She didn't know what was going on, but she wasn't going in unprepared.

Chapter Two

Selia locked her car and headed into Soren's office building. It was a two-story building, smaller than most and dwarfed by the skyscrapers that towered above everyone. Considering she'd been in only a couple of those cloud-reaching buildings a few times in the ten years she'd lived here, she was happy with her workplace. Her fear of no alternative escape routes kept her from thoroughly enjoying the views of the skyscraper owned by Angelo "Al" Lascari, the godfather to the Lascari syndicate, or any of the others the Family used and owned. She knew the proper incantation and energy manipulation to levitate, but it had costs. Nor, with as little practice as she'd had at that point in her life, did she want to rely on such a spell.

She slid her hands into her pockets, toying with the flash drives. Questions ate at her, but they would have to wait. Drawing a deep breath, she counted to ten as she let it out before unlocking the door and entering the building.

The security pad was on, making her feel a little better. Soren never left the security off for the main floor after hours, even if he was staying late in his office on the second floor.

The reception area was the same as every other office building. The floors were carpeted; dark curtains covered the windows, magazines covered the tables, and chairs were strategically placed about in small groups. A sofa sat against one wall, end tables to either side. In the center of the room was the receptionist's desk with doors on each side. The door to the right led into more offices, the door to the left to a flight of stairs. A small, narrow hallway hid the restrooms and an elevator. A few well-tended non-flowering plants sat in the windows and on the tables.

The office's waiting area normally had a homey feeling, but in the dead of night, it was creepy. Selia fully expected someone to jump from behind the doors at any minute, but no one did. She waited patiently for the elevator, her nerves on edge. The elevator doors opened, and she stepped inside and punched the button for the second floor. There was a soft ding before the doors closed, and the elevator began its rise.

Normally, Selia enjoyed the unique sensation of the elevator, but not tonight. Not after being chased by a pair of thugs and the surprising rescue by the city's most notorious vigilante. A smile played on her lips as she thought back to the strange meeting, but the doors opened before she could think too much about him.

The second floor was Soren's domain. Only the small night lights meant as a security precaution offered lighting to the otherwise darkened area. There was a long hallway, to each side ending at corners with windows that had a moderately good view of the area around the building. Selia looked out the window to the right as she stepped out of the elevator where a small garden, complete with a gazebo resided. The left offered a view of the street below. There were restrooms to the left and a single door with a black pad to the right. Ahead was the door to Soren's office.

Her nerves, however, didn't calm as they usually did if Soren was around. The door was open, and her heart quickened. She should have called, but it was too late for that now. Selia opened the door and found her fears were true: Soren, her supervisor for the last eight years and father for the past ten, was not in the room.

Instead, two burly thugs who could have made football players look like pansies stood on each side of the Soren's innermost office door, their mashed-in and scarred faces fixed in what she expected was a perpetual scowl. She saw Alfi Barboni through the open doorway as he leaned against the front of Soren's desk, flipping through a magazine, a bored expression on his otherwise handsome face.

Five foot nine inches tall, Alfi had been a thorn in Selia's side since she arrived in New Campania at the age of sixteen. She had experienced a huge culture shock going from a warring, magical island paradise where strength was tested and knowledge praised, to a place where she had to keep a low profile. Unlike her homeland, women on this continent were typically thought of as the weaker sex and she had to force herself to keep her unusual strength and knowledge secret. Magic wasn't believed to be real, let alone exist, in New Campania. Selia had been forced to keep it secret, for fear of standing out and becoming a target. Or, worse yet, be forced into becoming another weapon in Al's considerable arsenal.

Selia's docile act had fooled everyone, especially Alfi. He had immediately thought she would be an easy conquest, and that she would fall over herself to be another notch on his bedpost. Yeah, that hadn't happened, and ever since she had made her point, Alfi had hated her. He hated Soren, too, for taking her side and not punishing the girl who had dared insult a male member of the syndicate.

Selia wanted to stop just inside the outer room, out of the thugs' reach, but knew that wouldn't work. Alfi would take it as an invitation to open fire and she was a proverbial sitting duck, yet again. There was a slim chance that Soren would be coming later and Alfi wasn't here about the drive. So, she lifted her chin and strode briskly between the two thugs, just out of Alfi's reach.

"They aren't Soren's men," she said, instead of greeting him.

Alfi smiled, revealing a perfect set of pearly white teeth that would have made any dentist proud. The smile didn't reach his dark hazel eyes, but she had to admit, the smile made him look like a model. Dark black hair lay perfectly without a trace of gel, not a strand out of place. She smelled the faint whiff of hairspray, though. His charcoal gray suit was tailored to show off his perfect physique and she knew for a fact he went to the Family's gym daily. When it came to knowing the enemy, Selia didn't let any detail slip past her if it kept her from accidently crossing paths with said model-perfect, murdering bastard.

"You're absolutely correct, Selia." Her name slid off his lips, reminding her of a snake hissing. "They're my men. Now, give me the drive."

Oh, that wasn't what I wanted to hear, she thought. He, the dirty rat, had sent her after the drive. Not that the knowledge would do her much good right now.

"Where's Soren?" she asked, wanting to be certain.

"He's indisposed," Alfi replied, not moving from his casual perch on Soren's desk.

Crap. That could mean any number of things. Selia forced her lips to form a polite smile. "I'll wait until he's available."

Alfi's eyes narrowed and his dulcet, pleasing tone dropped a degree in temperature. "You may not have enough time."

Selia shrugged as she considered her options. There really weren't many. Maybe bluffing would work until another option arose. "The deal was I get the drive to Soren, nobody else."

"I'm Nobody Else," Alfi replied, his lips twisting into a malevolent smirk.

"Well, you're certainly nobody as far as I'm concerned," she conceded in a mocking tone. "That doesn't mean I'm giving you the drive, though."

"Oh, a wise ass," he returned, straightening and pushing away from the desk an inch.

Selia shrugged, refusing to give her ground. "I adapt to my environment."

"Better if you give me the drive, now."

Well, she always had been able to annoy him in two minutes or less. Though, usually, she had some sort of reinforcement to keep him from harming her. Pulling out the empty drive from her left pocket, she held it in the palm of her hand, just to the side of her body. It was time to get creative, even if it meant revealing she was more than just a pretty, shy, brown-eyed, brunette secretary with a demure smile and soft voice.

"I was instructed to give it to Soren. How do you know I won't destroy it instead of giving it to you?"

"You think you can do that with the three of us here?" he asked, nodding to the two thugs who hadn't moved from their sentry position.

Alfi had them well-trained. She wondered if he'd used puppy treats as reinforcement for good behavior.

"How do you know I can't?" she countered, keeping her voice even, despite her rising pulse and racing heart.

"Maybe I'd like to see that."

It was obvious to her that Alfi didn't believe her, but whatever. If he thought she was going to give in, he was crazy. Well, crazier than she had originally thought.

She replied, "Maybe you wouldn't."

Alfi gave a put-upon sigh and held out his hand. "Enough games. Give it to me."

Selia tilted her head to the side and pursed her lips as though considering his demand and shrugged.

With a shrug, she exclaimed, "Okay!"

Alfi smiled, but it turned to a look of horror as fire flared to life in Selia's hand, flash-frying the drive. She threw the flaming, melted drive into Alfi's face and ducked into a crouch as he screamed, throwing his hands to his face. Turning, she watched in detached fascination as the two thugs turned and fired towards where she had been standing. They were fast, but rather dumb because they didn't identify their target before squeezing their triggers.

Another scream erupted from Alfi as she scurried in a crouch past the two thugs who rushed to help their overlord. She glanced over one shoulder and smirked. One of the thugs had, apparently, managed to aim correctly. However, instead of hitting her, he had shot Alfi in the chest. Blood blossomed across Alfi's gray suit as the other thug punched in numbers on his cell phone even as she turned and ran like hell.

Pushing her thumb against the black pad, a green light flashed, and the door unlocked. Selia opened it far enough for her to slip through, pulled it shut, and raced down the private staircase. Sure, there was a safety feature to unlock the stairs if the fire alarm sounded, but there was no fire tonight and the elevator would take too long. Fortunately for her, Soren restricted who could use the staircase anytime without the need of a keycard.

There was a side door, hidden in the far corner with another keypad lock, along with a door to the right and left. The door to the right led into the main waiting area and the left opened into a side street. Fearing there would be more thugs waiting for her in the lobby or just outside the main entrance, Selia opted for the exit to the side-street.

The moment she exited the building, she ran. She didn't stop until her lungs threatened to burst from her chest, a good eight blocks from Soren's office. Even then, she continued walking at a quick pace, glancing around in the hopes of finding a store still open. Spotting a Starbucks, she ducked inside and chose a booth as far from anyone else as possible.

Pulling out her cell phone, she dialed Soren's number. The moment she heard his voice, she hunched over the table, hoping to hide from Alfi and his goons. "Where are you? You didn't send me an email asking me to pick up an envelope and then meet you at your office, did you?"

"No," Soren said. He sounded rather concerned and angry. "What happened?"

"I showed up at your office to give you the drive that was inside the envelope and Alfi was there. He tried to take it from me with extreme prejudice." Selia tried to keep calm, but it wasn't easy when someone had just tried to kill her. Twice.

"That figures about Alfi, but start at the beginning," Soren said, his voice calm and the sound of reason. He still sounded like he wanted to kill someone, though.

Selia drew comfort from his calm, steady voice and forced herself to keep quiet as she answered Soren's request.

"I got an email to go to Cerestes to pick up an envelope from the mailroom there. Since you were off, I figured it was legit. I know, I know; you've never asked me to do anything like that before so I should have double-checked, but the email looked legit. I had just finished when two goons showed up to 'escort' me. I escaped out a fire escape."

Selia dropped her voice and felt a blush creeping up her cheeks as she added, "I ran into the Sandman, who took out the pair, and went on to your office. I've already told you what happened there."

"You aren't telling me something," Soren said. He continued before she could reply. "You used your magic, but that doesn't matter now."

He muttered something in Italian about Alfi's mother. Typically, Soren kept his anger carefully hidden and tucked away. He had to be thoroughly pissed.

"You need to get off the phone. I'll contact you. Get somewhere safe. Nowhere you usually go."

That wasn't helping her fear. "What do you mean?"

"Do you honestly think the government is the only group that can track people by cell phone? Hell, I could Google where you are right now!" He took a deep breath and calmed himself once more. "Hang up, turn off your phone's GPS and get five miles away from where you are now. Fast!"

The call ended and Selia swallowed hard, doing as he told her. She emptied her pockets onto the table and sighed. She didn't have much. Her car keys, the flash drive, her phone's wall charger and cable she had stuffed into her jacket pocket for some dumb reason that didn't seem so dumb now, and her wallet. She flipped open her wallet and went through its compartments. Flipping through the contents, she found her bank card.

She looked around the Starbucks and her eyes landed on an ATM. If Soren knew where she was, then that meant everyone else could find her, too. If they already knew her location, using the ATM could do no harm.

Stuffing her pockets once more, she got up and headed over to the machine. If she was going to run, she would need to max out her withdrawal limit, since she only had about a hundred bucks on hand. Cash couldn't be traced; everything else could and would be.

So much for shoe shopping, she thought as she punched the buttons on the ATM and collected her five hundred bucks.

J. F. Posthumus

Chapter Three

Selia didn't use the subway very often, which was an understatement. She had no need for the subway when she had her own car and rarely went outside Soren's area of influence. That meant she didn't typically go into Tony Carenzo's territory on the North side of the city or the Southwestern area of the city that Lucien Vaschetti claimed. Nor did she visit the small area between the dons that the Sandman called home.

Keeping up with the crowds, Selia kept her head low and her shoulders hunched. She paid for a ticket to the edge of the city on the Northern Line. Boarding the subway car, she found a seat near the back and slouched, keeping her head low.

She watched as the train went above ground on the outside of Al's domain and into Tony's territory. Skyscrapers changed into townhouses and apartment buildings that ranged from modern and new to those that were boarded up or falling apart. As grocery chains and department stores passed by, Selia wondered if Alfi's actions had been sanctioned.

Though Selia wasn't knowledgeable of how the syndicate worked, she couldn't help but question why Al would have allowed Alfi to try to kill her. Maybe that was why Soren had told her to get out? To find out if Alfi's actions had been approved by Al? She sincerely hoped that Al hadn't approved it, since that would mean he had done a complete one-eighty towards her.

Watching the signs, Selia realized she was nearing the end of the line. When the subway car stopped, she disembarked, discovering she was in a business district. She wandered down the sidewalk until she found a little discount shop still open. Ducking inside, she happily discovered a selection of tourist-type clothing. Grabbing a jacket a size too big, a baseball cap, boring sunglasses, and several candy bars, she paid for all of it in cash.

Stuffing her hair beneath the cap, she pulled the jacket around her, zipping it shut. The candy bars she shoved into her pockets. Returning to the subway, she purchased another ticket, this one to a part of town she'd visited only once before, and that had been when she was seventeen.

Despite the fact Soren had told her to get further away, she couldn't bring herself to leave the city. It would put too much distance between her, Soren, and the only place she considered home. Instead, she was going to stay in an area where none of the Families had any influence: the self-declared "neutral territory" by all the dons, courtesy of the Sandman.

Not that this area had always been the Sandman's territory. It had, in fact, once been an area the Vaschettis and Carenzos had fought viciously to own. Then, the Sandman had stepped in and turned the tables. While the

Carenzo Family had been bent on taking out Lucien Vaschetti's people and the Vaschettis were intent on vengeance, the Sandman had taken out both. He busted drug deals and pimps breaking up their gambling, loan sharking, and protection rackets.

What better place to hide than in neutral territory that didn't belong to any Family and an area she wasn't known to venture.

Taking a cab was out of the question. Cabbies remembered their passengers and kept track of where people were picked up and dropped off. Instead, Selia hopped on a bus and when a low-budget hotel came into view, she memorized the route the bus took, hopped off three blocks past it, and took another bus until she came to a ritzy hotel. From there, she backtracked on foot to the cheap dive of a hotel.

Taking alleys and side-streets, Selia kept to the shadows, ignoring the clusters of people standing at the steps of townhouses and apartment buildings. She didn't keep her head low or hunched over. Instead, she walked with the swagger of an armed kid who knew her town and had business to take care of. Grabbing a couple sodas from a convenience store, she headed to the hotel's front desk where she paid in cash under a false name. With a keycard in hand, Selia took the stairs up to her room and settled in.

The room wasn't too small. There were two double beds, a couple of chairs, a large entertainment system and a fairly decent sized bathroom. Setting the small bag of drinks on a table, she pulled the heavy, boring pastel curtains away from the windows to find a small balcony overlooking the city street. Letting the curtains swing back into place, she grabbed one of the sodas from the bag and twisted the top off.

She took a long pull before recapping it and putting it on a small table. Standing in the shadows beside the window, she sank into the darkness and stared through the narrow opening, watching the people milling about on the sidewalk below. It brought back a memory of her childhood, when she had stood in the shadows of tall palms and lush jungle growth waiting for a deer to pass. She had been the hunter then, but now was the prey. It wasn't a pleasant thought.

A rueful smile tugged at her lips despite the unpleasant situation, and she sighed inwardly. That time was long gone. She'd never be allowed back to her island homeland. Her home now was this strange city of concrete buildings, automobiles, and technology. But was she going to keep running? As a child, she'd feared nothing and had stood up for herself. It was the only way to survive on Temeria. A person didn't have a protector or savior to step in when things got rough in her homeland. There, it was a matter of defend yourself, or be beaten senseless, or killed.

But her fearlessness had been driven from her when she ran away to Soren's ship in order to prevent herself from being killed. Soren had saved her then, and had continued protecting her, either by his hand or through his orders. She hadn't needed to stand up and protect herself, not when she had Soren. In fact, she'd been taught quickly to run from trouble so her secrets would remain hidden.

For once, she wasn't certain she wanted to run anymore. She wasn't certain if she wanted to turn to someone else to protect her when she could easily stand up and protect herself.

Her phone rang, pulling her from her troublesome thoughts.

"Text me the number where you're staying." Soren's voice was a welcome bedrock of security and safety. It was odd, she thought, how much Soren's confidence and stolid demeanor meant to her.

"Why didn't you just text me?" she asked.

"Are you really that naïve, girl? After all these years?" His tone was gruff and was followed by a click.

Blushing, she glanced at the phone and sent the number to him and waited with the patience of a hunter trained to wait for her prey. On the second ring, she picked up the receiver.

"I have your car, your gym bag, an extra set of clothes, and your laptop. What else do you need?" Soren asked, not bothering with a preamble.

"Cash would be nice, so I'm not killing myself here. I don't dare use any of my cards. They would be too easy to track and then they'd find out I'm still in the city." Selia twisted the phone cord around her hand. It wasn't like anyone else would see how nervous she was.

She could hear the smile in his voice as he replied, "You do good work for me. I'll bring you some cash. See you in two hours."

Two hours later, Selia was sitting in the middle of one of the beds, legs crossed, and hands curled gently against her knees. Her eyes were closed, and she was chanting in a hauntingly beautiful voice in her native tongue. A knock on the door had her rolling off the bed in a single fluid movement. Her hand went to her hip, and she realized belatedly she was in a hotel room waiting for Soren to arrive. Even more odd was the fact she had reached for a weapon, something she very rarely used, let alone wore outside of hunting or the shooting range.

Perhaps her former life on Temeria, where everyone carried a weapon, was starting to influence her once again. Strange how using her magic to protect herself was bringing back more lessons and instincts than anything else she'd encountered within the city.

Walking to the door, ignoring the strange turn of her thoughts, she heard Soren speaking in accented Temerian. He was giving her the old password they had contrived shortly after she had stepped foot on his ship asking for safety.

Your family is the homeland of your heart. She was now starting to understand what those words meant, even if she didn't know why he had made that the 'password' to prove it was him, should the need ever arise.

She opened the door, a grin on her face. "I never expected to be so happy to hear that phrase." She chuckled. "You did say I would need it one day."

Soren smiled and stepped into the room. He waited until she'd shut and locked the door behind him. "Yet you whined when I insisted upon it."

Shrugging, she had no response to that fact. Without seeming too brash, she grabbed her bag and dropped it as she pulled out the computer. She had the laptop open and booting before her duffle bag hit the floor.

"I haven't seen you move that fast since the day you stopped hiding on the ship, too afraid to come out for anything more than a late-night stalking," Soren commented, causing Selia to flush.

"You told me it wasn't something a normal person could do," Selia replied as she typed in her password. "But you always helped me better myself. I still don't understand why, though."

"I also spent a great deal of time educating you on how much you would need to hide your abilities," Soren retorted, but kindly. "I often wonder what you do on your own time. Such skills and abilities will atrophy if not used. That would be a crime and an insult to your heritage."

There wasn't a lot she did that Soren didn't know about. One of the few secrets she kept from him was her archery. Marksmanship with guns was something a person could learn and improve upon quickly and easily. Skill at a bow wasn't quite the same, though, and Selia had been taught from the moment she could walk how to use a bow. Her frequent camping trips had often been to go hunting. She tracked her prey with nothing more than her bow, a quiver full of arrows, and dangerously sharp knives.

She'd even purchased a license to hunt and fish without raising questions. Fishing, apparently, was an allowed hobby for a woman. She'd been 'allowed' to go hunting with a couple of the Family's enforcers before she turned eighteen and had earned herself a reputation as an expert hunter.

There had never been a question, at least to her, as to whether or not Soren had risked a lot for her. That somehow made everything that happened now, matter more than ever. Reaching into her pocket, she pulled out the drive and connected it. A minute later she was copying everything to her laptop.

"Why are you doing that?" Soren asked, settling onto the edge of the bed.

Selia glanced over to her father. "In case anything happens to you, gods forbid it does, I'll have leverage."

"Smart girl. That's one of the reasons why I like you," he teased. Reaching into the inside of his jacket pocket, he pulled out a stack of bills. He held it out. "There's two thousand here. It's not a loan."

Selia stared at the hand holding the bills and took it almost reverently. Staring at it, she didn't notice him pull out more items from his pocket.

"Use this to rent yourself a car. Don't trust public transportation. Keep in disguise." He paused as she took it, his other hand grasping hers as he grinned. "I think you'd look amazing as a blond."

Laughing, Selia leaned forward and kissed his cheek. "You already think I look beautiful."

"Yes, but I wouldn't recognize you as a blond," he countered, a twinkle in his brown eyes.

Shaking her head, Selia took a moment to really *look* at Soren. He was smiling and teasing her as he always had, but there was something different about him. His dark brown hair was slowly turning to a dashing salt-and-pepper. His face still held the same lines she'd known ten years ago, but his brown eyes were harder, and fury burned in their depths. He was handsome, charming, and could have been her father by blood.

But today he wore a black suit with a dark gray crisp shirt and a black tie. His shoes, polished and black, shone. For some odd reason, though, he reminded her of someone going to a funeral. Perhaps it was the black suit, along with the anger that wafted off him in red hot waves. Typically, he wore dark blue or light gray suits. Or, it could have been the fact there was a harder set about his jaw and he moved with the determination of someone set to kill. Despite the darker colors, and his hidden fury, he still didn't look as though he were in his late fifties.

Until now, she'd never questioned his age, or his heritage. She knew the rumors surrounding him that claimed he had a little bit of 'other' blood in him. Now she wondered if, perhaps, he had a little Temerian in him as well. Her people lived for centuries. At least, on the island they did, but her aging hadn't changed her appearance, so she guessed it was true for those off the island as well.

"I'll contact you in twenty-four hours," Soren said, interrupting her troublesome thoughts. "Keep low and be careful."

"I promise." Setting the items beside the laptop, she pulled the drive and handed it to him. "Was this sanctioned by Al?"

Do I need to worry about more people coming after me? She didn't say it, but she let the question shine in her eyes.

Soren shook his head, a frown on his face. "Al didn't know about anything. He likes you, Selia. You should know that, though I don't blame you for asking that question." He tucked the drive into the inside pocket of his jacket where he'd pulled out the money and her fake ID. "Don't worry about it, Selia. I'll handle this and you'll be home soon."

A gut instinct told Selia it wouldn't be that easy, but she ignored it. Trust was hard for her to give, but she trusted Soren with her life. She had always trusted him with her life and always would. Soren wouldn't let her down; he always kept his promises and his word.

She offered him a small smile. "I'll stay here until I hear from you."

Standing, Soren enveloped her in a hug. She surprised herself by not stiffening up or feeling as though she needed to push away from him, like she had many times before. This time, she hugged him back, thankful to have him in her life.

She'd been shy and skittish when she'd first met him, and Soren hadn't tried to change her into what was 'expected' by his society. He gave her distance, which meant hugs and kisses had been few and far between. They had become more frequent in the past couple years, but they weren't an everyday, or even weekly, occurrence. Not that she had never been on the receiving end of his affection; quite the contrary. She just hadn't allowed herself to truly appreciate it until she knew for certain he wouldn't betray her. Now, though, she appreciated the daughterly affection he offered, and she craved it.

She hugged him back, her arms tightening around him as she snuggled against his chest, like a daughter who hadn't seen her father in months, or even years. He was armed. She could feel the holster and grip of the gun beneath her, but that was normal. What wasn't normal was the hardness beneath his shirt, not that she would ask about that, either. Nope, she was going to enjoy this moment for as long as it would last. Besides, it was probably Kevlar and nothing to worry about. At least, not for her.

Chapter Four

Meditation was often a wonderful relaxing technique for the body and mind, but Selia discovered it only worked when one wasn't worrying about someone. For three hours, she tried to calm her nerves using various methods, and nothing worked. She tried hot chocolate, a long soak in the hotel's tub, complete with bubbles, then a hot shower, stretching exercises, and finally meditation. Nothing calmed her.

Soren should have contacted her two hours ago, but so far, nothing. Since nothing was helping her to relax enough to sit patiently and await his call or arrival, she turned to pacing the length of the room and glaring at the non-ringing phone. She had changed into a dark burgundy blouse cut so low she was afraid to bend over for fear of her ample cleavage falling out, skin-tight black jeans, and black boots.

They weren't the high-heeled style, either. These had wide, thick heels with heavy tread, and fit her snugly to just below the knees. The leather boots were supple and allowed for easy movement. In fact, the jeans allowed her to move easily, as did the blouse- even if it did have a dangerous neckline. Though, it certainly wasn't an outfit she would have chosen, which was probably why Soren had shoved it into her gym bag.

Even though she hoped there would be no need for it, she had also shrugged into her shoulder holster with the 9mm Glock snapped into place. A gift from Soren years ago, she kept the semi-automatic in her gym bag. Fortunately, Soren apparently hadn't seen a reason to deprive her of the gift.

A tap at the window broke her train of thought and she turned towards the balcony, gun in hand. Not seeing anyone, she walked cautiously towards the window, finger near the trigger, and pulled the curtain back. She dropped her arm and rolled her eyes as she opened the door.

"What are you doing here?" she all but demanded as the Sandman stepped into the room.

"May I use your bathroom?" he asked instead, a smirk in his voice as he removed his sunglasses.

To pass time the night before, Selia had done internet search after internet search looking for articles of the Sandman's outfit. Kind of obsessive, she supposed, but it helped to kill time. She had discovered, amongst other things, a brand of sunglasses that matched what he wore. She was now convinced they were infrared sunglasses, capable of being worn in any light situation, and he was wearing a lot of Kevlar.

"Sure, it's that way," she replied, thumbing towards the direction of the bathroom. "Mind telling me what you're doing here?"

He was a lot more dashing than scary in the dim light of the hotel room. His eyes were dark and still shadowed, but she could see his mask better and the change of his features beneath the fabric. He had a broad chest, his other features were similarly more fitting to someone sprinting down a playing field for a living, or into burning buildings. He'd have to be, to be able to do what he did. A study in all black, she couldn't help but wonder what he looked like beneath his disguise.

He chuckled and this time it was one of genuine amusement. "Actually, I'm here to rescue you. Again."

"Uh huh," Selia replied, as she glanced towards the still-silent phone. "Why would I need rescuing?"

"I liked you better as a brunette," he said, passing by her on the way to the bathroom. A flush, and a couple minutes later, he walked out holding a small hand towel.

Selia pulled the wig off, her hair pinned down in tiny, dainty, flattened curls. "It's a wig. I was trying to get used to wearing it."

"Glad you didn't cut it. You look good with long hair." He grinned, taking the shoulder-length blond wig from her hand, and examining it. His smile faltered when he tossed the wig back to her as he went to the door. "I found Soren. He was almost unrecognizable. Someone beat him to a pulp and left him for dead."

Selia gasped and felt the color drain from her face. He glanced back at her and when she didn't say anything, he nodded once and continued speaking, his voice low and even.

"His jaw was broken, busted ribs, broken arms, internal bleeding. He was shot as well, before being left. Would have been dead, too, if I hadn't found him." The Sandman turned his attention back to the hallway.

"Where is he?" she asked, a strange calm settling over her. Selia knew she should have been angry, furious, upset or even scared out of her wits. But she didn't feel anything but calm decisiveness. "Take me to him."

The Sandman looked over his shoulder at her. "He's safe. I took him to a hospital out of the way. The staff there knows how to keep quiet. Weren't going to fix him up until I told them to. He's far safer than you are at the moment."

"Fine," she replied. Turning away from him, she tucked her laptop into the duffle bag before snapping the gun back into her shoulder holster. "You're here to rescue me. So, rescue me. Then you can take me to him." She grabbed her oversized jacket and slid it on over her blouse, effectively hiding her holster.

"You know how to use that thing?" He nodded towards her concealed weapon.

Selia wasn't certain if he was joking or dead serious. "I wouldn't be wearing it if I didn't know how to use it properly. Soren taught me. He's the only one here who knows everything there is to know about me." A smile pulled at her lips and her face softened as she added, "I do him proud on the range."

He grunted and gestured towards the window balcony. She shoved the wig into the gym bag – blonde hair would be far more noticeable than brown – and shoved the cap back onto her head. The gym bag, she hooked onto her shoulders like a backpack, not bothered by the weight.

The Sandman gave a single nod of approval, put on his sunglasses, and stepped onto the balcony, effectively vanishing in the darkness. That was okay, Selia decided. She wasn't too bad at vanishing when she needed to, either. Magic made it easier, but she'd been taught how to do it without magic.

"Impressive," she heard him murmur as he grabbed the rope lying flat against the side of the building. "It took me years of training and practice to learn how to vanish like that."

"You aren't the only one with secrets," she murmured, leaning over and grabbing the rope easily, without causing it to sway with the movement. Okay, maybe she was showing off a little. "Up or down?"

"Up," he replied and the grin on his face was easily heard in his voice.

"Be sure to enjoy the view," she teased, her voice carrying only to his ears.

He chuckled and swatted her gently on her rear. "It's a guarantee. Now get moving. Let me know if you get tired."

She snorted. "How about you catch up with me?" With those words, she began climbing, hand-over-hand, up the side of the building.

Selia didn't fear heights. She had climbed higher as a child, and without the use of a net that many people favored. As a youth, you don't think of the dangers or have a fear of falling. Not if you've been taught well, and Selia had been a quick learner in everything she did. Magic might have been her forte and what she excelled at, but when given a task, she wanted to be the best at it, or as close as she could possibly get.

The rope didn't sway beneath her hands as she climbed. Once she reached the roof, she climbed over the edge, onto the flat surface, and turned to offer the Sandman her hand, only to find him right behind her.

"Where to now?" she asked softly, enjoying being only a hand's width away from him. "Or do you plan on keeping me entertained up here?"

"Trying to tempt me, lovely siren?" he asked, a gloved hand brushing across her cheek.

"I'm not a siren," she replied, smiling.

The attraction apparently went both ways. Either that or he was a damned good actor. She grabbed his hand gently with hers, holding it in place against her cheek.

She lifted her eyes to where his sunglasses sat, even as she tried to not lean into the odd warmth she felt from his gloved hand.

Swallowing hard, she said, "Take me to see Soren. Please."

He lifted his chin slightly, perhaps in a challenge, but Selia just kept her gaze level. A part of her wanted to stay with him, despite the fact he was technically the opposition, but he'd saved her twice. That meant something to her. The desire welling up inside her also said something other than 'enemy'. Unfortunately, with Soren being in the hospital and Alfi gunning for her, it didn't allow for a lot of conventional romantic opportunities.

The Sandman met her gaze before sliding his hand from hers and turning to look over the edge. She had to see Soren. Her father had the answers she needed, and she had the magic *he* needed.

"I could use magic to persuade you, but I'd rather not. I'm not like the rest of the Family, Sandman." She paused as he turned back to her. At least she had his attention. "Please, take me to Soren. I can help him, and I need to see for myself that he's alive."

Selia rarely pleaded. In fact, the last time she'd pleaded with someone, she had made a bargain and for nearly a year had felt as though she'd sold her soul to the devil. She stopped seeing Soren as the devil after only a few months with him, and that had been followed quickly by love and appreciation.

That hadn't stopped her from resenting Soren a bit because he forced her to glamour people to make his job easier, though. Free will was important to her, but she had made a bargain that included her using magic to force his influence on others. Eventually, she had learned that what she did was far better than the other possible methods Soren could have employed.

Nearly being killed and learning someone she had thought indestructible had nearly died put life into a whole new perspective. No, Soren wasn't an angel, but he sure as hell wasn't as bad as Alfi or many of the others in the syndicate. Soren had protected her when she'd needed it. His way of doing things, even using her magic to make his deals, agreements, and arrangements, kept people from dying or ending up wishing they were dead.

Her life was changing fast, once again, but she refused to lay down and die. Or run like a coward as she had a decade ago. The set determination of her jaw and the pleading in her eyes didn't waver, despite what she suspected was a frown hidden behind the Sandman's mask.

"I'll take you to him now," he agreed reluctantly. "But I want some answers afterwards."

She stepped forward and kissed his masked cheek. "Thank you." She smiled and glanced around before asking, "So, which way from here?"

Leaning down, he pulled up the rope and coiled it around a small grappling hook. He tucked the rope and hook away in a small compartment on his utility belt.

"This way," he said, moving past her and towards the opposite side of the roof.

Following behind him, their steps silent on the graveled roof, she watched as his coat swayed with each step, almost like a superhero's cloak. She knew better, though. The Sandman was no superhero. Not that it stopped her from admiring him.

He paused at the edge. "How good are you at jumping?"

"Average from where I'm from," she replied easily. "I can jump this without a problem. How about you?"

He pointed to a pair of metal poles lying near the edge of the roof. Walking over, he picked one up and hefted it experimentally.

"Good enough," he said before adding, "See you on the other side."

Turning, he strode back several paces and set off at a run, jamming the edge of the pole down on the roof and vaulting over the ten-plus-foot gap with the ease of an Olympian pole vaulter. She watched approvingly as he landed safely on the other side. Now it was her turn.

Counting the strides as she walked backwards, she paused and tilted her head. Turning towards the small building-type entrance to the roof, she narrowed her eyes, judging the distance. Closing her eyes, she held her breath before releasing it slowly. Taking a few more steps back, she took off running, arms pumping as she'd been taught as a child and, at the last moment, using the edge of the building to give an extra push, leapt from the roof.

Not looking down, she kept her eyes on the other side, legs spread as though she were doing a split in midair. Nearing the other roof, she brought her feet closer together and landed, falling forward in a crouch. The crushed rock scraped against her hands, tearing into her palms. Had it not been for the laptop in her gym back, she would have rolled with the fall, but it was too important to keep her laptop safe. She couldn't take the chance of rolling and possibly breaking it. So, instead, she took the pain with a warrior's grace.

Standing, she carefully picked the rocks from her hands and turned to the Sandman. Using barely a breath of magic, she healed her hands, leaving only blood behind. Raising her brows, she silently dared him to comment. Instead, he nodded once and moved towards the edge of the next building, leading her to a rickety fire escape. As their heads vanished from view, she heard the distant sound of men yelling and feet crunching from the other building. So far, so good, but she knew their luck wouldn't hold out forever.

She'd have to take a stand, but first she had to see Soren.

J. F. Posthumus

Chapter Five

The Sandman led her on a merry chase over rooftops, though alleys, and side-streets. Mostly rooftops, though. Selia discovered it felt strangely good to follow the Sandman. Running and using her talents of keeping silent and staying hidden in the shadows reminded her of her youth on Temeria when her magical training had been at a minimal and basic survival skills were at the fore. The Sandman led her for about four blocks until he descended a fire escape and led her around a corner to the hospital where he had taken Soren.

The outside of the hospital looked more like a large parking garage or some unusual office building There was no pretense or overblown architecture to the entrance, either. If a large sign at the ground level hadn't declared "New Campania Downtown Hospital," she might have wondered if the Sandman hadn't gotten lost or led her on a fool's chase.

They entered through an enormous receiving bay where medical supplies were being delivered. The staff consisted of three people in scrubs- two females and one male- who all nodded at the Sandman and her before going back to their task of checking the inventory and comparing their results against a ledger.

After a brief ride in a service elevator, the pair of them came out onto one of the upper floors. Selia noticed the shining floors of pale and muted colors, the half-circle shaped nurses' station, and the pair of nurses sitting at computers, likely entering their medical notes for their shift.

A sanitation employee walked about with a large cart, which was festooned with paper products, cleaning supplies, brooms, and mops. The Sandman nodded to each of these people, who did not seem to take much notice of her. Selia followed him as he strode to the back of the east hallway, confident in his destination.

In her homeland, the wounded were placed on comfortable bunks of feather and fine cloth. Bandages, blood, herbs, and potions would be normal to see. Each patient, no matter how minor or fatal the wound or ailment, possessed a strong nobility. Selia had never, nor would likely ever, get used to patients in the modern hospitals.

The strong disinfectants, the tubes, the monitors, even the gauze across lacerations and contusions, punctures and burns, seemed to belittle the patients laying on the metal and ceramic slabs that were called beds here. Even the lighting felt like it was designed to put the worst cast on the injured or sick. Selia had felt this from her first experience at the hospitals in this land, and the vision of her father, attached to every manner of machine and tube, solidified her feelings.

The lighting emphasized every bruise and cut; the multiple bandages looked yellowed and the blood days old. He looked like an animal that had been tortured and waiting to die. Yet the set of his jaw, though now crooked, was the same, and the grim set of his lips was the familiar expression of determination she knew well.

"Soren," she whispered, moving past her masked companion and to her father's bed.

Tears threatened, but they wouldn't help either her or Soren. Anger, though, was a powerful ally and Soren hurting in one of these beds certainly fueled her fury. She gently grasped his left hand in hers and didn't bother to see if anyone was watching. She had heard the soft click of the door closing.

She trusted the Sandman enough to know he would keep the door shut and they would be alone, at least for a short amount of time. Brushing her hand gently along Soren's jaw, she reached deep within herself and allowed her anger to flow freely, adding an extra boost to the magic she cast.

Healing major wounds was never easy, especially when done on someone else. One had to be certain bones set properly and everything had to regenerate correctly. Every mage had some knowledge in healing, but Selia hadn't been the typical mage. She knew more than the average student, but less than the Shamans or healers who typically cared for the fallen on Temeria.

Soren's jaw shifted and Selia could feel the magic fuse the bones back together. Loose teeth reattached themselves and the palest of his bruises vanished. The angry black and purple bruises slowly ebbed until they were a shade or two lighter. Carefully, Selia pulled the tube from his mouth and nostrils. She then moved her right hand down to his chest, following the pull of magic. She sensed his ribs shift into their proper positions before the broken and cracked bones fused back together. His bleeding organs healed before the magic faded. The worst of his injuries were cured to a point where the body could finish the process on its own. She smiled softly, tears finally forming in the corners of her eyes, but she refused to let them fall.

Moving her hand to the rail of the bed, she said softly, "I couldn't completely heal you. It would be too questionable, and I need to keep some power for myself. I'm sorry I can't do more."

"That's a very handy bit of magic, my dear," whispered Soren. His eyes were open. Reaching up, Soren rubbed his jaw and he smiled at her. "Good thing I didn't know about that one all these years."

Selia chuckled softly. "A girl's gotta have some secrets, doesn't she?" She leaned forward and brushed a feathery kiss across his cheek. "Who did this to you? I'm pretty sure I know who it was, but I need to be certain."

"Alfi and his pet gorillas," confirmed Soren. "Well, Alfi just pistol-whipped me after three of his men disarmed me. I'm pretty sure he's the *codardo* who shot me in the back after I was tossed onto the floor. He never could do anything the way it's supposed to be done. Two in the back of the head; how simple is that? And yet, he failed. Didn't bother to notice the wetsuit made of Kevlar I was wearing under my suit. Good thing. It's what kept me alive after I shot down two of his. Steel pipes, brass knuckles, and baseball bats aren't something you want to get hit with, sans protection."

"I'll take care of this," Selia said, holding his hand in hers. "I promise."

"Make sure you cover your tracks," he advised. "I can inform the rest of the Family that Alfi went rogue, but you cannot be fingered for anything. It would raise too many questions."

"Don't worry," Selia assured him. "I plan on taking out Alfi and no one will ever know I did it." She snorted. "Who would believe your little wallflower turned into a kick-ass vengeful warrior?" Soren grunted. Kissing the top of his hand, she added softly, "You're the only family I have. I... I love you."

"Love you too, kiddo." He winked at her. "Tell your masked boyfriend thanks... and that I have a job opening. If he's interested."

Blushing, she muttered, "He isn't my boyfriend, and you can tell him that yourself."

"Interfering jerk won't come into the room," Soren retorted, a smile tugging at the corners of his mouth.

Something flashed through his eyes and across his face, but Selia couldn't interpret what it was or what it meant. Ignoring it, she said, "Don't be too harsh on the nurses, okay?" She paused, a thought occurring to her. "Did Alfi get the drive?"

"Yeah, he's got it. My guess is he is planning on selling the info to a rival Family or is claiming I grabbed it and ran. Don't know if he has enough imagination for that last bit, though."

"Or he could be hoping to use it to usurp your position," Selia mused. "Doesn't matter. I can use that to pin his death on the Vaschetti family. You stay here, rest up. I couldn't heal you completely and if you move around too much, you'll undo everything I just did."

"I'm going to wait here for a nurse to notice I've taken out this tube and that my vitals are stable. That should get things rolling around here."

Giving Soren another kiss on his cheek, Selia smiled at him. "The Sandman is probably keeping them at bay. I'd better be going before someone gets wise. I'll be in touch, I promise."

"Don't trust him too much, Selia. Everyone thinks they're the good guy, but somebody always gets hurt." He nodded to her, and then closed his eyes.

"I only trust you," she whispered, letting go of his hand. She suspected that would change if she hung around the Sandman for too long.

It hurt so much seeing Soren lying there in the bed, hooked up to everything imaginable. She would cry and then she would avenge him. Turning away, she bowed her head and whispered an ancient prayer for the gods to watch over Soren and protect him.

Shutting the door behind her, she kept her gaze level with the Sandman. "Thanks for bringing him here. He said he has a job offer, if you're interested." She glanced away from the Sandman. "Keep him safe, will you? He's the only family I have left."

"If I didn't plan on keeping him safe and alive, I wouldn't have brought him here," the Sandman retorted. There was no malice in his voice, just a calm tone that could have been used by a teacher explaining the periodic table. "As long as he is here, I can guarantee his safety."

"I appreciate it," Selia replied, swallowing back tears. "He'll stay here, but I have work to do." She lifted her chin, ignoring the tugging in her chest. She hadn't been this upset when she'd fled from Temeria. It was amazing how close she'd become to Soren over the years. "I'm ready to go to your 'safe place', now."

Chapter Six

S elia wasn't certain what to expect when she followed the Sandman back across rooftops, through alleyways, and then through abandoned subway systems. He knew places she'd never heard of, and it gave her an insight into how the man traveled so quickly and easily through the city.

It was no wonder everyone feared him, but Soren's words, his warning, echoed in her head. She wanted to trust this masked man, but after a decade of not knowing who to trust other than Soren and a pair of her Family's enforcers, she couldn't bring herself to trust him completely. She couldn't, not yet.

They came up through a tunnel into a sub-basement and then the basement of a house. There was a quiet comfort to the basement that she hadn't expected. A coffee table sat in front of a sofa and there was a TV opposite the sofa. A full-length bar stretched across a far wall, and it was the bar Selia headed straight for. Well, more like the bottles of alcohol lined up on a shelf behind the bar. Spotting a bottle of tequila, she grabbed a shot glass and filled it before tossing it back.

The Sandman chuckled. Selia slid the bottle and glass to him before turning and walking to the sofa, dropping her duffle bag on the floor beside it. Curling up on the sofa, she laid her head on her knees and closed her eyes as the tears began to flow freely. She was tired and worn. She knew her body would eventually give out and she would fall into an exhausted sleep, but at the moment she didn't care.

The sofa gave beside her, and a hand rubbed her shoulder - a hand, not a gloved hand. She glanced over to find the Sandman sitting beside her, rubbing her shoulder and back. His gloves sat on the coffee table.

Turning slightly, she leaned against his chest, and he held her close, his still-masked chin on her head. His sunglasses had been removed and stowed somewhere. He said nothing and did nothing more than hold her, letting her cry silently against him. It was odd. She didn't trust many people, let alone confide in them, but she found herself wanting to confide in him.

Wiping her eyes, she felt him lean away before a couple tissues were offered. She smiled slightly, feeling better. The grief was gone, leaving in its place a cold, hard anger

"I don't know where to start," she said, wiping her eyes and nose with the tissues.

The Sandman got up and Selia turned to watch him go to the bar and vanish beneath it. He stood up again with two cans of soda before grabbing two whiskey tumblers and coming back to her. Popping the tabs, he poured the soda into the glasses and handed her one. Selia took a sip of the cold beverage. He pulled the bottom of the balaclava out of his shirt and rolled it up, so his strong, unshaven chin and wide, thin lips were exposed.

"Start at the beginning. Where did you come from?" he asked before taking a long pull from his glass. The question 'what are you?' hung silently in the air between them.

Why not? She thought. *After all, who was he going to tell?*

"I'm from an island somewhere in the Atlantic, near what you would call the Bermuda Triangle," Selia said, holding the glass between her hands as she stared at the popping, fizzing bubbles. "An island called Temeria and the home to a race of nearly immortal Amazonian-like women." She glanced at him sharply. "No jokes about a lasso and bracelets, please. We're more like your ancient Greek Amazons or, to be more accurate, Spartans, than your famed comic book character."

"Fair enough," he said, leaning back on the sofa. He appeared relaxed, but Selia could see the tension in his body.

"I'm as far from noble-born as a person can get, but I had a strong gift for magic. My mother claimed I could start fires at six months old. A rarity in any Temerian. So, I was sent to learn magic from the Temple once I turned six. That's not to say I didn't have to learn to fight, climb, hunt, harvest, and everything else a warrior and female Temerian would need to know about life. We aren't a peaceful people who enjoyed lounging around and having archery contests for fun."

Memories sprang to life. Unbidden but not unwanted. Selia remembered learning, at the early age of five, the proper way to kill a deer with only a bow and three arrows. She learned to fight and how to remain still for extended periods of time.

Punishments were swift and just, and the only time someone was sentenced to death was if one used the skills for evil. Killing and torture was as likely to get a person sentenced to death as readily as one who used necromancy.

Reading and writing were as important to the Temerians as learning how to kill and properly skin a deer. Being a mage, she had learned all the main languages used by her people and those who traded with them: English, Italian, Mandarin Chinese, and a few others. Knowing the languages of the traders who the mages and royal family dealt with on her side of the island had been a definite benefit when she'd been forced to flee her island.

The Sandman cleared his throat, pulling her away from the memories of another lifetime.

She continued, ignoring the warmth growing in her cheeks. "My gift was magic. Not just performing it, either. I could memorize a spell after reading it once and then perform it flawlessly. It wasn't unprecedented, but there had been no one like me for centuries. So, I quickly became a favorite of the teachers and given privileges few others were offered. My curiosity ended up being my downfall. Well, my curiosity and desire to protect the youngest princess of my ruling family."

"What happened?" the Sandman asked, his voice soft and encouraging. At least he wasn't bored.

Selia smiled ruefully. "I was sixteen. In two years, I would have taken my place as the youngest mage to ever become an advisor to my clan's ruling family. Princess Melia was to wed a minor noble who went through servants far more frequently than any other. One had just died, and I'd found a tome on magic that probably hadn't been used for several centuries."

She bowed her head, closing her eyes as she remembered that fateful day. "I went to what you would call our 'morgue' and used a spell that was forbidden. I raised the young girl from the dead and questioned her, learning her master had beaten her, forced her to do unthinkable deeds, and then killed her. The princess's consort was believed to frequently beat those who displeased her, often killing them for no other reason than mere amusement."

The Sandman leaned forward. "Why did you do that? If you knew the magic was forbidden?"

"The magic is forbidden because the necromancers used those spells for evil. Their intent was evil, and so the spells came to be thought of as evil and forbidden. Magic comes from life. They used it to kill, and not as defense, either. The necromancers would control people, forcing them to act against their will, often breaking their psyches in the process," Selia explained before taking a sip from her glass. "The spell I used didn't literally bring the girl back. It was more like speaking to her spirit, which is more of a gray area. Not that anyone would believe my thoughts about the spells, or even agree with me."

"That makes sense, I think," he said slowly. "So, what happened?"

"I told the headmistress what I'd learned, and she said they couldn't use the information because of how I discovered it. That I had to flee because she could sense the 'taint' of the spell I'd used on me and anyone powerful enough would sense it also. She said necromancy left a stench, and it would take years for it to wear off. Since the punishment for using those spells is death, she doubted I'd be able to hide long enough for my aura to cleanse itself." Selia shrugged, still not entirely believing what she'd been told. "The headmistress promised to find a legal way of learning what I knew to stop the wedding and punish the noble, but I had to run before I was caught."

A sardonic smile twisted her lips, and she paused long enough to take another sip of her soda.

"I had always been a favorite of the headmistress. She cared about me, more than she should have, I suspect. She told me to run to the docks, that the trader there might be able to help me. I collected a small bag of my belongings before running to the ship. To Soren's ship. I managed to get there before the bells started tolling. Someone else had learned what I'd done and had turned me in."

Selia set her glass on the table and stood, walking away from the sofa, her arms folded across her chest. Sitting still wasn't possible. She hadn't spoken of her past to anyone. Ever. Soren was the only other person who knew why she had traveled to New Campania on his ship. She doubted even Al knew the entire story behind her desire to leave the island. If he did, he'd never spoken of it.

"I was able to find Soren easily and asked… No, I should be honest. I all but begged him for help. He wanted to know why I'd want to leave the island and I told him the truth. For years I believed it had been a foolish choice, but now I think it was the right one."

"Why's that?" the Sandman asked.

She glanced over her shoulder at him. He didn't get up and try to console her, but rather stayed on the sofa, allowing her space and time. The man knew how to endear himself to her. From the genuine curiosity in his eyes, she doubted he knew what he was doing. Of course, he could also be an incredibly good actor, but something told her he was genuine.

"I think he already knew but wanted to know how naïve I was. He agreed to give me safety if I agreed to his conditions. I'd have to stay with him for three years, graduate high school, and do exactly as I was told before I would be allowed to live on my own. I had to promise to work for him as his personal assistant, and the job would include glamouring people into being receptive of his offers, requests, and demands." She turned around to face the Sandman. "I agreed, pretty much believing I was selling myself and my soul to a man who I saw as the devil himself. Not that I had a choice."

Actually, she'd been closer to capture than she was admitting to the Sandman. The fact her people knew she had read the tomes scared them all. She had just agreed to Soren's terms and been placed in a small room in his cabin before hearing the Royal Guards shouting for Soren. The thumping of their spears against the deck above her had echoed in the quiet office-like room. She'd heard Soren's calm voice and eventually they had come to where she'd been hiding.

Soren's voice never wavered from his ever calm and authoritative tone. The guards hadn't found her, and he had practically been forced to drag her from the small office to her own cabin that adjoined his. He'd later tried to coax her out of the small cabin. It hadn't worked. She, instead, chose to sneak out at night, silently creeping around the ship.

Curious yet fearful, she had obeyed Soren on the ship, allowing herself to hide in the lessons he had given her. When they docked, she followed him to his house, becoming his adopted daughter. Soren had introduced her to Big Al, as most of the Family referred to him, and been formally adopted into the Family. She had been sent to a small, exclusive Catholic school, learned to keep a low-profile and how to be a wallflower.

Soren had taught her everything she needed to survive in his world, from lessons about the society and her new homeland to giving her access to the best technology and training her on how to use guns and other weaponry. He had even made certain her 'babysitters' were enforcers who she had developed a close friendship with over the years.

"Yet you call him family," the Sandman said, breaking into her thoughts.

"He's been a father to me when I had no family at all. Even on Temeria, I didn't have anyone as close or caring as Soren. For a long time, I was afraid to think he truly cared, but he proved how much he cared for me when I snubbed Alfi. He had my back, and it cemented my belief that he wouldn't betray me."

That caught the Sandman's attention. His head lifted and his eyes brightened with interest. "You 'snubbed' Alfi? What happened?"

"Alfi thought I would be the pliant, willing mistress I appeared to be," Selia replied dryly. "I turned down his advances and then, when he refused to take 'no' for an answer, I made it more… poignant… by breaking his wrist."

The Sandman snickered. Selia took note of his smile, which was charming and not forced. He had even, white teeth and what she could see of his face was relaxed, comfortable with the conversation, and to some degree at least, her.

"No wonder he hates you."

"He's wanted Soren's position for years, even before I came to New Campania." Her smile grew darker. "Not that it will matter after he's lying lifeless in a pool of his own blood."

The Sandman bolted to his feet. He held his hands up in supplication or, perhaps, trying to approach her cautiously. As though she were a danger to herself or others and he was the one trying to talk her down.

"Wait a minute, Selia. I don't mind taking a life when there's no other choice." She raised a brow, and he rolled his eyes. "Do you know how many lives I've actually taken?" He gave a brief pause before answering his own question. "Seven. I've been accused of ten times that many. Mostly I cripple or destroy their livelihoods." He moved closer and grasped her by the shoulders. "Have you ever taken a life before?"

She gave him a pointed look, her eyes cold and hard. "I'm a mage with warrior training from a warring nation. Think about what that means." As realization flashed in his eyes, she continued. "As for Alfi? He goes down and I know how to make it look like it was done by anyone I want. Magic is a wonderful gift, especially in a world where it isn't considered real. I would prefer having your help in making it happen."

"Fine, since you'd no doubt attempt to do this on your own," he grumbled. "You can stay here. The sofa pulls out into a bed. We'll discuss details tomorrow."

A slow smile grew on Selia's face. It was nowhere near warm or benevolent. "Agreed. When this is over, I'll go back to being the quiet little wallflower I was trained to be."

"No, you won't," the Sandman said. "Please stay here, for your own safety."

He drained his glass, pulled the mask back down, and turned away. He headed up a set of stairs she hadn't noticed on the other side of the room. A door opened, then closed and she wondered briefly if he slept with the mask on.

A light-weight afghan lay over the back of the sofa. Tugging it off, her smile softened as she curled up on the sofa, not bothering to pull it out into a bed, and closed her eyes. The sofa was pretty soft and comfortable. The afghan was heavy enough to keep her warm. The morning would come soon enough, and she needed at least one night's peaceful sleep.

Chapter Seven

It was closer to noon when Selia finally woke up. No sunlight greeted her, but she didn't need it to tell the time. The clock on the TV stand did that job just fine and the clock read 11:38 A.M. Probably the longest she'd ever slept in, but that wasn't surprising, considering she'd barely had any sleep in the past forty-eight hours. She felt refreshed, and her magic replenished.

The door opened and she rolled to her feet, gun out and pointed towards the noise, even before she realized what she was doing. It caught her by surprise because she'd never before slept with the weapon, nor did she make it a habit to draw on someone opening a door.

Not that it was surprising, once the past two days-worth of memories caught up with her. She lowered the gun and slipped it back into her holster in time to see the Sandman putting the two bags with the logo of a local café on the coffee table.

"Interesting greeting," he said, not bothered by the fact she drew a weapon against him. "At least you didn't shoot." He glanced at the sofa, the fabric of his mask moving as he chuckled in genuine amusement.

"Always determine your target before firing," she replied automatically. It had been the first lesson a warrior learned, regardless of the weapon you used. She followed his eyes and added, "I don't need a bed to sleep peacefully. Temeria doesn't have the soft luxuries that you enjoy here in New Campania."

"Good rule to live by. I would have thought you'd be more accustomed to the pampered lifestyle of an underboss's daughter," the Sandman replied, setting the bags on the table before pulling out a breakfast sandwich and offering it to her. He wasn't wearing the sunglasses at the moment, or the fedora. "There are a couple of bagels and another sandwich in there. I wasn't sure what you might like. The other bag has some drinks."

Considerate, polite, and dangerous, Selia thought with a smile, *if I'm not careful, I could end up falling for this guy.*

To hide her thoughts, she reached into the bag and pulled out a drink before accepting the sandwich. Unwrapping it, she replied, "Oh, I enjoy the benefits, but I also go camping and hunting whenever possible. When I do, I leave the luxuries behind."

She bit into her sandwich and closed her eyes at the deliciousness that greeted her taste buds. Food was food and she wasn't a picky eater. Though, truth be told, she still preferred fresh food to processed, especially venison. There wasn't anything quite as tasty, at least to her, as a freshly cooked venison steak. She did love a good breakfast sandwich, though. This sandwich was hot and filled with cheese, bacon, ham, and scrambled eggs.

They were real eggs, too. Not the powdered or frozen stuff most places used.

"So, how did you find me last night?" she asked, as he pulled out two bottles of Coke from the other bag.

He glanced at her, and she had the impression he was smiling under his mask. It was something in his eyes. Or the way he looked at her. She couldn't figure it out, and to be honest, she was afraid to try.

He didn't eat, which meant he must have eaten already sans mask. "I'm rather old school. I found Soren's phone and checked the numbers. I then did a quick Google search for the phone number you sent him." He sounded nonchalant as he spoke. Selia guessed he wasn't lying about his method. "I took Soren to the hospital, then came to you."

"How did you find my room?" she asked between bites. She uncapped the cola and took a sip from the bottle.

He laughed softly. "I told them I was meeting my mistress there, that you already had a room, and described you. Tossed in a fifty for a tip and they were more than happy to give me the room number."

"Why am I not surprised?" Selia asked before taking a longer drink from her cola.

"Because you know all too well what people will do for money," he replied.

That was too true. People did everything for money or power, including making deals that often ended up with said people injured or dead. Sometimes they came out on top, but not always. She finished eating in silence, allowing her thoughts to wander where they would. Sometimes it gave her useful ideas, most of the time it just kept her sane. This time, realization dawned on her.

"Al doesn't know where Soren is," she said slowly. "Unless you cleaned up the mess…" She trailed off at the Sandman shaking his head before continuing. "Then that means the Family, at least those not loyal to Alfi, will be looking for Soren and me."

Soren wasn't just an underboss to Angelo 'Al' Lascari, who ran the Lascari syndicate. He was Al's right hand. Selia suspected Soren did more for the syndicate than Al did, but she never voiced it. She was all-too aware there were six underbosses, and then about three times that many captains below them. Each captain had about thirty or so men beneath him. That didn't include the 'mademen' or those who were Italian but weren't anything higher than thugs, cleaners, or who were base members and ran the day-to-day operations.

The pyramid always grew larger the closer you got to the bottom. Because of Soren's position, she knew the basics, even if she didn't know all the intimate details.

Soren's position kept him a step above the other underbosses. Selia figured it was due to his trading with

Temeria and being so close to Al. She didn't ask, and Soren didn't volunteer information.

She suspected Lucien Vaschetti's outfit had a similar pyramid, though with fewer underbosses, and wondered for perhaps the millionth time why they didn't join forces. In fact, according to one of the tales, the Lascaris and Vaschettis had once ruled the city of New Campania together with iron fists.

That is, until Vincent Lascari fell in love with a woman of untold beauty from another city, or land, depending on which version you listened to. Now, if it had just been Vincent who'd fallen head-over-heels for the dame, it wouldn't have been a problem, but Constantine Vaschetti had fallen for the same woman. It had turned into an all-out 'Helen of Troy' battle because the girl picked Vincent over Constantine and that hadn't sat well with Constantine. The war had occurred about twelve generations ago, and though Constantine, Vince, and Laurel were no longer amongst the living, the feud continued.

Selia didn't know if she believed that tale, or the other less interesting story where the two families had settled in the same city and competed with each other throughout the ages. Not that it mattered to her. She had been adopted into the Lascari family, which meant no rubbing elbows with the Vaschettis.

The Sandman pulled out the other bottle, pulled up his balaclava, and sucked down about a third of his drink. Selia watched as he swallowed. Somehow that simple, normal act had her thinking of many intimate ideas. That surprised her and she quickly looked away. Dating hadn't been forbidden, but her fear that someone would learn her secrets had kept her from getting too close to anyone. Not that him learning her secrets was an issue since she'd just told him almost all of them.

"So?" he finally asked, tightening the cap on his soda. "That just means you'll have to avoid them." Setting down his soda, he fitted his mask back into place.

"I'm not avoiding my Family," she muttered. "That will simply ramp up their search for Soren, which I won't allow."

"*You* won't allow it?" he asked, drawing it out.

Suddenly the room felt a few degrees colder to Selia. "No, *I* won't allow it. I know where Al lives, I know where he keeps his mistresses, and I even know where his secret stash of moonshine is kept. I spent the first three years of my life here learning about this city. I spent the following three years learning everything I could about the Dueling Dynasties thinking it would keep me safe. In many ways, it did. Now, it will help keep Soren safe."

"Dueling Dynasties," the Sandman said with a chuckle. "Nice. I'll have to remember that one. How do you know they didn't let you follow them?"

"When I don't want to be seen, I'm not," Selia said with a deadly softness in her voice. "I trained from an early age to hunt and kill. Not just animals, but people. I learned in the jungles, the villages… even the castle. Anywhere an assassin could enter, or battle could and would be fought, I learned in those places. Not just with weapons, but with magic also. Day or night, it didn't matter. Assassins don't care when they attack, as long as they think they can succeed."

He studied her for a few long minutes and Selia guessed he was at a loss for words. Finally, he reached over and ran a once-again gloved hand over her hair. "Your hair's a mess. Looks like a bird's nest. Want to freshen up?"

"You have a shower here in your secret lair?" she asked, her eyes lighting up with delight and mischief. "I could totally use a hot shower." He gave a soft groan and she grinned that much more. "Well, I hate being all sweaty for no good reason."

"Yes, there's a shower," he replied, his eyes darting away from her. "I'll show you where it is. You have a change of clothes?"

"Hoping I'll say no and be forced into wearing nothing by a bath towel?" she quipped.

Nudity wasn't a problem for her, though she had quickly learned upon arriving in New Campania that people here were embarrassed by a nude body. Something she'd found highly amusing.

When he didn't answer immediately, she let him off the hook. "I have a change of clothes and my dojo uniform, so no worries about me walking around in nothing but my skin."

Selia had no clue why she'd said any of that, but she couldn't take it back now. Her cheeks burned and a girlish smile played on her lips. She'd never been able to really flirt in high school or with any of the Family members. She'd had to dance around her words and be careful of what she said around anyone else she'd dated, also. Trying to hide one's self in the throes of passion wasn't easy.

This was different, though. This time, she didn't need to fear someone finding out her secrets and using them against her. It felt refreshing being able to tease and flirt with him without having to worry. Not that she expected anything to come of it. She was a part of the criminal organization he fought. No way would he be interested in her for anything more than a possible one-night stand.

"I was asking to see if I needed to provide you with clothes," he answered with an unmistakable laugh in his voice. "I would not object to you walking about sans clothing, but it's not a requirement."

"So does that mean I don't need to question your intentions?" she shot back playfully. "Where's the fun in that?"

"Question them all you want. I like to keep people guessing."

Selia laughed. It felt good to laugh after everything that had happened. "Perhaps I should, just to see what you would do."

"Well, unfortunately I wouldn't be able to enjoy the view for long," he said with a sigh. "I do have work to get to, and sleep, eventually."

"Pity," she teased. "Guess that means I'll have to go break into Al's house and talk to him without anyone else finding out where I am. I doubt he'll believe me about Alfi, but at least I can keep him away from Soren. I hope." She paused, and then became serious. "Or I could help you with your work. Doubt I could be much help for the sleep, though."

She thought a wicked little twinkle crept into the Sandman's eyes at that last part. He cleared his throat before saying, "I would welcome the help in gathering more information before either you or I move against anyone."

"All right," she agreed cheerfully. "Shower, torture you," she dropped a wink and bobbed her brows continuing, "then I'll visit Al and come back in time to help you gather information before we go to bed."

So, she probably could have worded that last part a little differently, but she was thoroughly enjoying the banter. Not like she'd ever get to do it with anyone else without worrying about serious repercussions.

Standing, she smiled serenely at the Sandman, hands clasped in front of her as she watched him with an innocent, wide-eyed, angelic expression. That twinkle reappeared in his eyes for a brief heartbeat as he stood, laughing softly. She leaned over and grabbed her duffle bag from beside her on the floor before turning back, still the picture of exaggerated innocence. The Sandman shook his head and chuckled.

"Come on, the bathroom with the shower is upstairs," he said, draping an arm around her shoulders and walking with her up the stairs.

Chapter Eight

The bathroom was huge, not quite as large as her old one with Soren, but it was still big. A claw foot tub sat in the corner; a white shower curtain hung around it like sheer veils surrounding a sultan's bed. The shower fixture shone, as though it were polished daily. Along one wall was a vanity and double sinks, cabinets on each side of the mirror that stretched nearly the entire length of the counter. The toilet was tucked away in a little hole to the side, probably to hide it and put the tub into focus.

Wicker shelving units were nestled in each corner to the right and left of the tub. The shelf to the left, farthest from the shower head, was filled with white and black towels. The one to the right was filled with a wide variety of shampoos, conditioners, and soaps. Small bottles and containers sat on a lower shelf, just barely in sight.

Stripping, Selia padded towards the sink, removing the pins from her hair as she stared at her reflection. A wry chuckle broke free as she surveyed the black smudges beneath her eyes and the hair that had pulled free from the pins. Her brown eyes were tired and there was an imprint of the holster on her shoulders and chest.

How the Sandman could possibly have been aroused despite her unkempt hair and black-smudged tired eyes, she didn't know. Of course, she wasn't entirely certain what did arouse a man's interest outside a scantily clad woman.

She had the typical Amazonian's figure: Firm, perky, full breasts, a narrow waist, and a firm derrière. Her legs were long and lean and though she had plenty of strength in her arms, it wasn't obvious. Soren had loved letting her dress up for his parties, and it had helped raise her self-esteem and grow into a confident woman.

Massaging her head with her left hand, her nearly waist-length dark brown hair falling around her in messy waves, she opened one of the cabinet doors with her right hand. Inside were toothbrushes, toothpaste, brushes, and combs. All were on their own shelf in neat rows. Was there anything this man didn't think of? She wondered as she grabbed a brush and began running it through her hair.

Tangles out, she turned to the tub, a broad grin on her face. A pity there wasn't time for a good long soak, she thought, as she stepped into the tub and turned on the faucets. Ah, well, maybe she'd have enough time later.

Thirty minutes later, she stepped from the bathroom, wearing a black blouse, black jeans, carrying shoes in one hand, and her duffle in the other. Her hair was pulled back into a braided ponytail, still a little damp.

The main floor was broken into several rooms, she discovered. The door to the basement was in the central hall. The bathroom was to the immediate left of that door. There was a door to the right, another halfway down the hallway, and immediately opposite the basement door was a small foyer. She wasn't sure what else the house held, but good manners said to not ask. That didn't mean she wouldn't explore the house, given the opportunity.

The Sandman had disappeared, and she couldn't hear him anywhere. Since she needed to find him, she went to the door opposite the bathroom and tried the knob. It opened to reveal a large gym.

It had been two rooms, she decided, from the arched supports in the center that had probably, at one point, been part of a wall. The gym had everything imaginable. She spotted equipment used for weight training and strengthening, a punching bag, and even a large, thick mat that reminded her of the ones at the dojos she'd gone to as a teen.

Reluctantly, she shut the door and padded down the hallway. She was about to try the second door when she heard a noise. Following the sound, she found a small office behind the open door. Bookshelves filled with books of all sorts lined the walls. There were a few tables, a couple chairs and lamps. The room was interesting, but what drew her attention was the Sandman, hunched over a computer screen.

"Anything interesting?" she asked, setting her duffle bag on one of the chairs. "I thought I'd find you before leaving to talk to Al."

"Yeah, that one actress that slept around on her last movie set is getting booted to the curb by her production company," he replied dryly.

She snickered. "Guess the film industry doesn't approve of that kind of thing, or at least not when it becomes public knowledge."

"My guess is that if they really wanted to keep her, they would." He scratched at his chin under the mask. "Other than that, no companies have suddenly folded, had wild swings in their stock, or lost any senior members. Also, the camera I've got planted outside of Big Al's house hasn't shown any visits from Alfi, or anyone else that would raise concern."

"He's at his penthouse?" she asked, pulling a pair of pumps from her duffle bag, and stepping into them.

"He's obviously not at his mansion. Not enough traffic or guards. For a cautious man, he never thinks to make it look more like he's at two places at once." The Sandman sat back and stretched. "My contacts at his penthouse have him receiving no guests for the past twelve hours. No phone calls from his landline. No clue about his cell phone since they're harder to tap. He's had three orders from room service. Last one was an hour ago, and the big guy was just fine then."

"Oh, good," Selia replied, her voice low and cool. "That will make getting in to see him easy."

"Getting into his penthouse won't be difficult, but it will require a change of clothing." He glanced back at her, looking her up and down. "You're a size six, aren't you?"

"Good guess," she replied, curious as to where this was leading. "You keep dresses of all sizes around for the women you rescue?"

"Nah, figured I'd buy you one. Want to keep the blond wig for the night?" he replied casually.

She laughed. "Well, considering how stocked the bathroom was, I had to wonder!" She added with a grin, "Only if you think I should."

"Well, I think it would be easier to get into the penthouse as the evening's entertainment and her charming handler, rather than punch or shoot our way in." He glanced at her with mischievous eyes. "As long as that doesn't rub your warrior woman ways wrong."

Selia shook her head, her smile not fading. "Nope, I think it could be fun. Though I will ask that you let me chat with Al alone, I'd rather not have to use my magic on him. But if I do, I don't want to chance you getting hit, also." She paused before clarifying. "Glamour, not fireball. Al's related to Soren, so hopefully I won't have to do anything other than talk him into not looking for Soren for a week or so."

"You presume that Soren didn't call his first cousin on his father's side shortly after you pulled your 'laying on of hands' hocus pocus on him."

"Yup, that's what he is," she replied easily. Just how much did this man know about her and her family? "He might have, but I'd rather know for certain. Besides, Al might have some knowledge that I can use."

It didn't hurt that Al treated her as a beloved niece. He had hosted parties for her, gave her birthday cards, presents, and had even gone to her graduation. They had never been super close, but neither had he ignored her.

"That's fine by me." The Sandman stood up and clicked his computer's mouse a few times. "I need to get out of this mask anyway. It's starting to itch. Let me make some calls to have the clothes delivered, and I'll take a shower. Then we can prep and suit up."

"Oh, so I get to see you sans mask?" She purred, her eyes twinkling and an impish smile curving her lips. "Unless you have make-up around here, you might want to add that to the shopping list."

"Unless you are allergic to the top brands in the business, I think I have you covered." He paused. "Pardon the pun."

He walked past her, opening a section of wall that she hadn't noticed as a closet. It revealed a large, old movie-style makeup table and chair, along with racks and racks of high-end cosmetics and facial prosthetics. There were small shelves with wigs as well.

"Try not to play too much while I'm gone, okay?" he teased as he pulled a cell phone out of his pocket and made his way out of the room.

"I think I'm in love," she said with a sigh, sitting on the stool.

She turned to ask him what color dress he was ordering but found only an empty room. Smiling, she began looking through the cosmetics: So many options, so little time. The man was an enigma and one she was growing attached to. Probably not the best idea around, but she hadn't always been known to be the good girl and do what was best. If she had, she'd still be on Temeria and an adviser to the queen and the princesses.

Of course, she wouldn't know what true affection was or learned the truth about a great many things, including what her people were really like. After all, until she'd had a long discussion with Soren, she'd have never known the rulers of Temeria dealt in human trafficking. It was a disturbing fact to learn.

She tucked her braid beneath her blouse and pulled on a bright red wig, tucking her dark brown strands beneath the edge of the hairnet. She studied her reflection and smiled. Red looked good on her, but she needed to do something about the dark circles under her eyes.

A doorbell rang sometime later, startling Selia. She glanced at the computer's old-style LED clock display screensaver and was surprised an hour had passed. She had applied foundation, hidden smudges, and finished her basic makeup routine before starting to explore the drawers and their contents. Selia was waiting to see what color and style of dress the Sandman was bringing her so she could match eye shadow and lipstick to it.

A door opened and conversation exchanged in muted voices. The door closed again sometime later. A minute after that, a man in a very expensive charcoal gray three-piece Armani suit walked into the room, carrying a silk garment bag. His hair was spiked blonde, his handsome face was covered with stubble a week away from a razor, and rimless glasses covered very dark green eyes. There was a mole just above the stubble on his right cheek. He smiled at her.

"Well, red does suit you." The Sandman, it couldn't be anyone else, had changed the pitch of his voice. It was higher, more energetic, and upbeat, almost laughing. Selia felt like she was about to be sold a large piece of real estate. "Good thing I bought a red party dress and matching heels, eh?"

Somehow, Selia managed to keep her mouth from dropping. She blinked a few times, trying to get her pulse to stop racing. Damn. He was appealing in the black outfit and mask, but he was downright gorgeous in the suit. Perhaps this was part of the reason Soren had warned her to not trust him?

"Um," she said, swallowing. "I... I'm glad you, uh, think so." Geez, she sounded like a high school teen who'd just met her celebrity crush. This was the Sandman. The same damn man she'd been teasing not long ago. That realization helped her. At least to the point of being able to talk. It did nothing for her racing heart and growing desires, though.

Great time for the libido to kick into overdrive, she thought. "Guess it's a good thing you did. Will I need help getting into it?"

He laughed, and when he spoke again, the voice was the Sandman, not some celebrity talk show host combined with a top salesman.

"I will be in the next room if the dress proves to be more than your considerable skills can undoubtedly handle. Before you start getting ideas: no, this isn't what I normally look like."

He dropped her a wink, handed her the garment bag, and stepped out. The door closed behind him.

"Oh, damn," she breathed. "If he looks that good like that..." She fanned herself with one hand before turning her attention to the dress. No man should look that handsome.

The dress was a strappy affair with a zipper back and straps that crisscrossed over the shoulders. The silk was smooth as water against her skin as she stepped into it. It had a gorgeous deep v-cut bodice, and with the built-in bra, there was no need for one. She zipped up the back to her waist and stepped into the heels.

Not quite twenty minutes later, she'd finished her make-up and double-checked the wig that she had redone while awaiting the gown. She studied herself in the mirror, making sure the floor length gown fell properly around her. She shifted it slightly and took a few steps back, pleased with the sexy show of her left leg as she moved.

Walking to the door, she opened it and posed in the frame. Jutting her left hip out just enough for her hand to fall onto it, she raised her right slightly above her, so her forearm rested against the frame.

"So? What do you think?" she asked in a soft, husky voice as she fluttered her lashes at him.

"I think you look stunning," he responded in a voice that was somewhere between the Sandman and the salesman. "I know I am sorry I didn't meet you under different circumstances."

"Thanks. I have to admit, I feel the same," she murmured, dropping the exaggerated pose. She reached out a hand and brushed his cheek ever so lightly. "Guess this isn't the time for ideas, huh?"

"No. Unfortunately, now is the time to go over weapons and tactics," he said with a sad smirk. He kissed her fingers and then placed a small cylinder in her other hand. It was fastened into a Velcro strap.

"Flash bomb. It's smaller than the ones you see in the movies, and the range is little better than six feet. But it's effective. Or would you prefer a compact .45 and a thigh holster?"

"Oh, a thigh holster?" she asked in a soft, purring voice. "That could be fun." She smiled shyly, adding, "I used to have a knife that I always kept on my thigh, at least until I came here. I've so missed the feeling of having something lethal attached to my leg."

The Sandman chuckled. He held up a small, hammerless .45 semiautomatic pistol cradled in a nylon thigh holster. The holster, like the gun and grenade rig, was black.

"It's got a six-round clip and there's one in the chamber already. Double action trigger set up. About a six-ounce pull. Good enough? Or would you like a little bit of time on the range with it, first?"

"I wouldn't mind outshooting you on the range," she teased, taking the thigh holster, and walking away towards one of the chairs in the room. She spoke over her shoulder as she propped up her left leg and slid the holster on. "But it's not needed. Soren let me try any weapon I wanted, and I do so love something that fits easily in a purse. Plus, it was fun seeing his reactions on occasion."

Chapter Nine

They took a cab to one of the high-priced, four-star hotels in the city. The entrance was somewhere between opulent and dull. A black eave covered the entire front of the hotel and a walkway the width of a car in front of the main doors. A pair of doormen dressed in black and gray uniforms stood to each side of the doors.

Selia might have been a part of one of the city's founding crime families, but that didn't mean she stayed in four- or five-star hotels on a frequent basis. So having someone open her door caught her a little off guard. Not that she let it show. Pasting a smile on her face, she barely glanced at the man, though she had no doubt he enjoyed the view of her low-cut, cleavage-revealing gown.

The Sandman met her on the sidewalk, not bothering with scooting across the seat. He nodded to the uniformed man and handed him a fifty with a smile. The doorman took the hint and returned to his post with a wink and nod. Selia flashed the Sandman an amused smile.

Together, they stepped into the opulent foyer of the Grand Hotel. A simple, yet exceedingly apt name, Selia decided. A wide staircase with lush, thick gray carpet and black banisters rose to a landing, where on each side, sweeping, curved flights of stairs led to the floor above them. Several chandeliers hung from the ceiling and there was an opulence that would have ensnared any newcomer.

Selia, however, didn't allow herself to stare. She did take it all in, silently admiring the beauty of it all as the Sandman led her to a pair of double doors off to the side. 'Sal's Place' was written in script across the glass window and Selia smiled slightly. It was one of Soren's personal businesses and no Family members were hired here.

They sat at the bar on high, leather-covered bar stools and ordered drinks. She sipped through a straw, careful of her lipstick, even though she'd brought the tube for touch-ups. The other reason she didn't drink much was she didn't want to have to visit the restroom while waiting. Too many things could go wrong, and she didn't want to take a chance.

She and the Sandman sat in silence for about twenty minutes before he got up, tossed a twenty on the counter, and offered her his arm. Shrugging minutely, she slid her arm through his, resting her hand lightly on his wrist. He escorted her to the main doors, where the doormen opened them without missing a beat or the Sandman having to pause in his steps.

Outside was a black stretch-limo. The chauffeur standing in his signature black uniform and cap held the door open. Limos were something Selia was accustomed to, so she stepped in and slid across the seat. The Sandman slid in beside her and she smiled at him, not saying a word. The door closed and she scooted closer to him.

Selia had to admit to herself, there were plenty of ideas that came to mind, if circumstances had been different. There were many ways of enjoying a ride around the city in a limo with a handsome man. Her smile and sidelong gaze must have given away her thoughts because that mischievous twinkle reappeared in the Sandman's eyes and he smirked at her, draping an arm around her shoulders, and pulling her closer.

Inhaling deeply, she forced herself to turn her gaze away from him, and instead looked out the window as they passed through the city. Part of her wondered how this man could afford all this. Limos weren't cheap, nor were the clothes she wore or the makeup at his lair. The rest of her wondered what he really looked like. It had been way too long since she had been attracted to anyone and her body was making up for missed time.

In an attempt to distract herself, she searched the sidewalks and road for Family members, both Lascari and Vaschetti. Though, if she were honest, she didn't know as many Vaschetti members as she did Lascari.

Sure, she knew those in charge of each layer of the hierarchy in the Vaschetti Family, but she didn't know every made man or enforcer. There were far too many involved in the day-to-day businesses for Selia to memorize. She knew the captains by description only and had seen the underbosses only a handful of times. Lucien, she had met once and once had been more than enough for her. The man was downright creepy.

Of course, even in her Family, she only knew all the underbosses, Al's advisor, a couple captains, and the two main enforcers. She knew the bodyguards the underbosses and captains used, and all the secretaries and assistants that came with them to the monthly meetings. The only place she knew everyone on a more personal basis was Soren's office where she worked.

She'd managed to spot a dozen people she knew from the Lascari family and two from the Vaschettis when the limo stopped outside a brick building that rose high into the sky. Far above them was Al's penthouse.

A doorman opened the limo's door and the Sandman slid out, offering his hand to her. She took it as she stepped onto the sidewalk, small red purse in hand. Not giving the doorman a second glance, she let the Sandman lead her into the building; a king with his queen. Or to be more accurate to the roles they were playing: a pimp and his woman. Inside there were a handful more of Al's people, keeping a watch on who entered and exited.

They received a few glances, or rather she did, but no one stopped them. They weren't even stopped when they went past the reception desk and strode straight for the elevator to the penthouse. The Sandman reached into a pocket and produced what looked like a credit card and Selia nearly laughed. Somehow, he had managed to procure the pass card for the penthouse elevator! No wonder he said it would be easy!

Resisting the urge to shake her head, she instead gave him a bright smile and stepped into the elevator next to him, a genuine smile on her lips. The door closed and she let out a soft laugh.

"That explains much," she murmured softly, barely a whisper.

"Indeed," he replied in an equally soft voice.

They remained silent as the elevator finished the climb and opened into a small foyer of the penthouse. The foyer opened into short hallway, which led into the main living room with a gorgeous view of the city. She took note of the emergency exit to her right, in case she had need of it later.

The last time Selia had been to this penthouse, she'd been with Soren. She had gone to the floor-to-ceiling windows and stared at the view of the city below them. Considering they were on the ninetieth floor, the penthouse held a pretty spectacular view. This time, Selia studied the man standing at the windows staring out across the city. One hand was in a pocket of his dress pants while the other held a whiskey tumbler.

She held the Sandman back against the other side of the door frame while she gathered her courage together. Angelo Lascari was a broad-shouldered, finely dressed man with classic Italian features, though those features weren't looking at her now. His hair was as black as a raven's wing and cut in a neat, timeless fashion. She suspected he dyed it, but she'd never asked anyone, nor spoken that suspicion aloud. Close to six-feet tall, her uncle cut a striking figure.

Letting out a breath of air, she stepped into the room and into the sight of Al's pair of bodyguards. The living room was lavish, with plush sofas, chairs, glass tables and a baby grand tucked away in a corner. A huge fireplace was against the left wall surrounded by sofas and a coffee table, while there was a wide-screen TV, larger than her sixty-two-inch at her apartment, on the right wall. She ignored all of the luxury, focusing solely on Al.

"Stop right there," one bodyguard said, and Selia didn't have to look to know he'd drawn his gun.

Selia stopped and felt the Sandman pause directly behind her. In that bright, smooth salesman pitch, the Sandman said, "Hey, man, I'm just here with the pretty lady."

Al turned around, his eyes narrowing. "What the hell is this?"

His voice, typically a low dulcet that could make nuns swoon and coax even the hardest person into agreeing with him, was now hard and cold. It was enough to make Selia shiver as though an ice storm had swept across the room. His dark eyes glared at Selia and her 'date'.

Al's voice dropped a few degrees more as he crossed the room. "I didn't order this."

Selia stood her ground, neither turning towards the goons or the Sandman, nor cowering before the don looming in front of her. Instead, she lifted her chin ever so slightly and allowed her Temerian accent to come out as she spoke in fluent Italian.

"Would you turn away the daughter of the night?"

The soft lilting accent of Temeria and the Italian language made for a strange combination. She willingly took the chance, and it must have worked because Al's demeanor swiftly changed and instead of glowering at her, he was examining every feature of her face with a hard intentness. She offered a smile with only the corners of her lips as she met his cold, black eyes.

"I know that face. You're not usually dolled up this much, but I recognize your face," he finally said, taking a step back. Selia could hear the men lowering their weapons, though they didn't put them away. "I liked you better as a brunette." It was all Selia could do to keep from rolling her eyes. She was saved from embarrassing herself by Al speaking again. "Who's your friend?"

"Oh, him?" She finally glanced over her shoulder at the Sandman who had his hands up, even with his face and palms outward. "Some actor I hired from a talent agency specializing in celebrity lookalikes. I don't know who he's supposed to be, but he was cute and got me past the girl downstairs. Batted his pretty green eyes at her and she didn't ask a question." She grinned and turned back to Al. "He's a cheap date and easy on the eyes."

Al snorted and waved away the guns. The goons slid their weapons into their holsters grudgingly. The Sandman slowly lowered his hands and shoved them into his pockets. He was the very epitome of a man obviously out of his element and fearful of having guns pointed at him.

"I'll have to speak with that girl, and the boys who let you by. It shouldn't be that easy for anyone to get up here," Al grumbled. He pulled Selia forward, draped an arm around her shoulders, and started walking her towards the hallway to their left. "Come along, dear, and we'll talk in private." He paused before adding, "Your 'date' will be safe as long as he doesn't leave the room or bother anything."

Selia smiled up at her uncle, showing the relief she felt.

"Thank you," she murmured as he led her down a hallway and into the master bedroom.

Once the door was shut, she dropped all pretenses and her forced-upon smile. Before she could say a word, though, Al pulled her into his arms, hugging her tightly. Surprised, stunned, and delighted, she returned the embrace. Selia hadn't even noticed him putting down his glass. Missing things like that could kill her, but at least it had been with someone she sort of trusted.

"Child, you worry Soren, which worries me," he finally said, breaking the hold. He held her at arm's length. "Soren called me and told me you took him to the hospital. That's fast thinking for a dame. It's more than what most women could or would do."

He gave her arms a squeeze before walking away from her and opening up a briefcase. Pulling out a stack of money, he turned back to her. "Use this for whatever you need."

She took the stack, only to discover it was three thick stacks held together by a rubber band. Looking up, she found Al holding out a small wallet. She took it and flipped it open. Inside it was a gas card, another fake id, and his business card. Sitting on the edge of the queen-sized bed, she tucked the money and wallet into her purse. A phone fell into it as she moved her hands, ready to snap it shut.

Looking up, she found Al towering above her. "Use that phone. It's a burner so it'll be safer than your cell. Soren has that number, if he needs to contact you. I'll let him know you're safe." He held out a small white business card with only an address on it, a set of car keys, and another set of keys that looked distinctly like house keys. "There's a rental car waiting for you. Go to this address. It's a bungalow outside town. The place is a safe house and is fully stocked with food. Stay there and keep low."

"All right, Uncle," Selia said slowly as she stood and took the proffered items. She asked hesitantly, "Soren will be okay?"

A small smile played across Al's face and his eyes softened. "He'll be fine. The doctors thought he had a broken jaw, but the x-rays were obviously wrong. It took a while, but he finally started responding to the medications and is in better shape than they expected, considering the short amount of time he's been there." Amusement filled his features, making him look about ten years younger and far more approachable. "You wouldn't know anything about that, would you?"

"Me, Uncle? What could I have done?" she asked innocently.

Other than Soren and the Sandman, Al was the only other person who knew her heritage, though he wasn't aware of her magical abilities.

Al chuckled and patted her on the cheek. "Keep your secrets close, girl, but keep your enemies closer."

It was an old saying and she knew Al approved of what she'd done. He and Soren were close and there was no threat of Soren ever trying to usurp Al's position. In fact,

Soren had countered several attempted coups in the past. A few had been ones she'd learned about and had informed Soren about. She didn't know how much Soren had told Al, but it was enough for Al to want to take care of her. There just was no way she'd ever tell Al as much as she'd told Soren, or even the Sandman.

"I'll be safe," Selia assured him. "I promise."

"Yeah, you will be," Al said, opening the door for her. "Don't play around with that toy of yours. The sooner you get to that place, the better."

"Yes, Uncle," she murmured, trying to not smile and failing only a little.

Al led her back to the living room, where the Sandman was sitting in a chair, hunched forward, hands clasped in the perfect example of a nervous man. He leapt to his feet the moment he saw her enter the room.

"Time to be going, John," Selia said smoothly, coming up with a fake name for her companion. She kissed Al on both his cheeks, and Al chuckled softly.

John, aka The Sandman, nodded quickly and met her at the doorway to the elevator. Al followed them. Selia and the Sandman remained silent, though Selia was smiling whereas the Sandman was not, as they stepped into the elevator.

Al gave her a final nod as he leaned in and hit the ground floor button. The doors closed and the elevator began its descent. Selia gave a subtle wave of her hand

and magic filled the elevator around them. A simple glamour for her to do what she needed quickly without fear of a camera recording her.

"Al gave me a rental car, phone, and cash along with the keys to a bungalow on the outside of the city. I'm to stay there and keep low. He also told me to keep out of this business."

She didn't take too much time to repeat everything Al said. The Sandman only needed the basics since he already knew about Soren. Pulling out the money, she tugged one thick stack of cash free from the rubber band and handed it to the Sandman, who was staring at her with a deep frown on his face.

"Don't worry, I glamoured us so the camera won't see or hear anything, but it won't last long," she assured him. "I need you to get me more clothes. You have good taste and know what looks good on me. I trust you."

"You shouldn't use your magic, Selia," the Sandman chided her.

"And if they're watching us? Do you think either of us would get out of this building alive?" she argued. "Keep whatever is left over."

"Fair enough," he replied, taking the stack and sliding it into the inside pocket of his jacket. "I won't mind spending blood money on a beautiful woman."

Selia felt her cheeks growing warm, even as the magic faded away and the elevator doors opened. Together they walked to the small parking lot to the side of the building. She paused in front of the car listed on the key fob Al had given her.

"A shame about the bungalow." She sighed. "Talk about a waste of money."

The Sandman placed a hand over hers, which was turning the key in the lock. "No, you have to show up there. They'll be watching you, and if you don't show up, one of two things will happen. Al will start a full-blown search for you. Or you'll be declared 'rogue'. Or possibly even both. I don't want to see you getting hurt or being on the outs with your family."

Selia smiled and leaned towards the Sandman. "Fine, I'll go to the bungalow, but I'm not staying there." She paused. "Keep my laptop safe."

"I'll pick you up an hour after darkness sets," he assured her. "Your bag will be safe."

An impish twinkle brightened her eyes as she leaned forward and kissed him. It wasn't a chaste, quick peck on the lips, either. The Sandman stiffened slightly in surprise before relaxing and returning the kiss, though he didn't lean into it. She felt his left hand lightly grasp her hip, even as she stepped closer, allowing the kiss to deepen.

Oh, gods, did she want more!

The thought snapped her eyes open and she slowly, reluctantly, broke the kiss. Her heart was pounding, and her pulse raced. She stared at him, lips parted, slightly swollen, and curved upwards into a soft smile. Blinking a few times, she finally lowered her lashes as she saw more than just mild interest shining back at her. He desired her, if that flicker of heat was any indication, and she definitely desired him, but this was not the time or place.

"I, um, guess I should be going," she finally said, trying to wrestle control of her floundering emotions. Inborn caution and wariness warred with desire, and so far, the desire was winning the battle. In a whisper, she added, "I'll see you tonight."

"Indeed, lady," he murmured, opening the door for her. "Hopefully, if he," his eyes shot upwards towards the penthouse, "catches wind of that kiss, he won't place extra guards on you."

Selia shook her head, the smile not wavering. "Don't worry about me, 'John.' I have a good reputation of not having lovers or boyfriends. At least, none that stick around for more than a date and goodbye kiss." Her face flushed at that acknowledgement of her inexperience, and she ducked into the car as the Sandman chuckled softly above her.

"Drive safe," he said. Just before the door shut, he added in a smoldering voice that had her breath quickening again, "You don't have to be dressed when I get there."

Chapter Ten

Her breathing had finally begun to quiet as she listened to the turn-by-turn instructions on the GPS in the car when the phone Al gave her rang. The destination had been an hour and a half away and she still had thirty-five minutes to go.

Glancing at the number, she breathed a sigh of relief. "Hello, Uncle."

"I hope you didn't give him the address," he said without preamble. "I'd hate for anything to happen to him."

"Oh, please, Uncle," Selia snapped. "I'm not that naïve. Everyone knows I don't have any boyfriends and you do not want to know how long it's been since I've kissed a guy. He was cute and I wanted a good memory after everything that's been happening."

Al did not need to know just how deeply that kiss had affected her. In fact, it was probably better he not know.

"Actually, I do know," Al said, drawing out each word in his usual dulcet voice. "You're still a child, so I'll ignore your *faux pas*."

How generous, Selia thought, *and not creepy at all.*

Al continued. "I spoke to Soren, to let him know you were safe. He's staying where he is and is glad to hear you're out of harm's way."

She could picture Al blowing out the smoke from his cigar as he spoke to her. The man loved his cigars. He wanted something, though. He hadn't called just to make a threat against her 'date'. Her uncle didn't make threats. He carried them out without bothering to speak to them.

Selia asked, not bothering with the typical games that were expected from the 'weaker sex'. "Is there something you want, Uncle?"

There was a long pause. Selia kept quiet, waiting for Al to speak. When he did, it was in a tone she had never heard him use before. It was flat, stark, and cautious.

"Do you know what Alfi had on that drive?"

"No," she replied uneasily. "The email was from Soren, so it never crossed my mind to look at it. Plus, I didn't have time to check it out, even if I wanted to."

There was another unusually long pause before he grumbled too low for her to understand him. "Don't worry about Alfi, Selia. I'll handle it. You need… you *have* to keep low."

Well, that's unexpected. I can understand him wanting me to stay low, but why is it suddenly imperative I do so? she thought, taking the road that led to the bungalow far on the outskirts of town.

"I'll keep low," Selia promised.

She wasn't about to promise to stay out of it, though. Honor demanded she kill the bastard that had hurt, nearly killed, the man she considered a father. If she'd been a male, it would have been her duty as a part of the Family. That was okay, though; since no one would believe a woman would step into a Family problem and eliminate the threat.

"You do that. How far out are you?" Al asked, changing topics, and sounding more like his usual self.

"Twenty or so minutes," she said, glancing at the Garmin.

"Good. There are some clothes there for you," Al replied. "I'll be in touch."

Then there was silence. The man didn't believe in farewells of any sort, unless it included a shot to the back of the head. Those were always pretty good, if not permanent, farewells. She tossed the phone onto the passenger seat and drove the rest of the way in silence.

Turning into the paved driveway, she followed the snaking road until it ended in front of a bungalow. It reminded her more of a homey cabin than something Angelo Lascari would own, but considering he wanted her to keep low, it made sense. She hopped out of the car and grabbed the keys, her purse, and phone. She climbed the four steps and unlocked the door.

The house was nothing to write home about. A small kitchen, complete with stove and fridge was to her immediate right. A kitchen table and four chairs were in front of the sink. She dropped her stuff on the table and locked the door behind her. To her left was a small living room with a TV, DVD player, two sofas and a long, wooden coffee table. Small end tables were shoved up against each end of the sofas.

The bathroom was a decent size. It featured a toilet, sink, and a jetted tub in the left corner that she knew she'd be putting to good use later. There was a shower stall tucked away in the corner opposite the tub. Oh, the hardships she had to endure.

Grinning, she turned to the door on the side of the living room. That door opened into a bedroom, as did the door on the other side of the bathroom. Both had the same, boring pastel curtains and quilted bedspreads. Each had a single dresser, closet, and armchair. A television was in the one nearest to the kitchen and she decided to make it her bedroom.

Opening the closet in that room, she discovered that someone else must have felt the same, because it was filled with dresses and blouses that were in her size. Narrowing her eyes, she examined the dresser and found shirts, socks, and jeans. There was even plenty of lingerie for her.

Selia really didn't want to know who had bought everything. Having some stranger buying her wardrobe was a bit too creepy, in her opinion. She didn't call the Sandman a stranger, considering he had saved her twice and knew her history. Closing the blinds and pulling the curtains shut in every room, she adjusted the thermostat, so it was a bit warmer and returned to the bedroom. Grabbing a pair of black, stretchy jeans, a snug black blouse, and matching lingerie that was far lacier and more expensive than what she owned, she headed for the bathroom.

The first thing on her to-do list was get rid of the makeup. She began scrubbing it off, thankful for the fully stocked cabinets. Free of all the makeup she'd piled on, she turned on the tub's faucets and began undressing as the mirror started steaming up. By the time she'd removed all the pins from her hair, the jets were bubbling, and the tub was full. Turning the water off, she sunk into the hot steamy water and closed her eyes.

As the jets pulsed, she allowed her mind to focus on her last conversation with Al. There was something more going on than what she'd first thought. It wasn't usernames, passwords, or anything minor that Alfi had placed on that drive. It was something that had even Al concerned. Obviously, Soren hadn't told Al she'd kept a copy of it. Why would it matter if she knew what it was? Would it make her a threat if she knew?

There were too many questions, and she didn't like not having answers. She needed to look at the data before going after Alfi. She would have to do that after the Sandman picked her up… in way too many hours from now. A smile on her face, she finally allowed the jets to relax her enough to fall into a light doze. Her last thought was of waiting for her unexpected savior in nothing but her bare skin and wondering what his reaction would be.

Chapter Eleven

Darkness fell at 6:45 p.m. Selia had been restless long before an hour lapsed. Hating the stagnant air inside, she stepped onto the back porch, her dark hair falling around her shoulders in soft waves as she stood in the shadows. The air was crisp and fresh. She pulled the long, black silk robe tighter around her as she inhaled deeply.

The smell of pines, dirt, and blossoms filled her lungs. She held it for several long heartbeats before slowly letting it out. The soft rustle of an owl's wings came to her over the breeze, along with the scuttling of small rodents and other nocturnal animals milling about the small forest line that meshed against the backyard of the bungalow.

The snap of a twig breaking caused her eyes to pop open and her head jerked towards the sound, but nothing was there. A hand fell upon her side, and she jumped, prepared to break away from her would-be captor, only to find the Sandman smiling at her from beneath his now-familiar mask.

"About time you showed up," she teased. "How did you manage that snap?"

He held up a small remote. "It's a squib. The kind used for gunshots in movies. I attached the small explosive to a fallen branch and detonated it with this remote." He glanced down at her body. "Planning on heading back to the city in that?"

"Nice trick," she complimented him. She gave him a soft, pouty expression, as she sighed. "Oh, I thought you wanted me to wait for you sans clothing."

He said nothing, opting to open the door instead and slip inside.

Chuckling, she felt a little guilty at her mischievousness, knowing full well nothing could come of her feelings toward him. She slid the robe off after following him inside.

"I'm sorry. I didn't have the heart to torture you by standing here in my bare skin. Not when I know..." She swallowed hard, looking away from him. "I know nothing could happen between us."

Gods, it hurt saying that and for some reason, more than it should have. What was going on with her?

"It's fine," the Sandman said in a relaxed tone. "It's probably better that I'm not distracted while driving. You can be very distracting, after all. No doubt more so... when you aren't hiding."

She blushed deeply and looked back at him. "I doubt a lot of people would agree with that," she murmured. Shaking her head, she raised her chin and tossed the robe to the side. "I'll grab a hooded jacket and your wig, and then we can head out." She paused before adding slyly, "Unless you have other plans in mind?"

"I doubt I could walk afterwards," he muttered playfully as he began checking the vents and lamps.

She realized he was looking for listening devices or cameras in the bungalow. She hadn't thought of that.

"Only one way to find out," she replied, heading into the bedroom she was using and pulling out a black, hooded jacket from the closet.

She ran a thread of magic through it, searching for any sort of tracking device and found nothing. Selia didn't dare use too much magic, even for a spell as minor as finding hidden cameras and 'bugs'. Magic flowed from a person's life force, and if used too much, it would drain the caster and leave them exhausted.

Grabbing the wig from the bathroom, she held it lightly in her hand as she returned to the bedroom and leaned against the wall where she watched him check the room. He was very thorough. After sweeping the room visually, he removed a small device from some hidden compartment beneath his coat and checked some spots a second time. When he was satisfied the room was clear, he nodded and sat down.

He noticed her looking at him and gestured for her to join him in the room. When she did, he declared, "This room is clean. I don't want to do anything, even talk, in the other rooms until they've been checked. Let alone... anything else." His balaclava pulled against his face as he smiled beneath it. "I don't know that I'd keep the mask on, and I'd rather not have Big Al or anyone else in the Family seeing my face on a homemade skin flick."

For a moment, it felt like her heart wasn't beating. Then it kicked into overdrive. Her eyes danced as she smiled at him. So, maybe there was a chance with him after all.

"Well, if not here, I'm certainly open for suggestions as to where..." She trailed off, blushing. "I doubt Al would have bugged this place, but the others..." She shrugged; her pulse raced from the thoughts swarming her. "As nice as this place is, I've got to admit to liking yours a lot better."

The Sandman stood up and walked to the door. "Never ignore a hint dropped by a beautiful lady, my dad told me. Off to my place we shall go. Are you ready?"

"Give me a minute," she said.

She disappeared from the room, grabbed her phone, and reappeared, attaching the case to a belt loop. Her wallet was tucked into a hip pocket. Selia knew the wallet Soren gave her wasn't traceable, but she didn't trust the one Al gave her. She had around four hundred bucks in the wallet and the fake ID from Soren.

"I am now," she said, brushing up against him.

She walked past him, pleasantly aware of his eyes taking in her figure as she walked ahead of him. The door latched and he moved beside her, then slightly ahead. She followed him into the woods, and after a five-minute hike, he stopped.

They came upon a black tarp hidden between some trees. The shape covered by the tarp was unmistakably a motorcycle of some kind. Selia wondered how she had not noticed the typically loud engine of a cycle in this quiet and somewhat secluded area.

The Sandman pulled off the tarp and began folding it. The bike was fairly large, with enough room for two on its single seat. It was all black and dark blues. Hard leather saddlebags had been attached at either side of the back of the vehicle. The Sandman opened the one furthest from her and placed the folded tarp inside. It was about the size of a folded-up flag, now. He straddled the bike and removed his right glove.

When he pressed his right thumb to a small oval of plastic set into the place usually reserved for an ignition key, a few muted lights came to life around it, including a display. Selia could now hear a soft whirring sound coming from the bike, but there was no exhaust.

"An electric motorcycle?" she guessed, not hiding how impressed she was.

"Yes, ma'am," he said, and she thought a little pride was in his voice. "I got those motorcycle guys on TV to build it for me. Okay, I got the old guy to do it. The son grates on my nerves." He revved the bike, which still hardly made a sound. "It will get up to one hundred and thirty. Climb on, and we'll get going."

He reached around and opened the other compartment. From it he pulled a full-sized helmet, with a darkened visor to conceal its wearer's identity. He held it out to her.

"Safety first."

She smiled and put on the helmet. As she was doing so, Selia watched him take off his wide brimmed fedora and, amazingly, folded it up until it was the size of a softball. He put it into the outside left pocket of his trench coat and produced an identical helmet to the one she was wearing. He didn't remove his sunglasses.

Obviously, he had that one hanging on the bike where she hadn't noticed it. Once he had his helmet on, she slid onto the bike behind him and wrapped her arms around his waist. She felt the taut muscles of his stomach relax a little, and then the bike moved forward. He moved confidently through the woods without lights on.

Yep, Selia thought after five minutes of driving in the dark, *he definitely wears infrared sunglasses.*

It wasn't until they were on a ramp, merging into the highway, that he turned the electric bike's brilliant headlight on.

An hour later, they pulled into a rental storage facility that allowed the patrons twenty-four-hour access. The Sandman parked his bike in the last storage unit on the row, put their helmets away, and replaced the tarp over the bike. Once done, he pulled the bundle of crumpled fedora out of his left pocket and tossed it into the air. It unfolded smoothly into its original shape and landed in his outstretched hand. He placed it on his head with a little flourishing gesture.

"Nice trick," she declared.

"Australians. They know how to make a practical hat," he replied. He locked the storage unit with the bike inside and looked at her. "Do you recognize where we are?"

"Yes, I do. I think I could even lead the way back to your lair, Mister Sandman," she countered.

"After you, then," he said with a small bow.

She led on, and in five minutes they were entering the sub-basement once more. She couldn't help but notice he was softly singing the words to the old song "Mister Sandman" as they went.

Chapter Twelve

Once they stepped inside the basement, Selia turned to the Sandman.

"I need my laptop. It's in my duffle bag." She closed her eyes and took a deep breath. She had to trust him, she reminded herself and found it was easier than she expected. "The information Alfi stole is on my laptop. I made a copy before Soren was roughed up." She opened her eyes, capturing his gaze and holding it. "Whatever Alfi stole is bigger than anything like offshore bank account information."

"I'll go get your bag, then," he offered as he tucked his sunglasses into one of the trench coat pockets and left the room.

She smiled after him and turned back to the room. Her jaw promptly dropped as she saw the clothes neatly stacked on the sofa, coffee table, and hanging on hooks against the wall. Weapons were neatly lined on the bar counter.

"Dear gods," she whispered. "Did he keep any of the cash for himself?"

She walked in a slight daze towards the bar, admiring the weaponry. There was an assortment of guns, ammo, and knives, but what caught her attention was the pair of swords that resembled short katanas.

She recognized the ebony-handled blades as kodachi swords. Temeria had something similar, only theirs were heavier and shaped more like short swords. Kodachi, Selia discovered during her first year in New Campania, were lighter and easier to handle, at least for her. They were also easier to hide than a short sword.

She picked one up, running her hand along the sheath lovingly before slowly unsheathing the blade to admire the shine of the well-honed edge. The blade was balanced perfectly, and she suspected, full tang.

"They aren't for show." The Sandman's voice interrupted. "They are battle ready and 'two-body' sharp. Do I need to explain what that means?"

"Not at all," Selia replied, glancing over at him. "Two-body sharp means they can cleave through two bodies with ease, to put it in simple terms."

She unsheathed the other sword and hefted it in her right hand. Twirling them slowly at first, she stepped away from the bar.

Moving with a dancer's grace, she wove the swords around her. An intricate series of thrusts, cuts, and twirls, she moved around the room in a blurring whir of silver.

When she stopped, the blades were mere inches from the Sandman. A quirky smile pulled at her lips.

"I would certainly hope they're battle ready. They aren't much good if they aren't," she stated. Pausing, she took in his wide eyes and laughed softly as she lowered the blades. "What part of 'warrior woman' did you not understand or get from my heritage? Really, Sandman, I'm not about to hurt you. Bite or nibble, maybe, but hurt you? No."

He laughed. "Maybe I like it rough. And that was an impressive display you just gave. Warrior woman upbringing or not."

Her cheeks burned even as she grinned. "Thank you." She gave a short bow from the waist. She nodded towards the bag he held. "I'll put these lovely blades away, if you'd be a dear and set up my laptop."

"But of course," he said regally. He placed her bag down and reached into it for her laptop. "Good thing I didn't purchase the spear," she heard him muttering. "Although the deerskin outfit would have been hot..."

She chuckled to herself as she returned to the bar and sheathed the swords. Now she knew what to get for Halloween. Perhaps she'd even knock on his door and ask for a treat.

Turning back to him, and the laptop, she said, "I can't help but feel as though you're spoiling me with all these lovely gifts."

"Think what you want. Perhaps I have money to burn and haven't had a lovely lady to spend any of it on," he countered.

She studied him, a curious smile on her face. "Perhaps, but I want you to know I appreciate it." She leaned over and kissed his masked cheek. "It isn't like I have handsome men giving me gifts very often. Well, those I don't consider family." She winked and typed in the password to the laptop, her fingers became a blur over the keyboard.

"At least you didn't make jokes about getting a young male ward and dressing him in bright, vibrant colors, instead."

She snickered as the laptop loaded. Clicking on a folder on the desktop, she turned her attention to him as it opened. "I can honestly say that thought has never crossed my mind: Unlike the idea of undressing you."

"You'll notice I haven't stopped you from doing that."

"That's just not fair," she complained. She leaned back, ignoring the laptop. "For a man who has worked hard at keeping his identity a secret, I'm rather surprised you'd be willing to... bare all for someone you just met. Someone who works for and is the adopted daughter of one of the crime families you typically work against." She paused. "You aren't planning on killing me to keep it a secret, are you?"

"I believe in a balanced relationship with women," the Sandman replied. "I have more than enough of your secrets. If you expose me, I expose you. It's simple, and it's fair."

She gave a slight nod of her head. "Fair enough. I have no reason to expose you." She turned back to the screen as she added teasingly, "Though, you didn't kiss me back, so I hope you'll forgive my lack of ravaging you like I want to."

"Oh, is that what it would take?"

"Well, it's not like I want to jump someone who's not that interested," she countered, a grin on her face. She really had no clue what was on the screen because the conversation was getting far too heated for anything else.

"You're just sore because you want me to take you like something out of a romance novel. I'd happily do that if we weren't trying to keep you safe." He pointed at the screen. "Unless you would rather get naughty instead of finding out what's on your laptop. You did ask me to bring it in here, after all."

"Oh, fine," she sighed, only half-serious. "Work first, play later."

She gave him a sidelong gaze that didn't hide any of her feelings for him before looking back to the laptop. Her eyes narrowed as she opened the first document. Coordinates were the first thing she saw. She recognized them as the nautical position for her homeland.

"Selia?" she heard the Sandman say. "You've suddenly tensed up. What is it?"

"This is information about how to get to my homeland. The names below? Those are the names of the ruling families and traders." She scrolled down to find a couple of paragraphs written in Temerian.

"What the hell?" she whispered, leaning forward even more. "Son of a..." She trailed off rereading the paragraphs to make certain she wasn't misunderstanding anything.

No, she hadn't misunderstood anything, and it didn't make her happy. In fact, it left her with even more questions. Leaning back on the sofa, she folded her arms across her chest.

"Damn, I wish I could talk to Soren without anyone listening in to our conversation," she muttered. She glanced over at the Sandman. "Do you want to know more about this or stay in the dark?"

"It's your choice to tell me or not. I prefer to know everything I can."

"That's fair." Selia said, turning her gaze towards the ceiling. "According to that," she waved towards the laptop, "There is, and has been for decades, an agreement between the Families and Temeria. It doesn't go into detail, which is really annoying. Only four people are supposed to have this information, but it doesn't say what happens if anyone else learns the information." She shook her head. "It's as though someone clipped out two or three paragraphs of an eighty-page contract."

"Are you sure it's all of the Families? Not just yours? I only ask because I got the impression that not a lot of shipping boats came to your homeland. I also can't see how other Families wouldn't have people like you on their payroll or... as workers, shall we say?" The Sandman scratched at his chin. "If the other families were as familiar with your people, wouldn't someone have recognized you for who you are, and made a move to take you or bribe you away?"

"I don't know. The two Families that matter in this city, as far as I know, are the Lascari and Vaschetti Families. Those names are repeated throughout this." She continued skimming over the document as she replied. "I do know there are several of my kind in the adult film industry. The Vaschettis deal in human trafficking and they buy the criminals of my homeland who aren't sentenced to death."

"That certainly explains a lot. But... the adult film industry?" He shook his head. "That makes some sense, I suppose."

"Beautiful women who don't age like the rest of the females on the planet? What wouldn't be appealing about that?" Selia asked with a shrug. "Soren and I had a long... discussion about it one time." Discussion or scolding, call it what you wanted, but the conversation had started because of her naïveté about her people, their ruthlessness, and how they compared to the Family. "I need answers, but I can't ask Al. I'll have to wait until Soren is better." She gave a heavy sigh. "Guess it's time to talk to Lucien about what he stole."

"Okay, so now you want to talk to the *other* most powerful male in this city." The Sandman sighed. "Sure, I always enjoy interrupting their nights. Got a favorite actor? I'll try to look like a bad impersonator of him."

Laughing, Selia leaned forward before shoving him over until he fell back against the sofa. She leaned over him, smiling down into his face.

"You do realize there are other ways to get someone's attention, yes?" she asked, one hand against the back of the sofa, the other on the armrest. "I do have his number, so I could just call him and set up a meeting."

She could see the challenge in his eyes as he spoke. "And he would just agree to a meeting with you because...?"

"Because he knows me, for one," she replied. "For another, I can offer him what he wants."

"What does he want, oh Amazonian warrior woman?" the Sandman teased. He was completely relaxed.

She scooted over until she was practically on top of him. Her eyes twinkled as she replied, "He wants what belongs to him: The data on that laptop. The problem is, he doesn't know I have a copy of it. So he'll be interested in what Soren's daughter can offer him." She shrugged. "Besides, he'll see it as a chance to sway me to his side." She paused and leaned down closer. "Wouldn't you want a chance to claim what belongs to you?"

"I don't get that materialistic. But I concede your point."

"You aren't like most people, especially those who are ruled by greed and power," she admitted, kissing his mouth lightly through his mask. She flopped back over onto the sofa, a smile on her lips. "At least you aren't asking why I have Lucien's phone number."

"I also haven't asked why you keep hinting about having wild, passionate sex and yet both of us are still wearing clothes." He stood up and went to the bar. "You haven't asked how I can afford all this. For all you know, I'm a member of one of the Families, trying to destroy them from within and without, to pay for their sins."

"You probably wouldn't tell me even if I asked," she mused aloud. "As long as you don't try to hurt Soren, I don't care what you do." She stood and watched him pour himself a drink. She furrowed her brows and sighed as she realized something. "I don't want there to be any questions as to why I want you. I don't want to be in the middle of us having wild, passionate sex only to have something happen." She turned back to the laptop, muttering, "Or have you decided you don't want someone who works for the Family you fight against."

"The pouting really doesn't suit you," he retorted. "If I felt that you or your adopted father were so bad, I wouldn't be helping either of you survive this not-so-little coup of Alfi's. I simply would rather focus on getting this situation handled, and then enjoy the full pleasure of a beautiful woman's company. Otherwise, as you suggest, something might happen, or other distracting thoughts could seep in."

Selia had the good grace to flush at his comments. "At least we're more or less on the same page."

She glanced back at him. He was a strange, unique man who tempted every part of her. Maybe it was more than lust shoving her along the path. She could deal with that. She hoped. Instead of dwelling on that line of thought, she pulled out the burner phone Al had given her. She had turned off the GPS even before Al had called her, so she wasn't worried about that. Punching in a set of numbers, she paced while waiting for Lucien to answer.

Chapter Thirteen

Selia had no clue why Lucien Vaschetti had chosen a graveyard of all places to meet. Well, to be more accurate, they were supposed to meet on the outside of the graveyard near the back entrance. Perhaps this was his way of trying to intimidate her. If so, he was failing miserably, because the dead held no fear for Selia.

The Sandman had driven her across the city, parked his motorcycle, and led her through a few abandoned subway systems and waterways before taking her over a series of rooftops. A good thing she kept in shape, or she would've been out of breath before getting a fourth of the way to the meeting place.

She was armed and wore a long black trench coat over her clothes, hiding her weaponry. The fact she now bore a strong resemblance to the Sandman in general appearance was slightly amusing. The Sandman hadn't liked the idea of her meeting Lucien, but he also hadn't had much of a say in the matter. Lucien had the knowledge she needed, and Selia suspected *she* was a key part to the whole problem. Or perhaps, her heritage was the key to it all.

A long, black limo sat pulled over in the grass, just far enough from the stone wall of the cemetery for the passenger doors to open. A black sedan was parked in front and another behind the limo. Two black-suited men stood at each sedan. They had the same never-changing, surly expressions that reminded her of golems.

Another two stood at the back passenger door of the limo. Selia kept her stride steady and confident. Each of these men had at least two guns and could draw on a moment's notice. Though they might not have an itchy trigger finger, she didn't plan on giving them a reason to think they needed to raise a weapon against her, either.

Behind her, in the shadows of an alley, the Sandman watched from a fire escape. Selia could sense his eyes following her and it gave her a feeling of safety, knowing she had backup if she needed it. She hoped she wouldn't require another rescue.

One of Lucien's bodyguards opened the door as she stepped into their cluster. Lucien Vaschetti stepped out but didn't move. No, he was waiting for her to come to him: A show of power. She knew how these games worked and she had to play them, or at least pretend to.

She paused and nodded to the man who led the Vaschetti Family. His hair was as dark as Al's, but was starting to gray at the temples, giving him an aristocratic appearance. His face held more lines, adding depth to the inch-wide scar running from the top of his cheekbone to his chin. Brilliant blue eyes were what she remembered most; cold and hard, yet mesmerizing.

Lucien was fit, despite the graying hair and lined face. He wore his tailored Armani suit well. A thick gold ring circled his left ring finger and a signet ring flashed in the dim light on his right hand.

"Ah, Selia Laios Lascari," he said, his voice as smooth as warmed honey. "You have grown more beautiful since last I saw you."

Flatterer, she thought. *Time to return the gesture.* "You're still as charming as ever, Lucien. Though I believe you have only grown more handsome over the years."

It wasn't a lie. Age had given his hard, cold face character and depth, something he had lacked the last time they'd met. Of course, she'd also been eighteen and still pretty naïve.

His smile didn't reach his eyes, though he kept his gracious posture. "Come, child. Let us speak in the privacy of the limousine. We are here as potential allies, meeting due to you unknowingly being drawn into a scheme by one of your former Family members, who has since gone rogue." He sighed. Selia suspected it was fake. "It is truly a shame when one so beautiful is used and then nearly killed due to blatant duplicity by one she should have been able to trust."

Yes, after all, everyone in the criminal underworld is trustworthy, she thought as she resisted the urge to roll her eyes. Selia didn't give voice to her thoughts. Instead, she forced a smile to her lips as she continued toward Lucien.

"Unfortunately, it's all true. I must confess, I'm surprised you're aware of everything that has transpired," Selia said, accepting Lucien's outstretched hand. "I sincerely apologize for the theft from your business."

Lucien kissed her knuckles like an old-time gentleman before stepping to the side and gesturing for her to enter the limo. She stepped into the vehicle, not liking it, but knowing she couldn't refuse and still learn what she needed.

"Your apology is accepted," Lucien replied, following her into the limo. The door closed and he turned, leaning against it casually. "However, I do not feel you were responsible. You were following orders, showing loyalty to your own Family. Those of us who still appreciate the old ways cannot fault you."

The old ways of this country and Italy believe that women have no mind of their own. A man told them what to do, and as long as they did it, they were good little girls, Selia thought bitterly, but she continued to smile at Lucien.

"You seem exceedingly knowledgeable about me and my movements."

"My dear, surely you know we have eyes everywhere. Not only myself and my organization, but yours as well." He leaned forward and from somewhere pulled a wine bottle and two glasses. "Would you care for a drink?"

"I'm afraid I don't drink," Selia replied. It wasn't quite a lie. She never drank in a social setting. Only where no one else would see her and know. Lucien should have known that fact, so she suspected he was testing her. "I shouldn't be surprised by your knowledge, but considering my position within the Family, it isn't something I think about often."

"Ah, that is right. Such a pity," he said, pouring himself a glass. "You are a wise girl. Most women aren't satisfied with just doing their job. They want more."

"I'm loyal to Soren, Lucien," Selia said softly. "It's no secret I do as he bids and am happy with my position. It's a good life."

Lucien gave her a sharp glance and his voice became colder. "Everyone has aspirations. What are yours?"

"To survive," she replied simply. She paused and leaned back against her side of the limo, giving a relaxed appearance. "Why don't we drop all the pretenses and games? I met you in the hopes you could explain what is so important about what Alfi stole. I also have a deal to offer you."

That caught Lucien's attention and he perked up like a hound dog catching the scent of its prey. "Indeed. I like a forthright woman. What sort of deal could Soren's little flower offer me?"

Selia bit back the first response that came to mind. Insulting a potential ally wasn't the wisest choice, so she settled for a less defensive answer.

"Even a rose has thorns, Lucien, and some of the deadliest plants are the most beautiful." Selia kept her tone light and casual, as though they were discussing the weather. "Answer my questions, and then we'll discuss your missing data. It's very possible that I could retrieve it for a small non-monetary price."

"I'm intrigued," Lucien said, and he sounded genuine to Selia. The don took a sip of his wine and settled back against the seat again. "Ask me your questions, little belladonna, and I'll consider the agreement."

Belladonna, the name for deadly nightshade, was a poisonous yet beautiful flower. Selia found it interesting that he compared her to that, despite the fact she had kept a very low profile for the past decade. Perhaps he knew more about her than she originally believed.

"Okay," she said slowly. "What was the information Alfi stole? Why is it so imperative it's retrieved by either you or Al?" She paused before adding, true curiosity ringing in her voice, "And why do you not question my ability to retrieve your information? Twice, I've been told to stay out of this, yet you aren't. Why?"

Lucien nodded slowly. "You aren't here trying to gnaw my ear off with useless questions. I like that, so I'll answer your questions. First, however; what of this payment you spoke of?"

"Ah, yes," Selia said softly. "The payment for my delivering what Alfi stole. I want the Vaschetti Family to claim responsibility for the death of Alfi Barboni." She paused and studied Lucien with a calm, cool gaze. "I'll do the deed, but your organization admits to it. Not by rumor, either. I want you or one of your underbosses to directly contact Al and make the declaration. Since Alfi has been declared rogue by Al, I doubt there will be an issue."

"Deal," Lucien said without batting a lash. Selia wondered if he even thought about it before agreeing, not that it mattered. "No need to worry about me upholding my end of the bargain, Selia," he assured her. "Should Alfi fall by your hand, I'll be certain the Vaschettis accept the glory of his death."

"And again, you don't tell me to not kill him or interfere," Selia said, keeping his gaze. "Why?"

"You are right to question my intentions. Perhaps I am hoping you will die. Perhaps I have a nefarious plot to steal you away from Soren and Angelo. But no, little nightshade, I plan neither. I'm aware you are a Temerian. I am aware you arrived in the port upon Soren's ship and hidden in his house and a cloistered Catholic school, where you graduated, perhaps not with honors, but with high grades."

Lucien swirled the wine in his glass before taking another sip. "The information Alfi stole was nothing minor. No, what he stole from Ignacio's computer is something even you would, or at least should, wish to keep silent." Lucien's hard blue eyes captured her gaze and held her in place. "The coordinates and information for your island homeland of Temeria is what Alfi stole. Including the names of the ruling families and who we trade with on the island, as well as what we trade for. He doesn't want it for himself. He is taking it to Azyre House."

Selia could feel the blood drain from her face. The fact Lucien knew so much about her wasn't overly surprising. Spies were everywhere in this city and if the price was right, loyalties could be bought. Being told the coordinates of her island homeland might be made public, however, was beyond frightening: It was horrific and troublesome. There were secrets there that did not need to become a part of the whole wide world.

She suspected the reasons the Families kept it silent was because they wanted all the imports, and thus the profit from the island, for themselves, but it could be catastrophic if news spread. Raids would happen, invasions, and the entire way of life on Temeria would be disrupted. Not to mention the ecology.

Selia knew what the foolish humans around the world did to their own ecologies, decimating and causing the extinctions of animals and plants for no reason other than greed. She did not want to see that happen to her homeland.

"That's right, Selia," Lucien continued when she didn't speak. "Alfi plans to sell it to the highest bidder. It doesn't matter. We want the return of that information, since he managed to wipe it from the computer at the same time it was downloaded to the flash drive." He again turned his eyes to her. "There are only four people with the knowledge of your homeland. Myself, Angelo, Soren, and Ignacio. We wish to keep it that way."

"Very well," Selia replied. "I'll get the information back to you. What about the other questions?"

"Tenacious." Lucien sounded like he approved. He probably did. She kept silent and Lucien chuckled before continuing. "As someone who was trained on the island, you are skilled, far more skilled than any of us, in the art of war. Angelo is a fool for not using your talents."

"Now, now, that is my beloved uncle you're speaking poorly of," Selia said, her tone light, yet warning. "I prefer keeping a low profile. Had Alfi not pulled me into this storm, I'd still be keeping a low profile."

Lucien laughed. It was the kind of laugh that starts in the belly and bursts forth in true merriment. "Ah, girl, you are amusing. Something would have eventually lit your fire and you'd be stepping out away from the wall, just as you are now."

He shook his head, setting the glass into a holder. "I didn't get where I am today by believing foolish ideals. Someone who was raised to fight would never remain in the background their entire life, not when it wasn't their choice. You remained against the wall, pretending to be a docile lamb out of need. Now you step out due to need: the wolf reclaiming its true nature. You won't be the same after this and I'm looking forward to seeing what carnage you will bring."

So that was it, Selia realized. Lucien was hoping she'd step into the limelight and bring chaos down around her and the Lascaris. And during that chaos, he would be able to step in and take over the Lascari territory.

That wasn't going to happen, though. Sure, there were warriors in her homeland that thrived upon laying waste to everything around her, but she had been taught control. She controlled her desires, not the other way around. Well, at least the violent desires.

"Only time will tell," Selia stated. "Did you need any more answers, today?"

"Yes, I do." Lucien leaned in and for a moment she thought Lucien was going to try and kiss her. Instead, he asked, "Without knowing what the information was, you came to me to offer its return and the death of those responsible. Why?"

Selia knew she should have expected a question of that sort. Just how honest should she be with Lucien?

"Alfi nearly killed Soren," Selia replied slowly. "He stole from you, and I've been told to stay out of it by Angelo." She smiled slightly. "You have the most to lose and the most to gain by my offer."

"If Soren had not been injured, do you think you would be here, making such offers?" Lucien countered, without answering her question.

Selia tilted her head to the side, considering the possible scenarios that could have occurred before coming to a conclusion.

"Does it matter?" she finally asked. "I'm Temerian, Lucien. We don't reflect on knowing the impossible. We reflect on the decisions we did or didn't make and their consequences, so we might make better choices in the future."

Lucien took a long moment to ponder her words before nodding. "I think that is not the answer I was looking for, but it will do for the time being," he said, and that seemed to be the end of the conversation.

"I have one last question: How did the Families learn of Temeria?"

"Now that is a tale only to be told over a long meal," Lucien replied slyly. "There were journals and diaries that told the whole story, but they've been lost for decades. The truth, however, is known to those who take over the business. Perhaps you should ask Angelo, and if he doesn't desire to discuss it, come see me. I'll treat you to a feast and a tale worthy of the meal."

Or she could just look for the journals and diaries. That idea appealed to her far more than asking either patriarch the story of how they discovered her homeland. She had what she wanted, though, which was enough for her. At least for now.

"I appreciate your time and troubles, Lucien," she said formally. "When Alfi is dead and I have your information, I'll contact you."

"I'll be looking forward to your call," Lucien replied smoothly. "I do have one final question for you." Selia nodded and he gave a sly smile as he asked, "How did you happen to have the Sandman rescue you?"

That question made her laugh. She replied, "I batted my lashes, flashed my boobs, and cried on his shoulder."

"Ah, you spotted him nearby and used your magic," Lucien said thoughtfully.

Selia shrugged, uncomfortable with the fact Lucien was aware of her magical abilities. "Maybe, maybe not. A girl's got to have her secrets, doesn't she?"

Lucien laughed heartily. "I'll give you that one." He rapped on the window and the door beside Selia opened and a hand appeared in the doorway. Selia nodded again to the Vaschetti patriarch and accepted the proffered hand.

"Oh, and Selia," Lucien called. Selia leaned down to look into the limo and Lucien added, "I'll keep my men out of your way. Perhaps you shouldn't get too enthusiastic and kill any of my boys, hmmm?"

"They'll only die if they get too close," Selia replied. "But I assure you, my only target is Alfi."

Lucien nodded once and turned away from her, a dismissal if she'd ever seen one. She straightened and nodded to the bodyguard before striding back the way she came.

Once out of earshot, she said softly, "You get all that?"

The Sandman's voice filled her ear, almost as though he were inside her head. "I'll wait for you on the roof."

Selia smiled into the darkness. "I'll meet you there."

Things were getting more interesting. The stakes had risen, but she wasn't ready to call. Not yet. There were plenty of questions for Soren and she'd have to eventually tell him about Lucien. Her thoughts were on the information she'd just received and figuring out where to go next.

J. F. Posthumus

Chapter Fourteen

The Sandman wasn't on the roof by the time Selia got there. Puzzled, she walked the perimeter. Pulling out the small ear bud he had given her from a pocket –she hadn't seen a reason to keep it in when she was about ten minutes from him, not to mention it felt weird- and replaced it.

The sound of scuffling and a sharp yelp that didn't sound like the Sandman greeted her immediately. Rolling her eyes, she held up a hand and spoke the words to a spell. Finding her companion, she decided, was far more important than waiting around for his eventual reappearance.

She used a simple locator spell that required only a name and some knowledge of the person she sought. The more powerful her connection with the person, the better the spell worked. Considering she had a great deal of affection and trust for the Sandman, she had no doubts about whether the spell would work.

A small blue dot formed on the palm of her hand, near her thumb, which was currently pointing towards the opposite side of the building. As she jogged across the roof, the blue dot moved closer to the center of her palm and grew brighter. She looked down, ignoring the sounds of the fight in her ear.

She didn't bother searching for him, and instead started running down the fire escape as quickly and silently as a jungle cat. Though a slight rattle sounded out every so often, she was nearly as silent as the Sandman had been upon their first meeting. Of course, she also didn't have as much experience with metal stairs as he obviously did.

Pausing about halfway down the stairs, Selia now had surround-sound of the fight: One half from the ear bud, the other from the fight directly below her. That, however, wasn't why she stopped. Selia knew she needed to hide her features.

Shoving a hand into a pocket, she pulled out a scarf and wrapped it over her hair, above her nose, and around her neck, pulling it tight against her skin. Though the scarf made for a flimsy disguise, it was the best available. Something was better than nothing.

Ignoring the drop- it was shorter than most she'd dealt with on Temeria- she jumped over the edge and landed in a crouch. Standing, she lightly dusted her hands together, dispelling the magic. The brilliant blue light from her hand drifted away into the darkness.

Moving towards the back of the alley, Selia realized she was heading towards the back of a business near the loading dock. She paused as she neared where the Sandman fought, hearing voices to her left.

"Hey, that's the Sandman taking out our competition!" a youthful voice exclaimed.

"Yeah, but once he's done, he'll be tired," an older man replied, authority in each word. "We can take him, then, and the families will have to respect us."

There was a murmur of about five different voices, all in agreement.

"Looks like there are some others who have the same idea," another voice suddenly said.

"Come on, let's get him and them." It was the youth again.

That's right, kids, Selia thought, slowly sliding the swords from their sheaths. *Go on past me and we'll see who is taken out.*

She'd worn the blades upside down, secured on her back beneath the trench, for just this reason: The ability to unsheathe them with ease and as little noise as possible.

Peeking around the edge of the building, Selia saw the newcomers a few feet from the Sandman, who was breaking wrists and ankles. The fight was intricate, and the Sandman systematically laid the thugs out at his feet. Though the fight was taking far longer than she would've allowed. Of course, the attackers would also probably all be dead, too. Dead people don't tend to get back up to attack again.

Rolling her wrists, Selia kept her head down as she moved forward. Each step was silent until she stood directly behind a wanna-be thug who looked like he should have been going door to door trying to sell hair potions to balding men. Behind the thugs was not where she wanted to be. So Selia crossed the street and jogged ahead of them. Once in position, she paused in front of the leader, head bowed.

Their leader was a scraggly haired man who had more scars than lines on his aged face and wore a stained jacket that recked of cheap cigarettes and beer. "Out of our way," the man demanded, pulling a blackjack, and thumping it against his hand.

She just shook her bowed head, staring at the thug.

The man lifted his head and his crew of eight goons closed in around her.

"Move or we'll move you," the leader said, and the group of men grinned at her like a pack of jackals, thinking they'd found an easy target. Each person held a weapon of some sort.

She shrugged and shifted to the side, giving the appearance she was going to let them by. The man grinned and began laughing at her. Selia smiled beneath the scarf and promptly spun around, slicing through the two men nearest her before dropping and rolling behind them, even before their bodies fell to the ground.

That got their attention, and the idiots howled their rage, spat some rather rude phrases, and rushed her. Her trained mind counted more than eight, so apparently, she'd become the bigger threat.

Her blades sung in the night air, unleashing blood and body parts. The leader had allowed three males to get ahead of him. Selia cleaved through the one on the left, using her momentum to cut through the one on the right in a sweeping arc that finished at the man's throat. The arterial spray from the exit hit the third man just before Selia rammed one sword into his abdomen, to the hilt. She took a moment to sever that one's carotid artery before shoving him to the ground.

The leader stood next, surrounded by the four other men who had planned to gang up on her. None of them looked thrilled with the idea, now. She let out a war whoop, knowing she was smiling fiercely, and they couldn't see it.

A pity, she thought vaguely.

Moving swiftly, she crossed the swords in front of her and viciously pulled them apart, eviscerating the leader. Her right leg came up, foot connecting with the jaw of the still-healthy man closest to it. The jaw gave way and he stumbled back. Selia took the opening to swing past him, slipping the blade in her right hand between the ribs of the thug directly behind Mr. Broken Jaw even as she severed the spine of the thug to her left. Pulling both blades free, she put the screaming broken-jawed man out of his misery with a downward slash that split his skull and sank halfway through his head. A hard yank freed the blade as she looked to see who was left.

As the last man, the youth who'd spotted the Sandman, ran away, Selia merely stood still, swords pointed outward, hands slightly away from her sides with her feet planted shoulder-width apart. With her head was bowed slightly, and though no one could see it, she was grinning. For a moment, the fleeing survivor turned while running and appeared as if he was going to point a weapon at her, but he shifted back to straight out running a second later.

She straightened as the night grew silent around her and she studied the bodies that now circled her. Blood stained the ground and she nudged one body slightly with a booted foot. It gurgled and she gave a dismissive shrug.

Turning, Selia gave the Sandman a low bow, bending only at the waist. It wasn't an easy feat to do, but she had been trained and her muscles weren't strained at all. This had been more of a workout than a true fight.

"We need to get you back to the cabin," the Sandman finally said, hitting the long, metallic cylinder against the brick wall near him. It fell in on itself and she recognized it as a collapsible baton.

"Why? The night is still young, and I need to clean the swords," she replied, wrinkling her nose at the blood that was sliding off the blades.

"I'll take care of the blades for you this time," he said. "Don't even try to argue."

Selia sighed. "Fine. You don't do anything without a reason. Let's go before I change my mind."

The Sandman chuckled as she wiped most of the blood off on a corpse before sliding her swords back into their sheaths.

"I'm sure I could change your mind," he replied in that tone that had her melting. From the smile pulling at his mask, she knew it, too.

"I have no doubt," she replied, falling into step beside him. "Not going to scold me for killing so many?"

He tilted his head in a curious fashion as he replied, "It isn't my place to scold you."

Chapter Fifteen

The return was quiet, and no one had been waiting for them when they had arrived. The Sandman had walked her into the bungalow, checked to make sure she was safe, and then bid her a good night. Five minutes after a quick shower, she was snuggled in bed, asleep.

Sometime later, the ringing of a phone woke her. Groggily, she reached over, grumbled about the time – a little past three o'clock in the morning- and unlocked the screen before managing a sleepy, "Hello?"

"Where are you?" Al's voice broke through her sleep-addled stupor.

Rubbing her eyes, she replied, "In a bed that isn't mine."

"What?" Al drew the word out and his voice held an unspoken threat.

Opening her eyes, Selia rolled over onto her back, and stared up at the ceiling of the bungalow, grumpy at being awoken at such an absurd time.

"I'm in the bed at the bungalow you sent me to," she explained. "Obviously, it isn't *my* bed, which happens to have a nice soft feather mattress, equally soft feather pillows and a nice, warm, snuggly comforter. This bed has none of those." She stretched languidly and stifled a yawn. Her voice grew concerned as she asked, "Why are you calling so early, anyway? Soren's okay, isn't he?"

"Yeah, yeah, Soren's fine. It's you I'm worrying about. Seems someone decided to join leagues with the Sandman, and it resembled you," Al replied. He didn't give her a chance to object before continuing, "I'm sending some boys to check up on you. They'll be at the bungalow soon."

"Guess I'd better get dressed," she said through a yawn. Another exclamation and she grinned, glad she was able to annoy him in a way where he really couldn't retaliate. "Really, Uncle, do you think I'm going to meet them at the door in just my skin?"

"I didn't need to know that," he nearly groaned, eliciting a laugh from her.

"You're the one questioning me," she retorted. "Stay on the line while I try to find something other than one of those sheer lacy things your people left for me."

Not waiting for a reply, she sat the phone down and opened a drawer and began digging through the clothes. Finding a long, silky red night gown with long sleeves, she pulled it over her head. It hit just above her ankles and felt smooth and warm against her skin. She picked up the phone again as she heard a knock on the door. Grabbing the gun that had been kindly left in the nightstand, she padded towards the front door.

"I hope those are your people, Uncle, otherwise they're going to be shot and you'll be the one cleaning up the mess."

Al chuckled. "Yeah, they're my people. Bernie and his brother, Alex."

"Should I invite them in for popcorn and a movie?" she asked dryly.

"You should be hospitable, yes," he replied.

"Well, since you were kind enough to send a pair I actually like, I'll be nice and let them poke around to satisfy you." There was a pause, and she could almost see him frowning. She asked, "So what brought this about, anyway?"

"Alex has a laptop for you. Check out the pages already loaded," he said.

She sighed. "Okay, Uncle. Want to stay on the phone while I greet the boys or what?" There was silence. Sighing again, she said, "Fine."

Al's top enforcers stood on the porch, smiling pleasantly at her as she opened the door. Despite the early hour, Selia was actually glad to see the brothers as she took in their attire. Both were wearing dark clothes and were obviously siblings. They had dark brown hair, brown eyes, and chiseled features, but that's where the similarities stopped.

Bernie was the classic enforcer with a square build perfect for a boxer. He had a square jaw to go with his roundish face, a small pug-like nose, and thick lips. Instead of a suit, Bernie had opted for a black t-shirt and jeans, to go along with his preferred leather jacket that hid his shoulder holster and preferred weapon, a Judge, from sight.

Alex, however, looked as though he should be an accountant. Taller than his brother by a few inches, he was around five eleven and all lean muscle. A narrow, boyish face, he preferred polo shirts with his dress pants, even in his off-hours. There was nothing to show he was deadlier than Bernie, but that was probably the point. He was the innocent looking one while Bernie looked like he'd like to pummel you into ground beef.

"Hey, ya, Selia," Bernie said. "The boss wanted us to be sure you were okay."

"Sorry to have woken you," Alex added. He dropped a wink and lifted the briefcase-like laptop bag. "We brought a peace offering."

Selia laughed. "Come on in. Al was just telling me you guys were coming. I just hadn't expected you so soon." The brothers glanced at each other as they walked past her. She put the phone back to her ear. "As you heard, they're here and I'm here. Satisfied?"

"For now," was the curt reply. Then he hung up.

Rolling her eyes, she shut the door and turned to the brothers. "Well, since you're here, care for anything to eat or drink? The place is pretty well stocked."

Eyeing the gun in her right hand and phone in the left, Bernie raised his brows. "We'll pass, but thanks."

"I know you guys have to look the place over, so let me know if you find any cute guys hiding somewhere. I could use the distraction from boredom," she quipped, setting the gun and phone on the table before looking pointedly at the laptop. "Al mentioned a laptop? Please tell me I get to keep it."

Alex laughed as Bernie headed for the bedrooms. "Al said it's yours. I'm guessing he means you can keep it." He sat the briefcase on the kitchen counter and opened it with two clicks. He pulled out a laptop and booted it up. Alex asked softly, "You've been here all night, right?"

"I'd better, since I had to get up so damned early," Selia muttered before glancing at him sharply. "Where else would I be, Alex? I'm pretty sure you know that I'm not here for a vacation."

"Don't know, but someone who looks a lot like you, was seen with the Sandman." Alex's bland, emotionless voice stayed low and soft. It was the tone he used when he was talking to someone he was about to kill. He leaned closer to her and whispered in her ear, "I don't want to have to kill you, Lia."

The desktop loaded and then a photo of her, in her trench coat and swords with the Sandman behind her looking into the camera stared at her from a webpage.

The caption read: *There's a new playmate in town and she's sided with The Sandman.*

Selia didn't bat an eye. Instead, she tilted her head to the side and studied the picture like anyone who found carnage interesting.

"For a vigilante, he's cute," she stated. "Pity he's against the Family. She, however, makes *him* look like a kitten." Alex snickered. Selia pointed to her disguised self in the picture and the bodies on the ground. She asked, making sure her voice sounded incredulous, "You think *I* did *that*? *Al* thinks *I* did *that*?"

"Yeah, well, you got to admit, that looks like you," Alex said, his voice no longer dead. Instead, he sounded as though it was the dumbest thing he'd ever been told.

"She's around my height and has darkish eyes. So what? I can't be the only woman in this city with dark eyes and is just over five feet." Selia went to the fridge and pulled out a can of ginger ale. She popped the top and took a sip. "My car has been outside since I got here. The overpriced tracking and road-side service feature that came with it can confirm that. Just call their toll-free number or check with the rental agency. I answered the door as soon as you got here and wasn't out of breath or sweating, so obviously I wasn't in a hurry. Al woke me up, so it's not like I was in the midst of changing from that," she pointed to the laptop, "into this." She gestured towards her nightgown.

Alex's eyes swept over the clingy red gown and her tangled bed hair. His eyes then went back over her figure once again, this time slower as a smile pulled at his lips. "Those are all good points."

"Besides, that sort of carnage isn't something I could learn overnight," she added, tilting her head back and swallowing more of the drink. Considering Alex's eyes didn't stray from her throat, she was pretty certain he didn't believe that she was the person in the picture anymore.

"Yeah, that's true. You might know how to use a gun and fight, but I've never seen you go near a sword," Bernie said from behind Alex. Alex glanced over his shoulder to Bernie, who added, "Place is clean."

"Well, damn," Selia said, snapping her fingers. "I was hoping you'd find some handsome guy tucked away somewhere."

Alex and Bernie laughed, and she smiled. She pondered for a second, and decided to be a little stinker, as well as make sure of something.

"You boys didn't put any naughty little cameras around here, did you? Keeping me safe by making sure I sleep in the nude?"

Bernie paled while Alex looked mortified.

Yep, Bernie had argued to have that happen, Selia thought.

"No! No, ma'am! We wouldn't do anything like that!" Alex went from mortified to almost panicky as he spoke. "Big Al would consider it a poor way to treat a lady! It's just, with this new player in the game, and her… um… kinda looking like you…"

Selia laughed, making sure it sounded good-natured.

"It's okay, Alex; I was just teasing. I understand Al's caution, and need to make sure. There can't be that many women he knows that might be capable of going bad-ass, vigilante style or otherwise. I'm flattered he even thought of me." She took another sip of her soda. "But do you see that woman-" she gestured at the photo of herself on the laptop- "cracking open a ginger ale for celebration after a good bout of ass whuppin'?"

Alex and Bernie laughed again, harder than before. She felt she had convinced them, for now, at least. Her phone chose that time to ring, and she glanced down at it.

"It's Soren," she told them.

"We'll head on out, then," Alex said. "Enjoy the laptop and be safe." He walked over to her and gave her a hug. He whispered in her ear, "Stay away from the Sandman, girl." Louder, he said, "Sleep well, Lia."

Bernie shoved his brother out of the way and pulled her into a bear hug. "Take care of yourself. We'll watch over Soren for you."

"Thanks, Bernie," Selia replied, picking up the phone, which was still ringing. "Drive safe!"

The pair nodded again to her and left, turning the lock behind them. She answered the phone. "Hey, Soren! How are you feeling?"

Chapter Sixteen

"Are they gone?" Soren asked abruptly.

"Yes, they're gone," Selia replied, walking into the spare bedroom, which opened onto the porch. She stood at the door and stared out into the darkness. "It's safe to talk."

"Don't be so sure," Soren said a little too sharply.

Selia sighed. "Trust me, okay? I know there's nothing in this room."

"How?"

"Do you really want an answer to that?" she countered. "I saw the photo. Al sent over Bernie and Alex, who told me to stay away from the Sandman. I think Alex was sent to kill me."

"You think? Selia, you had a photo taken of you fighting side-by-side with the Sandman. In the city, after you were told to stay in that damned bungalow," Soren hissed. She was a bit surprised he was able to keep his voice so quiet. "The Sandman works against the Family, girl; and you were seen as his ally. That kind of thing doesn't go over well with most members. They tend to see it as being a traitor and they deal with *that* with extreme prejudice." He paused before adding in a very soft, warning voice, "I told you to stay away from him."

Her eyes flared with anger, and she stared at the owl looking in at her. Its dark eyes never blinked, even as it turned its head sideways.

"He saved your life. If he thought you were so evil, why would he have done that?" She asked, her voice soft. How she managed to stay so calm, despite the fury welling up in her, she didn't know. "I told you that I was going to take care of Alfi. It's a matter of honor. As for the Sandman…" A smile pulled at her lips despite her anger. "It's more like he's working for me. Well, more like he's my sidekick, than anything."

A heavy sigh sounded from the other end. It was a sigh of acceptance and resignation. At least Soren knew it was a losing battle to tell her to not go after Alfi or be around the Sandman.

"Get yourself a better disguise if you're going to be around him," Soren finally said. He didn't sound too happy, but Selia knew Soren understood. He didn't have to like something to accept the reality of the situation. He continued, his voice pure business. "I hope you know what you're doing, Selia. You're playing a game where you're likely to get burned and burned badly. I can't protect you from Al. If that doesn't matter to you, how do you think Al will look at me for having you made a part of the family?"

"Alfi is planning on selling the information on how to get to Temeria," Selia said. There was a sharp intake from Soren, followed by a few Italian curses. "Now you know why I have to do this. We both have a stake in this. If any of my former Temerians discover I'm still alive and where I am, not even Al can protect me. Especially if they think I had anything to do with the island being sold out. Never mind that old business that sent me running."

"Just don't get attached to him, Selia," Soren said softly. "I don't want to see my daughter with a broken heart, because you know you can't see him after this is done."

"Now you shouldn't have said that," Selia said with a sigh. "You know I don't take orders very well." There was a snort and grunt of acknowledgement. "Bernie and Alex were satisfied. Al will be satisfied as far as the Family is concerned. If he personally thinks I'm getting cozy with the Sandman, he'll just keep an eye on me and wait for proof."

"Maybe," Soren muttered. "Al can be pretty unpredictable."

"I've never said this before, but you *are* a father to me. So, my dearest father, let me reassure you about a few things. One, Lucien agreed to take the credit for Alfi's death. Provided he gets the information back and I'm the one who kills Alfi. Two, I have no reason to *not* wear a disguise. I don't want to be identified by anyone else. If there are witnesses, and I really don't plan on leaving any, there won't be anything pointing towards me, or you. Three, I'm not going to run away this time. I have to take a stand at some point. *This* is that 'some point'." Selia paused and watched the owl fly into the darkness. "You can yell at me later about meeting up with Lucien, but I have what I need now. I also have someone willing to have my back when I'll need it the most."

Soren sighed again and she heard him rubbing his face. "All right, Selia, all right; I'll do what I can to keep our men out of the way. Don't tell me anything and keep yourself disguised. We both know what you're capable of, and that sidekick of yours is probably a better choice than any of our men." There was a pause and when he spoke again, there was a catch in his voice. "I don't want anything to happen to you."

"Nothing will," Selia assured him. "I love you, so you better stay there and get well again."

Soren chuckled. "Keep safe and I'll be in touch."

Selia stifled a yawn. "I'm going back to bed. I need some sleep if I'm going to be of any use to anyone."

"Sleep well, *piccolina*," Soren said softly.

"You, too, Papa," Selia said, swallowing the lump in her throat, finally allowing herself to call him her father. She could hear the smile on his face before the click of the phone. She wiped away a few tears.

Hanging up the phone, she now understood why her people on Temeria didn't form affections towards others.

Loving someone created an attachment that could hurt those around them. It could be used against you, and if you weren't careful, could cause you to make foolish mistakes. She'd once heard that 'love was a fool's game'. Well, she had just become one of those fools. First towards the man who had managed to become a father to her and then again towards the man who had saved her from two thugs, and who hadn't stopped saving her since.

Selia stared out into the darkness for a long time after hanging up with Soren. So much had happened in the last few days, she was beginning to wonder if her life would return to normal. Or if her life had just changed as dramatically and permanently as it had that fateful day she'd been forced to flee Temeria.

J. F. Posthumus

Chapter Seventeen

Selia didn't wake until late. Though she awoke well past noon, there were still several long hours before she'd be able to meet up with the Sandman. A pity, too, since she could have used his companionship, but she knew there couldn't be anyone at the safehouse. So, she walked out into the woods and began a little old-world style fun. She'd have to thank Al later for owning a place that had a nice long expanse of forest.

A newly made spear, a fairly decent bow, and several arrows later, she stood on the back porch practicing her aim. It wasn't the same as using the bow she had purchased, but it was definitely more comfortable and far more familiar.

In fact, the hand-made bow brought back memories of her days as a child on Temeria, when she had still been living with her mother and sisters. It felt as though it were a lifetime ago, but the memories still brought a smile to her lips as she notched the bow, pulled the string back, and loosed the arrow. The feathers had been a bit difficult to acquire, but she'd managed it after three hours of hard searching. The time spent had been well worth the effort.

She was surprised how quickly making bows, strings, and arrows had come back to her. Of course, having a craft shop fifteen minutes away that stocked yards of silk and paraffin wax made the process a lot easier than having to make her own cloth and wax, as she'd done on Temeria. She could have bought feathers there, but they weren't the "real" thing, and she could not bring herself to use them.

The arrows shot across the distance and into the makeshift target of a cardboard cereal box and she smiled. The laptop currently had a wide history of DIY pages, in case anyone became too nosey, with the excuse of being bored and this seemed like fun.

Not that Selia could tell anyone the truth. She didn't have access to her duffle bag and the collapsible bow she kept there, along with the full quiver that was also in the bottom of the duffle bag. A natural-made bow and arrows was far more difficult to use than the manufactured ones a person could buy, and her skill was far better than any amateurs would have been. Not that it mattered. She was the only one who ever went hunting with a bow, anyway.

She notched another arrow, pulled it back as she lifted it to her eye and loosed it. The arrow landed square in the center. Soon, the box wouldn't be usable, but she'd done enough, and the sun was setting. Gathering up her arrows and the box, she headed back inside and to the kitchen where the *penne rigate* was boiling. The white sauce was simmering, and it all smelled delicious. She'd fixed enough for two but figured the Sandman wouldn't be staying to eat.

By the time darkness was creeping in, the second serving of pasta was in a container in the fridge, dishes had been washed and put away, and she was sitting on the porch watching the fireflies blinking in the backyard. The same black silk robe was wrapped around her, and her feet were bare. Her gun sat nestled in her lap alongside her phone.

Al had called her back as she'd been eating, reminding her to stay at the bungalow, and to let her know Soren was doing better. He had also assured her Soren had agreed to stay in the hospital until everything blew over and Alfi had been taken care of.

She'd teased him about believing she was the woman in the photo. He had grudgingly said it couldn't have been her, since she'd been at the bungalow and couldn't have known the picture had been taken. Selia hadn't known, but the Sandman had noticed it. Not that she had shared that bit of information. Instead, she had brushed off Al's former suspicion as though it wasn't a big deal. The call had ended, leaving her wondering how the Sandman could have noticed the photographer and glad that Al no longer thought she was a threat.

Closing her eyes, Selia opened her senses to the night air, allowing old skills left unused for far too long to come to the fore. She slowed her breathing and allowed her body to relax as she listened.

Small twigs crunched under barely-there feet that belonged to a raccoon waddling through the forest looking for dinner. The soft sound of feathers followed by the rustle of leaves was an owl settling down on a branch. A gentle whoosh of wings, a squeak, and a branch creaking again signaled the owl catching a mouse and returning to its roost.

A gentle breeze brushed against her, and she inhaled the scents. Leaves, dirt, flowers all filled her lungs. She listened closer, allowing her senses to expand, and smiled.

"You can stop sneaking around," she said to the night, her voice low. She opened her eyes and looked directly at the still-hidden figure of the Sandman. "You were right about getting back here last night."

Though she hadn't seen him, or even heard him, Selia had somehow known the Sandman had been walking towards her through the trees. Maybe she knew he was there due to the lack of animals rustling up their dinner, or the barely heard sound of the owl flying off. Not only was she puzzled by her ability to sense him, but also irritated by the fact she had allowed her senses to dull so much over the years.

A hunting trip by herself was definitely going to happen so she could sharpen the skills that had been honed from the moment she could walk. *When* she'd stopped depending so heavily on her warrior skills, she didn't know. That was soon going to change, though, if for no other reason than to be able to sneak up on the man who loved sneaking up on her.

"You've seen the picture, then?" he asked as he walked silently toward her. "I think it's poorly framed as a study on your magnificent breasts, but it was a thug with an outdated iPhone running for his life. I suppose considerations have to be made."

"Um, thanks," Selia said, blushing. "Yeah, I saw the photo. Al called around three this morning as Bernie and Alex showed up at the front door. Alex gave me a laptop, which had the photos already up and ready for me to see." She snickered. "I might have managed to embarrass Al in the process, too. By the time the Caruso brothers left, they were satisfied it wasn't me in that photo."

As he neared the porch, she stood; the gun in one hand and phone in the other. She dropped her voice into a husky whisper, "Care to step inside, handsome?"

"Why, yes; yes, I would." He countered with a deeper tone in his own voice. She wondered what was going on behind those sunglasses and balaclava. His gloved fingers traced the curve of her jaw.

She closed her eyes and sighed, leaning into the touch. He really shouldn't have that effect on her. No one else caused her heart to nearly jump from her chest, shivers to race down her spine, or make her legs feel like jelly with the touch of a hand, gloved or not.

"Not fair," she whispered, as her hand with the phone fumbled for the door.

Somehow, she managed to open the door, and when she opened her eyes, he was already slipping past her into the house. One of these nights, that mask was going to come off, along with the rest of his clothes.

Following him inside, she tossed the robe on the bed. She wore a very short skirt and a short-sleeved blouse beneath the robe. A pair of ankle boots sat on the floor next to the bed.

"Very nice. What are you wearing beneath it?" the Sandman said cheerfully as he gestured to her outfit.

Heat flared across her cheeks, and she was pretty certain the blush went down to her cleavage.

"Why don't you find out?" A sly smile pulled at her lips as a dare sparkled in her eyes.

He actually approached her, removing his sunglasses, and tucking them into his trench coat as he came closer. He pulled off his right glove, slowly, and it disappeared into his trench coat as well. His fingers, rough but warm, brushed against the exposed flesh of her breasts and a shiver of delight raced through her. He leaned in close to her.

"Take off the mask and see what happens," he invited.

Dares were always something that got Selia into trouble because she could never back down from them. His words sounded an awful lot like a dare to her. Hesitantly, she searched his face for any sign that would tell her to stop. Not seeing anything that would signal she was overstepping bounds, she lifted the edge of his mask and slowly pulled it up to his nose. She swallowed hard as she stared into his eyes, her lips quivering in anticipation and excitement, wondering if she should continue or stop there.

His lips quirked upward into a smile as his eyes brightened. She watched, as though from a distance, as his face lowered to hers and her lips parted. Her eyes closed as their mouths met and she melted against him, her hands wrapping around him as the kiss deepened and their tongues danced together, exploring each other's mouths.

The kiss was heaven on earth and all thought evaporated from her mind, desire taking its place. She felt him turn her, his hands roving over her body even as she pressed against him. He tasted like coffee and cream, with a hint of mint. She suddenly decided coffee wasn't so bad, after all.

The Sandman slowly moved her towards the bed, except some part of her didn't like that idea. She turned him around and shoved him onto the bed. With a wide, brilliant, almost feral grin, she pulled off the blouse, revealing a black bra with lace fringing the edges and tossed it to the side.

She was crawling up the bed overtop him, when she heard a crash and her brain suddenly caught up with what she was doing. Looking to the side, she saw the lamp was on the floor in pieces, and the bulb shattered. Blushing fiercely, she ducked her head before looking towards the Sandman with just her eyes. He leaned up on his elbows and began chuckling, which caused her to giggle a little.

"Well, should we take that as a hint to stop for now, or shall we just trash the place?" he said with a killer smile.

Selia groaned and curled up on the bed beside him, draping herself across his side. She kissed his chin even as her hand played across his chest.

"We probably should take the hint," she sighed, tilting her head back to look up at him. "If Al sends the boys back, I'd have a hard time explaining how I managed that feat, not to mention the reason why." She nuzzled up against his neck, enjoying his unique scent. "I can't tell them the truth," she whispered, "Though I would most definitely rather be enjoying you."

"I'd like that as well," he said with a smile. He paused, considering something. "I can get a replacement lamp here within an hour. Let me make a call. That will negate you needing to explain anything. Now, if we can just get this mess cleaned up, perhaps get a cold shower..." He trailed off with a laugh.

She giggled and had to force her eyes from darting down his body to find out just how aroused he was. "Very well," she finally said, kissing his jaw lightly. "I'll go find a broom and dustpan while you make your call."

Sitting up, she scooted towards the edge of the bed and paused. Glancing over her shoulder, she teased, "So... you plan on letting me take the initiative, huh?" She dropped a wink. "I'll keep that in mind."

"What can I say? Vigilantes like strong women," he replied. "It cuts down on the need to rescue them."

She snickered before replying, "Takes all the fun out of it for the girl, though." Standing, Selia headed for the bedroom door. Pausing in the door frame she added over her shoulder, "I wouldn't object to being grabbed and ravaged. Especially since I know you can leave me weak in the knees and putty in your hands."

"What made you think I'd let you keep the initiative after things got started?" he retorted with a wink.

Selia swooned in the doorway. Oh, gods, the man was evil. She turned to look at him with desire filling her eyes. "Mmmm, good point. Guess we'll have to find out, won't we?"

"At some point, yes, we will," he agreed.

Selia smiled and left the room. If she stayed too much longer, the phone call wasn't going to get made and they'd probably still be there at noon the next day. A delightful and thoroughly enticing thought, even if it wasn't a very practical or safe one.

As she searched the kitchen for a broom and dustpan, Selia had to admit she was somewhat thankful chaos had crashed down around her. If it hadn't, she wouldn't have been able to meet the Sandman, let alone discover such an overwhelming attraction for him.

A part of her knew there was something more than a physical attraction, but her saner side refused to examine it and figure out what it was.

Locating the items, she padded back to the bedroom and found the Sandman standing by the door, his mask back in place. Such a pity. He had such handsome and strong features. When he saw her, he must have read something in her expression.

"I didn't want to keep the mask halfway on, it's not comfortable. If I took it off..." He shrugged. "I'd be tempted to kiss you, eventually even getting back to your lips."

"More's the pity," Selia murmured, as she knelt beside the broken lamp.

He sighed and gestured towards her bra. "Would you mind putting those away? They're more dangerous than your swords."

Looking up, Selia's face flushed. "I, umm... I'll go grab another blouse," she replied.

Picking up the largest, almost-intact bottom of the lamp, she dropped it in the small trash can in the room on her way out. Smiling, she darted to her bedroom and grabbed a dark blue blouse from a drawer and pulled it on over her head. The blouse had small cap sleeves, a deep scooped neck, and was practically a second skin.

Returning to the bedroom, she said, "Whoever filled out the wardrobe must have thought Al was putting up a mistress. I doubt think there's anything not scandalous in that closet!"

She crouched near the mess and began piling the rest of the large pieces on the dustpan before using the little broom.

The Sandman hadn't moved from the door, which was far from annoying. All things considered; it was probably a good idea. In fact, she found it difficult to not think of his lips on her, his hands roving over her body as he explored with warm, light kisses.

Standing, the dustpan full, she turned to find him directly behind her, and her breasts now brushed up against his chest. *Why did the fabric of her blouse have to be so damned thin?* she wondered as she smiled softly into his eyes.

"I think it's time I made that call," he said, a little hastily. He pulled out what looked like an armored flip phone, opened it, and began scrolling through numbers, moving away from her suddenly.

All Selia could do was nod. The mess was cleaned up and she somehow managed to dump the dustpan of pieces in the trash can without spilling it on the floor. Leaving him to make the call without her as a distraction, she stepped into her bedroom and sat on the edge of the bed. Running her hands through her hair, she fell back onto the mattress and stared at the ceiling.

What in the names of all the gods was going on with her? The Sandman wasn't the first man who had aroused her, but no one else had ever affected her as strongly. She didn't understand it, but then, she hadn't dated a lot, either. Drawing in a deep breath, she rolled off the bed and decided to search for shoes.

By the time she'd found a halfway decent pair that wasn't three-inch high stilettos, she had managed to calm her nerves and bash down the nearly overpowering desire to rip every piece of clothing from the Sandman's body and carry out every promise and threat she'd spoken so far.

Restraining herself became considerably easier when she remembered Soren was in the hospital and Alex said he didn't want to have to kill her. She returned to the main bedroom to find the Sandman tucking the phone away, and once again, looking outside.

"So, how long before the lamp is delivered?" she asked, interrupting his thoughts.

"It should be here within an hour. It will be coming from a nice Hispanic family business. They barely speak English, but that's a positive thing when you want to keep a low profile." He glanced at her. "Yes, I'm fluent in Spanish."

"I'm just a bit envious," she replied with a smile. "I can get by, but I'm nowhere near fluent in Spanish. Italian, yes. Spanish? Not so much."

"I won't tell you the other languages I'm fluent in, then," he said with a shrug. "I spent two years going through those computer language software programs. You should try them."

Lowering her lashes, she didn't tell him she was fluent in Latin, Russian, Hebrew, and German. She even knew enough French to be more than a passing tourist due to the high school classes she had taken. Those were in addition to the languages she'd learned on Temeria, due to the pirates her people traded materials with.

"Perhaps I should look into that," she replied. Turning her eyes back to his, she added, "So… what shall we do until the lamp shows up?"

"What did you have in mind for tonight?"

"Well, I'd like to see Soren again before checking out Azyre House," she replied. "But I need your help in coming up with a disguise that will fool even him." She sank into the single chair in the room and leaned back into it like a queen on her throne. "I have an idea, if you're interested."

"I've been interested in all of your ideas so far," he conceded. "Go ahead."

Selia smiled softly and leaned forward, excitement and delight etched on her face. No one would recognize her. Not even Soren.

Chapter Eighteen

Selia followed the Sandman into the hospital, once again taking the backdoor. Again, no one stopped them or spoke, though a few did give her a second glance before smiling and turning back to their work. She didn't bother keeping her head down; what was the point when she was with the city's most notorious vigilante?

The Sandman stopped outside Soren's room and leaned causally against the wall. She paused, her hand on the door handle and gave him a quizzical frown.

"You coming in?" she asked.

"Nah, you need the time alone with your dad," he replied, hands in his pockets.

Her face smoothing out, she smiled, leaned over, and kissed his masked cheek. She'd eventually get used to the unusual texture of his balaclava, but that was okay. There was plenty of time. Opening the door, she slipped inside, allowing it to ease closed behind her. Soren glanced towards the door before doing a double take. A smile grew beneath her scarf as he stiffened and began searching for a weapon he didn't possess in a panic.

"Who the hell are you?" he demanded, as he twisted on the bed, still trying to find a weapon, or rather something that could be used as a weapon.

Selia giggled. She couldn't help it. Seeing Soren unable to find a weapon of any sort was too funny, especially since he was in a hospital bed and clothed in one of their gowns. He paused and looked closer as she walked towards him.

He sighed and collapsed back against his pillows, finally recognizing her.

"Selia, I should take you over my knee for this."

She giggled again and took off her neoprene gloves before taking his hand in hers.

Soren gripped her hands tightly with his left hand as he shook his head and gestured towards her outfit with his right. "You're using that as a costume?"

She freed a hand and fingered the wavy, shoulder-length blonde hair of the wig she had chosen from the Sandman's vast collection. Her brows were now blonde, and she had changed her eyes to green, thanks to contacts. She'd used enough eye shadow and liner to make her now-green eyes pop even more before applying blood-red lipstick that wouldn't come off without makeup remover or a lot of scrubbing, even if the scarf she wore did hide her lips.

The scarf wrapped around the lower portion of her face, allowing only her eyes and forehead to be seen. Somehow, the Sandman had procured a Kevlar vest that managed to reveal plenty of cleavage, and she wore a plunging V-neck black blouse over it. A wide utility belt emphasized her narrow waist and the black leather jeans made her legs seem even longer. Black waterproof boots completed the basic ensemble, but it was the black trench coat that truly brought the entire outfit together.

Of course, the gun tucked into a shoulder holster and the twin swords beneath the trench coat, didn't hurt, either. A small Keltec was snug inside her left boot and a very nice set of throwing knives were tucked in her right.

"It fooled *you*, didn't it? And you know me better than anyone else," she countered, her eyes dancing with laughter as she looked down at him.

Soren raised a brow, the smile fading slightly. "Really? Is that still true? What about your not-so-little sidekick?" Selia blushed hard, and though she opened her mouth to speak, nothing came out. Soren's smile grew. "Only three shades of red? You must not have said, or done, much."

"Not for lack of trying," she muttered, glancing away as her face burned.

"Maybe you shouldn't bother telling me details." He paused, squeezing her hand before changing topics. "What have you learned about Alfi's plans so far?"

"Nothing more than what I've already told you. He's been in touch with, Azyre House, and plans to auction the information to the highest bidder," Selia replied, feeling guilty for not knowing more.

"That's unfortunate. You need more intel before you can act against him. Otherwise, killing him might not prevent what he has planned." Soren shook his head, relaxing further into his pillow.

"I could learn more if I wasn't relegated to the bungalow," Selia grumbled.

She didn't bother to hide her annoyance. It was pointless when Soren knew her moods better than anyone else. She may have had an excellent poker face, but Soren had been around her long enough to know her little tells.

He snorted. "Oh, yeah. You're really staying at the bungalow. It doesn't look like you've been restricted to the bungalow to me."

"I'm not? Tell that to Al when he sends the guys to check up on me daily." Selia retorted.

Soren grunted and shifted in the bed. "Not sure what I could do to help about that."

"Don't worry about it, Papa. I've still got a few surprises in store."

Soren chuckled a little before a yawn interrupted him. "You need to go, or I need some coffee." He stretched, laughed, and then yawned again. "And you'll have to take off that damned scarf."

"I'll let you get some rest, Papa," Selia said, finding it easier and easier to call him that endearment.

Probably because she'd finally allowed herself to consciously acknowledge what she'd been feeling ever since she'd realized he truly cared about her. She pulled the scarf down and kissed his cheek.

Soren returned the kiss and smiled up at her. "Take care of yourself, *piccolina*, and be careful."

"I will," she promised before turning and walking away.

Soren's voice stopped her as she went to open the door. "You have a name for this… persona?"

Selia smiled and looked over her shoulder at him, pulling the scarf back into place.

"Nightshade," she replied, and Soren's laughter followed her as she left the room.

"I'll take it he's doing well," the Sandman said as the door cut off Soren's laughter. He nodded towards the room. "Care sharing the joke with me?"

"He asked what I was calling myself," Selia replied sweetly.

"Yeah?" the Sandman asked, the fabric of the mask stretching to hint at the smile beneath it.

"Nightshade," Selia replied impishly. She lowered her voice until only he could hear her. "He didn't recognize me, so I think this should be a safe disguise."

"Good," the Sandman replied. "We have a detour to take before we can make a visit to Azyre House."

"Oh?" Selia asked, intrigued. "Did you learn something?"

"Yeah, I learned there's going to be a bunch of drug dealers using a rave near here as a cover to meet and sell their goods. I plan on busting them up."

There was a darker edge to his voice and for some reason; it made Selia want to jump him that much more.

"Well, then? What are we waiting for?" she asked. His brows rose above his sunglasses, which made her smile widen that much more. She slid an arm through his as she explained, "Well, I hate being late for a party."

Chapter Nineteen

Selia had never been to a rave, so it took her a few moments to orient herself to the cacophony and visual overstimulation. Over a hundred, possibly closer to two hundred, people aging from sixteen to forty gyrated, undulated, and writhed about the open floor. They probably thought of it as dancing.

Clothing seemed almost optional. She noted a number of topless people decorated with strategically applied paint that was iridescent with the black light that poured in from all sides. Strobes, set to different timers, flashed in time with the constant pounding of percussion. Songs changed, but the drumming rhythm seemed to be nearly the same, with barely a pause in between.

The exception was when the DJ on the raised platform took time to shout out to the crowd and rev them up. She could smell and see alcohol being consumed, along with burning tobacco and less legal substances. Vials and pills were being passed about. Noses and mouths were being filled with chemicals and derivatives of plants that grew freely in her homeland.

On Temeria, such plants were grown for their medicinal purposes, but here, she did not see anyone suffering from near-fatal wounds or debilitating disease. The only sickness Selia could detect around her was the poison of over-indulgence and a complete lack of restraint.

The smell of intimate contact was also strong. Selia knew all of these things happened in this city, and that in some ways her employers fueled it. But she had never seen it all in the same place, so highly concentrated. It took a bit to regain herself and to be fully alert to her surroundings.

What grounded her the most was the Sandman's hand as he gripped her left forearm. His touch was the only familiarity in this place. He leaned over and whispered in her ear.

"Are you going to be okay? It's a lot to take in the first time."

She dimly realized he wasn't whispering; he was almost shouting. The volume of the music was loud enough to require it. She nodded her head. Turning, she spoke into the Sandman's ear.

"I'm fine. Just a little amazed at the pandemonium."

He nodded and looked into the window. They were perched on the roof of the warehouse that housed the party and looked into the skylight. "Just blend in if you want to go inside. Move your hips, look dazed, don't make a lot of noise, and you won't be noticed. Well, you'll get noticed because you're beautiful, but that can't be helped."

"Why can't I take part in your little drug bust?" she asked.

"Oh, you can make your way to the back alley whenever you like," the Sandman replied with a smile. "But you'll be a little too memorable for anyone who's around to give a statement to the police."

"Still planning to leave witnesses, eh? How have you kept a low profile for so long?"

The Sandman didn't answer, aside from rolling his eyes and moving to the back of the building, disappearing down the fire escape.

Selia supposed she would stand out, dressed in head to toe black. Even if she removed the mask across her face, an athletic blonde in a skin-tight black outfit and swords would stand out pretty well down there.

Maybe, she thought, if she stripped down to her expensive underwear…

Deciding that she would rather take part in the violent aspect of the evening than dance with a bunch of strangers, Selia watched the people below for a while longer. She was confident that once the real fun began, she'd hear something. She snickered at a stray thought that she'd wait until she heard the Sandman cry for help.

The scene below soon began to bore her, however. Once she was used to the chaos taking place, there was very little to interest her. A final glance into the throng did provide one bit of interest for her. Several girls were grouped together, all of which had light colored hair, except for the tips, which each girl had dyed a different color. She pondered on how intrigued she was by that as she made her way to the fire escape the Sandman had gone down.

As she came to the top of the ladder, she heard grunts and yells cut short. From the roof two stories up from the alley, Selia witnessed the Sandman in fighting form. He spun from foe to foe, the extended steel batons cutting through the air before impacting on weapons, limbs, and the occasional skull.

Four men lay on the pavement around the Sandman. Two more were in the midst of falling to join the unconscious. There were three more men, armed with guns, who continued to fight with him. None of them were far enough to make a clear shot without risking injury or death. They seemed to be waving their guns at the Sandman, as if he was going to do them the courtesy of holding still long enough for them to shoot.

The sound of a breaking forearm was followed by the clatter of a firearm to the pavement; one less weapon to worry about. Even as she waited with keen interest to see what method the Sandman would use to disarm and undoubtedly subdue the final pair, Selia's eyes caught movement a little further away. A good fifteen feet away, two more people, a male and a female, were entering the alleyway from an adjutant street. Both wore denim and leather clothing, lean of build and confident of stride. They saw the Sandman in action and moved simultaneously. Semiautomatic handguns, looking too large to be comfortable for either of the newcomers, came out of their jackets and pointed at the Sandman's back.

Selia didn't think. There was a moment of remembering that the Sandman was dressed, literally, in head to foot Kevlar that would prevent anything short of a high-powered rifle round from puncturing his body. She pondered how many similar situations the Sandman might have faced and survived.

She just leapt from the second story roof. Her arms went wide as her legs tucked together. Wind blew against her body as she plummeted to the couple who were even now discharging their weapons. Her eyes and mind locked onto the sight of the Sandman being slammed forward by the impact of both guns. Her eyes were sharper than they had ever been since she came to the city.

The puckered holes that appeared in the material of the Sandman's trench coat burned into her mind. The sound of his batons falling from his hands onto the street sounded horribly clear. The impact of his body as he hit the street seemed to be pressing against her own flesh. She screamed as she fell the last few feet into the ones who had shot the Sandman.

Her forearms smashed into opposite shoulders of the female and male just before her feet touched the pavement between them and her knees bent to absorb the impact of the fall. Selia came up, swinging her fist into the male's face. Her knuckles struck the man's face just below his right eye, and the bones of his skull gave slightly an instant before the force of her blow forced the man to his knees. Selia grabbed the female by her medium-length blonde hair and pushed her face down into Selia's rising knee. The woman's nose broke, and Selia felt teeth come loose against her Kevlar-reinforced knee.

She pulled back on the woman's hair and was momentarily surprised when the woman's hair came up without the woman attached to it. As the woman slid to the ground, groaning, Selia recognized her as one of the young girls whose hairdos she had been admiring earlier. This one's tips had been dyed a brilliant shade of jade. The green appealed to Selia in some distant corner of her mind. The wig went into her trench pocket as she moved swiftly past the fallen pair.

She was only a few steps from the Sandman, trying to get up, when the two men he hadn't had the opportunity to dispatch opened fire. Selia moved confidently forward, noting the clumsy and shaky aiming of the two young males who might not even be out of high school. She also noticed that people were pouring out of the back entrance of the warehouse, and smartphones were pointed in her direction.

Hell, she thought, *I'll give them a show.*

Continuing to move forward, Selia seemed heedless of the bullets being fired at her, which wasn't hard, in her opinion. The guys were horrible shots. She knelt, grabbed the Sandman's dropped batons, and flung the one in her left hand at the nearest shooter.

The baton hit the gun and the fingers that gripped it. There was a collection of muted crunching sounds. The gunner howled as the gun dropped from his broken fingers. Even as this was happening, Selia threw her body down into a half-roll, half-flip and landed on the ground past the injured gunner. The momentum carried her on, and she rolled up into a crouch before the second shooter, whose arm was still outstretched past her. He was aiming where she had been, more or less, seconds ago. Selia brought the remaining baton in a full swing up between the gunner's legs.

The growing crowd around the back exit all shouted "Ooooooh!" in mock sympathy; the final gunman could only manage a soundless wail. His knees buckled, his hands coming to his crotch. The gun discharging was obviously not a reflex, but rather a matter of the gun still being in his hand as both fists clenched.

Unless, of course, the gunman had some strange notion that shooting himself in the knee would improve how he was feeling. Some shrieked at the sound of the gun firing, but more laughed at the result. Selia saw some of the crowd push in for a better view, their smartphones held in front of them.

Reaching behind her, Selia retrieved the baton she had tossed. She hefted both weapons and thought, *Nice. I see why he likes these.*

She rose slowly to a standing position.

"Hey, Nightshade," a familiar voice called from behind her. She turned around, facing the Sandman. He stood three feet behind her and asked casually, "Mind giving those back, now?"

She tossed the batons to him, underhanded. He caught them deftly, but she could read the stiffness in his movements. He was in a lot of pain.

"Hey, Sandman! Dude!"

This call came from someone in the crowd milling outside the warehouse's back entrance. Selia glanced over even as the Sandman looked past her to the crowd. Selia estimated at least half the rave was either in the alley or trying to get there.

"Take a picture with you and your sidekick, man?"

A tall, gangly male with blue hair that was cut short on the right and covered most of the left side of his face was holding up his iPhone. His wrist was festooned with glowing bracelets, and he had a hopeful smile on his face. Others were shouting that they, too, would like a photo-op. The rest were just staring, videotaping, taking pictures, or furiously texting. A handful were going "old school" and actually talking on their phones. The phrase "O-M-G! You are not gonna *believe* what just happened!" rang out in several voices, overlapping one another.

"I'm… not the Sandman." The Sandman said in an almost serious, carrying voice. "And she isn't my sidekick." There was a long, awkward pause as the sound of smartphones snapping pictures filled the silence. As if he couldn't handle the spectacle and silence, the Sandman all but blurted a final statement. "Don't do drugs, kids; they're bad for you."

"If you loved the show, make sure to buy the graphic novel!" Selia suddenly shouted in a loud, absurd voice. She didn't know what was coming over her. She also realized that she was waving at the crowd like she was Miss America on a parade. For some reason, she couldn't stop herself. "Tonight's entertainment was brought to you by the owners of the establishment and that awesome DJ! Give 'em a hand!"

Most of the crowd turned to face the open door and began applauding.

Selia moved towards the Sandman, who was already ducking into the shadows. She took a chance and cast the spell that made her undetectable in shadows, taking care to cast it wide enough to affect the Sandman as well.

She looked back to see the crowd trying to find them. She knew the spell wouldn't show up on a camera- it didn't produce any light or visible energy, and they were both in the darkest part of the alley. She followed after the Sandman, knowing they were heading toward the motorcycle for a fast trip to his lair, and an even faster trip back to the bungalow outside of the city.

Chapter Twenty

She was mostly right. They were on the eco-friendly and silent motorcycle within minutes. But the course that the Sandman took was not what she expected.

"Ummm... you just missed the turn-off for the lair." She yelled through her helmet, leaning against the Sandman's.

"We are heading straight to the bungalow. Can you keep that 'hiding' spell on us while we're traveling? We need to get there as quickly as possible and not every cop is going to look the other way for us." The Sandman's voice carried back to her, aided by the wind.

"Sure," Selia replied. "It's a spell any novice can cast. I was a year away from being granted master status when I was banished."

Magic came from life and the living, and the stronger the caster, the more powerful the spell. Or, with the lower-level spells, the longer they could be held before tiring the mage. Though Selia hadn't cast a lot of magic out of fear in the last ten years, she was still strong in the arcane. It wasn't something that would just vanish from not being used.

Grow rusty like a tool left unused, sure, but not disappear. Considering she had been using some magic, mostly novice, apprentice, and initiate level spells, she was able to use the less-frequently used spells without worry of being wiped out by them.

"Good. Hold on tight," he warned, and the bike lurched silently forward.

The on-board speedometer display jumped to 110. She had to really concentrate to work the spell. That was going to be a challenge when her arms had to be locked as strongly as possible around the Sandman's waist.

"Why the rush to get back to the bungalow?" she yelled, confident the spell would hold long enough for the question.

When this was over, she was definitely going to delve back into her mage craft that she'd let atrophy for almost a decade. Odd that she'd been so diligent those first two years about keeping up her training before allowing this new world to overcome a lot of it.

"How long did it take Big Al to freak out and send goons to the bungalow when a single picture of you playing Mrs. Sandman showed up on the internet?" he practically shouted at her. "How long do you think he's going to sit on a whole page of YouTube video clips before checking to make sure you weren't lying the first time? You'll be lucky if he doesn't have you tailed twenty-four seven after that fiasco!"

The spell flickered for a few seconds as what he said hit her like a brick wall. She spat out one of the many curses she'd learned in Italian as she gripped his waist tighter. Love, anger, and even fear were powerful emotions that could be used to fuel spells. Selia pulled her annoyance and fear of them being caught together and fed it into the magic. Some lessons, it seemed, were returning with a vengeance.

Fortunately, the forest to her temporary home was coming into view and they were slowing down. Even before the cycle stopped, she jumped off and grabbed the cover from the side. Using a touch of magic, she had the bike covered the moment the Sandman slid off the seat.

Selia took off at a run, pulling off her coat even as they neared the back door, the Sandman on her heels.

Pulling him into the bathroom, she yanked the door shut before shoving the jacket into his hand.

"If... *if* you are right, it won't take Alex and Bernie long to show up here. Even shadows can be seen in a dark house," she said by way of explanation, as she tossed her gloves on the sink's edge. The bathroom was the only room in the house with no windows. She tugged off her belt, followed by her boots.

A knock on the door sounded even as she was wiggling out of the skin-tight leggings she wore beneath the Kevlar pants. A few more softly spoken curses and she kicked the Kevlar pants and leggings towards the Sandman.

She stuck her head out the door and yelled, "Just a minute!" She yanked out the pins in her hair and tossed the blond wig in the sink. Quickly, she removed her cosmetic contacts and set them carefully on the edge of the sink. Smirking, she pushed the Sandman into the shower stall, shoved her weapons against his chest, and turned on the water.

"Stay put and shut up," she told him as she shut the door and raced to the 'clean' bedroom while jerking on the bathrobe.

Running to the door, she was a bit surprised the door hadn't broken in, from the sound of the insistent pounding that hadn't stopped. She turned the deadbolt and lock, and threw open the door, a scowl on her face.

One hand held the robe shut, and she knew her hair was a mess, half-pinned and half-falling around her head. Her makeup was smudged, and considering what her reflection in the mirror had been, she looked as though she'd be in the middle of something pretty intense.

"Make this quick," she growled. "You just interrupted what would have been a very... enjoyable… shower."

Bernie's hand was in mid-knock, and he stared at her, his eyes wide and his mouth dropped half-way open before he snapped it shut. Alex was doing his best to not stare at her, though his eyes kept flicking back to her hair, face, and where she was grasping the robe just at her neck.

"Um, we, uh…" Bernie stuttered.

"We're here to make sure you weren't out... anywhere... tonight," Alex said, his eyes staring at the living room window.

"Uh, we might need to see your... guest," Bernie managed to say as he stepped carefully past Selia before nearly running into her bedroom.

"Fine," Selia said, shifting seductively. "I'll be right back."

She turned and sauntered casually back to the bathroom, opening the door just enough for her to slip into it. She walked to the shower and opened the door.

It took everything in her to not burst out laughing as she stared at the Sandman.

Standing in the middle of the falling water, he was grinding his teeth. Frigid water splashed out and she realized belatedly she'd only turned on the cold.

"Well, you did say you wanted a cold shower," she whispered, which only got her an even angrier glower and more grinding of teeth.

"Sweetheart, it seems some friends have come over to see if I'm safe. I haven't the foggiest idea why, but they said they might need to see you." Selia continued, her voice loud, seductive, and apologetic.

She held a finger to his lips, getting her wrist wet. She placed her other hand at her throat and used just a touch of magic to change her voice.

When she spoke, it was in a higher, playful voice, nothing like her own. "Aww, but I was hoping to have you all to myself, darling." She paused, grinning at the fury burning in the Sandman's eyes. In the 'other woman's' voice, she added, "Are they going to be joining us?"

Selia dropped her hand and dispelled the magic. In her normal voice, she replied. "I don't know, honey. I'll have to ask them."

She leaned in and kissed the Sandman on the cheek. Giving him a purely wicked grin, she closed the shower door. Returning to the living room, she ran her wet hand over her now-damp hair. Both men stood with slack jaws and bulging eyes. Alex gathered himself into a more respectful pose and expression within a second. Bernie continued to gape, although a very chauvinistic smirk was pulling at one corner of his mouth.

"So, do I need to tell my friend she needs to dry off and we make it a party?" Selia asked with as much innocence as she could muster, tilting her head slightly.

"Uhhhh..." Bernie said, before a teenage giggle erupted briefly from his mouth. He actually slapped his left hand to his mouth.

"No! No need for that!" Alex said quickly. He actually put his hands out as if to ward off something. "It's very nice of you to ask, but we can see you've been busy, and are going to be busy for a while."

"We actually can't see, so maybe we could-" Bernie began.

"Shut up!" Alex roared at Bernie. "Do you *ever* think before you speak? Soren would put your balls in a vase if you so much as-" Alex stopped suddenly, looked back at Selia, and gave her a nervous smile. "We'll be leaving, now," he said in a much calmer voice.

"Hey, just so we know..." Bernie said, that smirk still on his lips, "... your friend is..."

"Karen. Her name is Karen. She's a hot little redhead. A ballerina. No, you can't see pictures," Selia said; her voice laced with warning and pride.

"You and Karen enjoy the rest of your evening." Alex offered. "I'm get the walking tool over here out into the cold air, so he'll calm down. After that, we're a memory."

"Have a good night, boys," Selia drawled. "I know I will."

Bernie opened his mouth to say something, but Alex grabbed him by the collar and gave a swift yank. They shared a look, Bernie looking a little annoyed and Alex giving him an expression that was clearly a warning and a threat. With a final nod towards her, they turned and left. Selia locked the door after them before padding back to the bathroom, not bothering with holding the robe closed anymore.

Opening the shower door, the Sandman had moved to the far side of the stall but was still getting soaked; she reached in and turned the water off. Not that he could have done anything; his hands were still full of her stuff.

"They're gone," she said with a bright, cheerful smile, despite his glower. He remained silent as he stepped out of the shower. "We're all alone again, darling," she continued in her best seductive voice, still trying not to giggle at him.

"Well put a red wig on me and call me 'Karen', sweetheart," he said, deadpan. "You realize I have to clean every single one of these weapons, and the contents of my pouches, immediately? Otherwise, it's all rust and unreliable equipment?"

"I know," she replied, still trying to not giggle. "I'll help. I even have a robe you can wear while your clothes dry."

Chapter Twenty-One

After an extensive and time-consuming search of the living room, kitchen, and her bedroom for bugs and cameras, Selia and the Sandman sat on the living room floor cleaning their weapons. She wasn't surprised to find the place clean of bugs. After all, why would Alex and Bernie be sent to check on her if they'd bugged the place?

She glanced over and rolled her eyes. "Do you really have to wear that towel?"

He was wearing a tight pair of boxers, and a large, fluffy white towel that was wrapped around his face and head. Only his eyes and the bridge of his nose were visible. But she could swear he was grinning underneath the fabric.

"Man of mystery: Gotta stick with the *modus operandi*," he replied easily. "Besides, you haven't earned it yet. Not after that shower gag."

Selia giggled. "Well, it was either that or I conceal you with magic and chance it would collapse with them here." She turned her gaze back to putting the gun she'd just cleaned back together again. Stifling a yawn, she said, "I'm sure I could find a way to get back into your good graces. Alex and Bernie won't be back until at least tomorrow."

"By tomorrow the internet will be replete with rumors that we're getting our own reality show called 'Crimes of Love' or something worse."

She snickered. "Or thinking it was all a publicity stunt for a graphic novel in which you get a girlfriend to spice things up."

"Forgive me for not being thrilled if I have that option to think of as the best," he grumbled. "You know, I've been operating for over a year and barely been more than a rumor within certain circles. I met you and now I'm going to have to hire a publicist."

Laughing, Selia lifted her gaze to meet his still-angry eyes. "Yeah, well, this is probably why Soren drilled into me the importance of keeping my head low. He knew if I allowed my heritage to show, it wouldn't be missed." She yawned and stretched. "Another reason to want Alfi dead, yes?"

Secretly, she enjoyed allowing her true self to shine through. It felt right and natural, whereas keeping quiet and in the background had felt wrong. Even before she'd been pulled into this disaster, her life had felt wrong, as though she were living a lie.

"It's so nice that you are enjoying yourself. I wish I could have known you when I first started," the Sandman interrupted her thoughts with his irritated tone. "With all the publicity it would have garnered, I'd be pulling in mad merchandising royalties by now and living large off the interest rates of my Swiss bank accounts."

Her mouth dropped open, and no words came out. Her mind seemed locked by his statement and obvious disapproval.

"Oh, good. I have your attention," he continued with a faux casualness. "So, how do you see this all playing out? Should I just expect to spend the rest of my chosen career planning around driving you back and forth from your secret identity and your life as a Mafioso princess who couldn't harm a fly? No, that's not progressive enough. I'll put in an order for a matching electric motorcycle. Or do you want yours to have some extra style so people can tell who's coming on the scene?"

Anger curled inside Selia, and she carefully set the gun down and stood. She had to move away from the weapons, or she might be tempted to use them on him. Something she didn't want to do; she was a bit surprised to realize.

"I didn't ask for your help," she bit out. "I'm sorry if the thought of you being killed caused me to bring you into the limelight. That wasn't my intention." No way was she going to tell him there might be more than just a physical attraction between them. "If you prefer, you can walk out that door and I won't cross your path again."

The phrase was frequently used as a promise to never see anyone again on Temeria. If that was what he wanted, she'd do it. No matter how much it might hurt.

"No, you didn't ask for my help; but that's how it works." He continued, adopting a cartoon caveman voice, "See defenseless person running from goons, me go help, ugh. Sandman is good guy. He not know woman in high heels just want to corner goons so she can kick butt and dazzle a crowd." He dropped back into his normal voice. "Before you assault me or get righteous, explain how you've gone so long without lashing back at the life you chose?"

"Soren saved me from death. He took me into his home, kept me safe, and watched over me. Something he didn't have to do. He protected me when I had no one; showed me warmth, affection... love," she said, walking to the window in the kitchen and staring out the window. "I obeyed him first out of fear, then loyalty, and finally love. I saw no reason to disobey him. I actually feared that if I did anything, it would hurt him, and I couldn't betray the person who I owe so much. Someone who taught me so much and showed what a parent should be like to their child."

She glanced at the Sandman, who was watching in silence.

"Children in Temeria aren't shown much affection. My mother cared for me and my sisters, but there were no gifts given, no shoulder to cry on if a pet died. Nothing other than the distant caring like that of a bird that raises her chicks before kicking them out, to either fly or die."

"Fine. I can see why you were with Soren." The Sandman put aside the last weapon he'd been cleaning. "But I was referring to you being such a recluse. Obviously, you haven't gone ten years without keeping yourself in shape. I don't think the bow and arrows you keep in your gym bag are merely for sentimental value. You've been keeping yourself in training for a reason. Your true nature is screaming to get out and stay in the open."

She jerked away from the window. "What do you want me to say, Sandman? That I was waiting for a chance to wear a mask and that suit to storm the night?" She shook her head. "I couldn't do anything in the open. Sure, I keep in shape and keep the less obvious skills sharp, but that doesn't mean I was waiting for a chance to turn back into a warrior." She shook her head, not sure if he would even understand. "Soren encouraged me to honor my heritage, but that doesn't mean I could let it free." She sighed heavily. "I'd still be hiding my true self if I hadn't been forced into this ludicrous cat-and-mouse game."

The Sandman laughed, but it wasn't cruel. It was good-natured and it took her off guard.

"Selia, think back to the first time you started acting this way. I am not complaining, dear lady. But please... think back."

"What? The group was going to ambush you." She shrugged. "I couldn't let that happen, so I stepped in."

"I've been doing this for over a year, Selia," he said with a voice that was like a teacher explaining something to a slow but promising student. "Do you think that would have been the first time I got blind-sided? How many other... sidekicks, assistants, partners, whatever, do you think I've had?"

"You've had exactly zero," she replied with confidence. She didn't eavesdrop on the meetings Soren and the other underbosses had with Al for nothing, and the Sandman had been a frequent topic.

"Precisely," he replied, nodding. "So, how have I survived this long without you? Did you just happen to be there on the one night when things got too heavy for me?"

"No," she replied. "I was there because you took me to meet Lucien."

"You still don't understand," he said with a sigh. "I've been in much worse situations than the one you joined in on. That's not macho posturing, Selia. I was the one who interfered with the large shipment of illegally imported animals last fall. The police were alerted and did the cleanup. They took the credit. But that group of thirty crewmen that were 'apprehended'? The police didn't have to subdue a single one of them. You might have seen the hospital bills for those guys, since it was your 'family' that hired those guys. Think they were all standing in a single spot when I got there, and I threw a super-sized stun grenade at them?"

Selia gave a dismissive shrug. "That was one of the other underbosses." Then, it dawned on her and a look of understanding and comprehension crossed her face. "I get your point, I think. You didn't force me to step in. It was my choice. I could have easily stayed out of it, but I didn't. I entered the battle without any other thought than taking down the enemy."

Dear gods, did she just say that? It was almost a direct quote from her instructors on Temeria when she was learning the art of war. Talk about scary. She hadn't thought of those lessons for years.

"That's exactly what you did. You just saw an opportunity that you'd been secretly waiting for, and the rest was instinct and passion." He nodded to her. "When you jumped in, I actually had to think around *you* more so than the arrival of more goons. I appreciated the help, even more so at the rave. But your style is very different from mine. Some part of you wants to be a spectacle, to show what you are capable of. I want to be able to do what I chose to do without ever escalating odds against me. You can't do that when your enemies know who you are, what you look like, and how you operate."

Selia met his eyes with hers and kept his gaze as she asked in a completely emotionless voice, "Do you want me to stop? I'll still go after Alfi, but I'll leave the city to you if you desire it."

"I want you to respect the danger you put us both in." He began putting away the gear into the compartments of his belt, which was on the floor in front of him. "I enjoy working with you, and spending time with you. I'd like to think we can continue to spend time together after this mess with Alfi is done. I don't intend to kill more casually because you do. Nor am I going to lecture you about how you deal with adversaries. We will either find a way to work together; or we won't." He paused. "I'd prefer that we do."

"So would I," she replied softly. "I can't change who I am or how I was raised for sixteen years." She offered a soft smile. "At least you aren't going to be targeted for as many murders with me around."

"How do you figure that?" The Sandman rose up off the floor, the now repacked utility belt in his left hand.

His batons, gleaming with oil, hung from the loops made into the belt's webbing. He placed the belt on the table and went to the bathroom door. Both of their outfits were hanging inside to dry. He peeked in and nodded.

"Oh, come on," she replied. "There is photographic evidence of me with bodies at my feet. I was raised from the crib to kill and took my first life when I was eight. That, I might add, is considered 'old' for my people." She paused before continuing. "I come from a race who have been killing for generations. It's bred into us. That's a part of me that isn't going to change. If and when I fight, the probability of corpses is far greater than leaving people unconscious, bound, and gagged."

The Sandman chuckled. "You are incorrigible. I was referring to how do you figure I'll be targeted less? You came onto the scene after me. The body count has just increased by, oh, at least one thousand percent. For those who think you are my sidekick, I will be held accountable. For those who think you're my boss, I'm a way to get to you. Anyone disbelieving in you at all is just going to hold me responsible for the deaths you caused."

She considered what he said and tapped a finger against her lips. "I'll know for certain once things calm down and Soren is back at work." A smile pulled against her lips as he glanced at her with a raised brow. "Soren likes taking me along wherever the meetings are for the Family. I might not be in the room, but I certainly have enough spells under my belt to eavesdrop on any room. Soren knows it and likes having me take notes for later... use."

She'd never questioned his methods, but now she wondered why Soren asked her to do that. She now also wondered what he did with the notes she kept and if he acted against the things he had often objected so strongly to.

"I'll try to curb my more deadly tendencies. Perhaps if I had a pair of batons like you used," she offered with a smile.

"I've got a spare pair in the bike's compartments, along with replacements at the lair," the Sandman replied cheerily. He went into the bathroom and emerged with their outfits. "All dry. Now, what shall we do with the rest of the evening?"

"Are you going to take off that towel and leave the mask off?" Selia asked, her eyes twinkling.

"Nope, you haven't earned it yet," he replied, smirking.

"You jerk," she said, laughing. "Fine, how about a movie? Unless you prefer taking the chance of sleeping with me?"

"How do you feel about horror movies?" he asked, his dark eyes laughing.

Chapter Twenty-Two

Selia woke up to the smell of bacon, coffee, and the sound of something sizzling in a skillet. Her stomach grumbled and she slid from the bed, running a hand through her loose hair as she followed the smell into the kitchen. Her stomach rumbled even as she blinked her eyes trying to remember how she got into the bed. The last thing she remembered was being curled up on one of the sofas beside the Sandman watching an old horror flick.

At some point he had pulled her into his lap, and she must have fallen asleep. The memory brought a smile back as she remembered the steady beat of his heart and the warmth of his arms as he held her close. The fact she fell asleep in his arms spoke volumes, at least to her, about how safe she felt around him.

Come to think of it, it had taken her nearly a year before she'd allow herself to fall asleep anywhere near Soren. It was so odd seeing The Sandman in his outfit with a dish towel tossed over one shoulder and a spatula in one hand.

"Ah, so the sleeping beauty awakens," he teased, glancing at her over his shoulder. "Go grab a shower. I'll keep the food warm."

"Do I look that bad?" she asked, not the least bit bothered.

He raised his brows. "Go see for yourself."

Laughing, she did as he suggested. Her laughter grew as she stared at her reflection. Her hair was a tangled mess, half her lipstick was gone, and the rest of her makeup was horribly smudged. She was surprised he hadn't laughed or given her a look of disgust. His appeal just jumped a few more notches.

Using the makeup remover in the cabinets, she quickly washed her face. For a brief moment the horrified thought that Alex and Bernie had noticed her blond eyebrows crossed her mind. Her mind began to form a plausible explanation to give if they asked. Then she remembered their eyes never stayed on her face for more than a few seconds because they'd been far too distracted by her 'guest' and her supposed lack of clothing. Stepping into the shower, she decided that a hot shower would definitely make her feel a lot more refreshed.

Twenty minutes later with one towel wrapped around her body and another covering her hair, she padded into the bedroom and pulled a slinky white summer dress from a hanger. Thin straps crisscrossed over her shoulders, and she smirked at the fact it had a built-in bra as she dressed. A pair of equally strappy sandals completed the picture. Satisfied, she brushed out her hair and let it fall in wet curls.

When she went back into the kitchen, the Sandman was filling a plate with bacon, eggs, and sausages. A tall glass of juice and another of soda sat on the table. A nearly empty mug of coffee was near him on the counter.

"Impressive," she said as he turned towards her. "How is it no one has managed to snap you up? You're handsome, charming, and can cook. You have impeccable taste in clothing and weaponry. I might be a bit naïve when it comes to dating and many things about men, but I do know those aren't common traits."

"I don't socialize much," he said with a shrug. "I married early to a controlling, mentally ill woman. After five years, there was no doubt that I would ever give her enough, so I left." He looked to the ceiling and shook his head. "I never made enough money for her or did everything she wanted. She expected me to live off the welfare of others without her. Well... she was almost right."

He laughed once, and then continued. "I write articles, you see. Mostly for websites, now. It's a decent living, but because I don't chase celebrities or write sensational articles to back up absurd or baseless theories, it's not the most decent of incomes. Anyways, two years ago, long after my ex had gotten all she could in the divorce settlement, I won the lottery... literally."

Accepting the plate of breakfast food, despite the fact the sun was setting, Selia sat at the table. The Sandman sat across from her; his mask pulled up just far enough for him to drink his coffee.

"You won the state lottery," she repeated. "Nice. So, you stay hidden wherever you live when you're not bashing bad guys and saving the occasional damsel in distress." She speared some scrambled eggs and sausage on her fork. "I'm not foolish enough to think you live in that cozy little lair of yours." Dropping a wink, she turned to devouring her food.

"No, I actually live in the townhouse next door; the one that connects to the lair. I had that installed. This one, I bought from the neighbor who occupied it for thirty years. In fact, I bought most of the block. The biggest problem for people who suddenly get a large sum of money is that they don't really know how to use it wisely. Sorry, am I boring you?"

Selia shook her head, a bit in awe and amused by his freedom to tell her so much. She swallowed her mouthful of food.

"Not at all! A bit surprised that you're telling me so much about yourself," she replied. "I have a nice nest egg saved up and a good deal of money invested in a portfolio. Part of it is from Soren's generosity and part from my salary from working for him." She filled her fork up again. "Yes, I get paid the same amount as any other secretary and no, generous gifts of thousands of dollars are not an everyday occurrence." She tilted her head to the side. "So, what did the ex-wife do when she found out you hit the jackpot?"

He laughed. "She doesn't know. No one knows, except my parents, my first accountant, and the state lottery people. Oh, and now, you. I'm not breaking any laws by not telling my ex. It's not income she has any legal claim to. But, also, I didn't want people to know. I don't want any of the attention having access to large amounts of money can get you. My friends and the few associates I have in my... uh… normal life, think I'm just a very frugal guy who helps others when he can. The fact is, I made sure that I paid back my parents, friends, anyone who helped me out when I was struggling."

He took a sip of coffee before continuing. "I have very sensible parents, who never had a lot of money. It wasn't possible to pay off their mortgage for them without telling them how I could afford it. They supported me while I was dealing with the divorce, and the strain my settlement took on me. They want grandchildren but have figured I'll find another woman and settle down when I've found someone who's really good for me, and vice versa. Anyway, after paying off my debts to everyone- my ex doesn't get any kind of support and we had no kids- I made sure I paid all my taxes, had bank accounts set up to make sure I could pay all future taxes with the interest, but I still had a really, really big chunk of money left over."

"The first thing I did was buy this stretch of townhouses from my landlord. I grew up here, and this is my city. I wanted to have an income that didn't depend on writing articles. Writers don't exactly have a 401(k) to pay into. And I didn't want to rely on the lottery money. Silly, maybe, because it was enough to live in the way I was comfortable with. But, that's me. I didn't want to live like a rock star or a movie star, travel the world and throw money everywhere. Can you understand that?"

"It makes a lot of sense." Selia nodded, feeling very fortunate to have so much of his trust. She picked up a piece of bacon and nibbled at it thoughtfully. A smile tugged at her lips as she added, "You'd make a good father."

"If I'm as good as my dad is, I'll consider myself lucky," he said softly. Picking up a piece of bacon, he took a bite, chewed slowly, and swallowed.

"I don't know your parents, but I know you and you are a good man. Whoever you choose as a mate will be very lucky indeed," she said in almost a whisper. "The children will be even more fortunate." She gave a smile. "Sorry, please continue."

The Sandman shrugged off her comment. "After I bought this block, I hired a manager to take care of it. It's an old friend of mine. We've known each other for decades. We made sure to keep this neighborhood as free of drug dealers, pimps, and gang members as we could. But with all the options in the world, I decided to keep to myself and improve myself. Instead of going to a gym, I had my accountant set up credit cards for a small business that was responsible for all the landlord business. I bought gym equipment and lost forty pounds. At the same time, I did online college courses for business, communication, computer repair and service, learned seven languages... and all the while, becoming more dismayed with what was happening to people in this city."

He shook his head, lost in memories.

"After that first year, I got to spend a lot of time with another old friend who had become a cop. We talked, and still do, about what was happening, and how badly the police were handcuffed by rules and loopholes. I decided I would make a difference. I'm not a billionaire and I don't have a thing for bats, but you get the idea. There's a lot of stuff you can get that gives you an advantage over criminals... or even police. I hired another accountant who's never met me personally and set up other businesses that make money in real estate, housing, and computer technology. I have some major stock in the big computer companies. But they give me an income to buy stuff that makes me the Sandman. All bought legally, and from companies that have as clean a record as you can and still stay in business. Anything I get that isn't for plain old me is bought through the company I had built to fund The Sandman's efforts." He coughed and blushed a little. "Geez, I'm talking too much. Um, any questions?"

"You aren't talking too much." She assured him before pausing to take a sip of her juice. She continued, almost shyly. "I have only one question. What's your name?" She blushed deeply and rolled the glass of juice between her hands. "My name, my birth name, is Selia Nitetis Laios, not Selia Laios Lascari. I don't even think Soren knows my true middle name. I don't think I ever told him."

"Oh, I'm William. William Brendan Fredricks. Not a very exciting name. But pleased to meet you, Selia Nitetis Laios."

Selia laughed softly. "Perhaps not an exciting name, but it fits you." Her eyes twinkled as she lifted the glass to her lips. She added over the rim, "Tis' a pleasure to meet you, also, William Brendan Fredricks." Allowing the lilting, musical accent of her homeland to return to the fore as she spoke, it made his name sound exotic and enticing.

She picked up her plate, tilted the chair back precariously, and slid her plate into the sink. Allowing the legs to touch the floor again with a soft thud, she winked at her companion. He hid his laughter behind his mug. The ringing of her cell phone kept her from teasing him.

"Oh, look! Soren's calling."

Picking it up, she answered cheerfully. "Good evening, Papa! How are you doing today? Feeling better?"

"As a matter of fact, the doctors are amazed at the speed of my recovery," replied Soren. "Of course, they're surprised I'm recovering at all, considering the condition I arrived in."

There was an amused quality to his voice that Selia hadn't heard in a while. It reminded her of happier times when she was younger.

"I can't tell you how thrilled I am to hear that!" Selia exclaimed, delighted by his words and his tone. "Hopefully you'll be able to go home soon, and things will go back to normal." *Or at least, as close to normal as possible*, she added silently.

She smiled at the Sandman and decided that normal was a very relative term. Even after she resumed her place as Soren's secretary and personal assistant, she'd still return to the Sandman.

"Now, can we talk about your new nightlife?"

It was impossible to not giggle. "Uh, what about my new nightlife, Papa?"

Maybe she could distract him a little with the endearment. She kept her eyes carefully locked on the juice in her glass.

"You promised me you were going to be careful," he said in a teasing tone. "I should have made you promise to lay low and not bring attention to yourself. Of course, you didn't listen to me when I told you to stay away from him. So, what other disobedience can I expect from you?"

"I'm surprised you aren't yelling at me," she replied, not giving into nervous giggles, though she knew her laughter was evident in her words. "Does putting the fear of you into Alex and Bernie count as disobedience?"

"Not at all." Soren chuckled. "I mean it this time when I say it: Keep a much lower profile. For the love of the Virgin Mary, all of the hospital staff is talking about 'Nightshade' and her sidekick the Sandman."

At that, she did laugh. "That might make him a little happy." She raised her gaze to the Sandman, her eyes crinkling with suppressed laughter. Maybe that was why he was in such a good mood? "I'll try harder, Papa; I promise. Have you heard anything from Al about Alfi or, um, 'Nightshade'?"

"No one has seen Alfi." Soren grumbled. "Al has people keeping an eye on the auction building, but once the business starts, it's really too late to do anything but kill him. There are too many guards and too many witnesses for any kind of comfort." There was a pause. "He hasn't been to any of his usual haunts or his home. Hell, his mistress hasn't even heard from him. Al was actually quite complimentary about the lady of the evening; said it was good that she was keeping the Sandman occupied with other people's business."

Selia snickered. "Yeah, well, that wasn't exactly how it happened, nor was it planned on my part." She paused before adding, her smile growing as she spoke, "Yet Al sent the boys over to make sure it wasn't me. I can only imagine what's being said about me, after their visit." She took a sip of her juice as she kept her gaze level with the Sandman. "Guess someone else will have to visit the auction house and dig up some clues."

There was a long, heavy sigh from the speaker.

"Selia, careful doesn't even cover what you need to be. There is something else at play in all of this and none of us knows what or who it is. I don't care how trained or determined you or your friend is; this is all a bad scene." Soren sighed again. "Your cover for being at the bungalow has sent more than a few tongues wagging. Al wanted to know if you were aware the Church viewed such activities as a sin."

"Al can take his view and shove it. He knows exactly where I came from and in my homeland, such a thing is not considered a sin, or an abomination, or anything other than normal." Selia's temper flared. and she forced herself to tamp it down. "If he needs a reminder, I'll happily give it by speaking in my native tongue the next time we meet." She breathed deeply. "As for the rest, I'll be careful and inform him what you said. I swore vengeance and I will honor that vow." She added playfully, "We take that sort of thing serious back home, you know."

"I recall it very well," he said in a chiding tone. "When this is all done, you better be alive, and I want to hear all the details. Love you and be careful."

The line went dead.

She made a sour face at the phone and put it back down on the table where the Sandman had left it to charge; he must have plugged it in the night before for her. She just couldn't bring herself to call him by his real name. Not yet anyway.

"Papa said there's someone or something else involved in this, to be careful, and also confirmed my suspicion about needing to get into the auction house." She blushed and glanced away from him as she added, "He also said my little, um, acting last night has tongues wagging and that Al doesn't approve." She smiled at him slyly. "Guess after this is all over, I'll just have to be seen with a handsome, charming guy. Wouldn't happen to know someone willing to help me with that little problem, would you?"

The Sandman smiled. "I could probably whip up someone. Do you want a blonde, brunette, redhead, or bald?"

"As long as it isn't bald, I'll probably fall into his arms at first sight," Selia replied impishly. She laughed softly, as she confessed, "You left me breathless the night we went to visit Al. I have no doubt it will be a constant thing with you, no matter what you wear."

"Oh, such flattery! You can't be from around here," he said in an exaggerated tone, and batted his eyelashes.

She laughed. "Don't make me smack you. I know for a fact you have an incredible physique." Standing, she shook her head at him. "I'd best go get dressed before I disrespect your desire for privacy and prove my point."

She leaned over, kissed his masked cheek, and sauntered into the bathroom to change for that night's escapade.

Chapter Twenty-Three

A zyre House was a six-story building a few blocks from the docks. It wasn't overly elegant or extravagant on the outside, instead looking like a tall brick building with revolving front doors. A pair of guards walked the perimeter of the building. The Sandman pulled out a baton, but Selia placed a light hand on his arm before he could move forward.

Both had dressed at her bungalow, so there had been no short detour to his lair before going to the auction house. That meant they had more time to look for something that would tell them when the auction was going to be, which room, and possibly something about where Alfi was currently hiding. A pair of guards patrolled the outside, crossing by each other before continuing on along their path.

"I'll take care of this," Selia murmured. The Sandman narrowed his eyes at her, and she smiled. "No need to harm them," she whispered, a promise ringing in her voice. "Just watch."

Not bothering with hiding in the shadows, she strode across the small alley they'd been hiding in and approached the guard who was moving towards them. The other had already moved towards the next side of the building.

Just to be theatrical, Selia waved a hand in a sweeping gesture as the guard looked towards her, his hand falling to the gun at his hip.

"You don't need to do that," she said, her voice low, sultry, and commanding. The guard stopped and his hand fell to his side. She paused within arm's reach of the guard and motioned for the Sandman to join her. Even as she heard his steps nearing her, she continued speaking to the guard who was staring at her with unblinking eyes. "Now, you're going to let us into this building without activating the alarm and give us the keys that go to this building. After that, you will forget everything about this conversation and the pair of us before continuing your patrol as though nothing has happened."

The guard nodded and did as he was bid. He unhooked the round ring of keys from his belt and handed them to her, followed by a pass card from a pocket. Turning, he punched in a code to the door and held it open. Once she and the Sandman were inside, the guard let the door shut. Selia watched him move off before it closed completely. She gave the Sandman a sweet, innocent smile.

"I suppose I have nothing to worry about in the way of camera footage?" he asked.

"Nothing to see here but static."

"I'm just going to call you Obi-Wan from now on," he muttered under his breath.

Selia giggled and admitted, "I did tell you that Soren had me use my magic to coerce his clients into agreeing with him. This wasn't very different."

They had entered into the back of the building, which also happened to be the loading area. Shelving units went from floor to just a foot or two below the ceiling and the shelves were filled with boxes and bubble-wrapped items. Crates were stacked against the entire length of one wall and forklifts were lined up against the opposite. To the left of the door they had just entered was a narrow hallway and there was an office to their right.

"According to the floor plans, the offices are on the fifth and sixth floors," the Sandman said as he strode to their left. "Which floor do you want to take?"

"I'll take the fifth floor, you can have the sixth," she replied. "How do you suggest we keep in contact?"

The Sandman reached into his pocket and pulled out an ear bud; probably the same one she'd used before. She took it and slipped it into her ear. She asked under her breath as they started up the stairwell. "And you couldn't have given this to me back at the cabin?"

He chuckled and she swatted him lightly on the back of his head, making him laugh that much more.

"You jerk," she teased.

Sharing smiles, they fell into silence as they continued up the stairs. When they reached the fifth-floor landing, Selia nodded to him and opened the door, vanishing into the dark hallway. They had gone over their plan as they'd dressed at the bungalow. There were only a handful of offices on both floors and one of them had to hold the information they needed. Fortunately, the doors had not only a number but also names and descriptions of what was behind them.

Selia picked one door that stated it belonged to Aubrey Landress and used her magic to unlock the door. Aubrey Landress was a name she'd heard on occasion by some of the other underbosses when they were talking about who would deal in certain types of stolen goods. She was a cut-throat when it came to deals and had no problems using strong-arm tactics against anyone who dared cross her. Crossing to the desk, Selia began carefully looking for her day planners, schedule book, or anything she might keep names and dates.

"Find anything interesting?" she asked softly as she found a small black book and flipping it open.

"Not yet," the Sandman replied. "How about you?"

"I might have something," she replied, her eyes scanning the finely written notes quickly. She jumped ahead to the current date and flipped forward until her eyes found Alfi's name and a time. "Yeah, I think I found something useful."

What came back to her, however, were the sounds of a wrist breaking and a yelp of pain that didn't belong to the Sandman. She snapped the book shut, replaced it, and ran for the door as a crash filled her ear. It took every ounce of self-restraint she possessed to not talk to him as she threw open the door to the stairs and ran up them. By the time she reached the sixth-floor landing, silence met her ears.

"Sandman?" She asked, keeping her voice low. "Are you okay?"

Silence was her only answer. That wasn't a good thing, especially since she felt dread curling in the pit of her stomach. She crept down the hallway, checking each room carefully. He wasn't behind any of the doors. All right, she decided, time for a spell. Holding her hand up, she cast the basic locator spell she'd used before, fully expecting a blue dot to form on her palm.

When it didn't, her heart plummeted, and she stared at her hand in disbelief. Only one thing could prevent that from happening: another mage. Even if he were dead, the spell would have allowed her to locate the body.

Selia shook her head and headed back to the stairs. Instead of going down, she went to the roof. The moment she stood on the top of the building, she walked to the center and knelt like someone preparing to propose to their betrothed.

There was only one spell that she knew of that could possibly work, but she didn't know if it *would* work. It was one designed to find a mate. Not a mere spouse or lover, but a life-mate. It reminded Selia a great deal of the bald eagles of this land that took only one mate in their entire lifetimes and wouldn't find another until one of the pair died. Except for some Temerians, it lasted even after one of the pair died.

If it didn't work, she had no clue how to find him. If it did work, it meant she had a lot of explaining to do and was probably even more screwed. Somehow, she doubted she could tell Al that her mate was the Family's nemesis who went by the name of the Sandman. Personally, though, the idea was both frightening and exciting. It was something she'd figure out later, provided the spell worked and the Sandman was alive to discuss it with her.

Of course, the spell might also point her to the first boy she'd kissed when she was thirteen. If the spell led her to the ocean, she'd have to figure it wasn't tracking the Sandman.

Taking out the small knife from her boot, she nicked the heel of her left hand's ring finger. Once blood dripped onto the blade, she placed it in the palm of her left hand, the point at the tip of her ring finger and the hilt at her wrist. The left-hand ring finger had long been called the 'vein of love'.

Drawing a deep breath, Selia let it out slowly. Chanting the words to the spell, she allowed her affection, amusement, and yes, love for the Sandman, fuel the magic. The magic engulfed her, and she felt as though she were standing in the middle of a burning inferno.

Gasping, she whispered his true name. "William Brendan Fredricks."

The fire slowly abated to where she could breathe and every memory she had of the Sandman flashed through her thoughts. His smile that made his eyes twinkle and the way he teased her. The fire that burned in his eyes when they were filled with desire. The fury that blazed when he was angry. Their first meeting. His helping her escape the hotel. The disguise he used to escort her to Al's penthouse.

His unique scent that was a husky smell of pine and cloves mixed with something sharp yet sweet. Almost as though he wore cologne or aftershave that blended with his skin to create a smell that enticed her at every turn. She remembered his touch and the way it made her desire more than a mere caress. The fire finally abated, and she opened her eyes to find the knife glowing a blue silver.

Apparently, the spell worked. Selia pushed down the urge to give out a shout of triumph.

She felt a distinct pull towards her back and she stood slowly, holding the knife's hilt tightly in her hand. Turning, she realized which way she was being pulled.

Chapter Twenty-Four

Either the Sandman had been taken to somewhere closer to the docks, or her mate was back on Temeria, and she was truly screwed. Shrugging, she decided there was only one way to find out. She tucked the still-glowing knife back into her boot and started running towards the edge of the roof before jumping across to the building opposite the auction house.

From there, she descended the fire escape and began a steady run towards the docks, allowing the pull of the spell to lead her through a maze of alleys, up and over rooftops, and towards the docks. The pier came into view as she left an alley. She rolled her eyes, about to give up when she felt a harder pull to her left.

A smile crossed her lips as she cast a cloaking spell and began down the wide street to another large warehouse. Large double doors appeared to rise up, like huge garage doors with a smaller door beside them. A pair of large windows were high on the wall opposite the smaller door.

The magic pulled her towards the side where a small stairwell led up to a door about eight feet above her. She crept up the stairs and looked through the window but couldn't see anyone inside. Strange that the spell hadn't led her directly in the main door. Though he had to be inside somewhere.

Knowing better than to enter an unknown area, she looked around, but didn't see another way into the building, at least from her current position. Descending the stairs, she walked around the building, searching for another option, but no other buildings had fire escapes or provided easy access to the roof.

Shrugging, Selia returned and used a touch of magic to unlock the door. Peering around cautiously as she slipped inside, she didn't see any sign of people. On a table in the center of the room were the Sandman's tools, coat, and belt. Against one wall was a table with a coffee maker and amenities, which stood beside several snack and drink machines. She gathered up the Sandman's stuff and headed out the door directly across from the one she entered. Opening it, the magic pulling at her grew stronger.

A long hallway with windows to the right overlooking the area below met her eyes. Fortunately, it was dark, and she was still using the cloaking spell. She stood in front of the window and looked down to finally see the Sandman in a maze of boxes piled a good eight to ten feet around him. The Sandman was in a chair wrapped up by glowing ropes. He struggled furiously, and the ropes were only getting tighter the more he struggled. There were guards, or rather thugs, holding weapons and acting as sentries. She wasn't concerned. She had magic on her side.

Continuing down the hallway, she found the stairs that led down into the bay area. There was no door to open, so she walked between the guards at the door without a thought. Mazes were only confusing if you didn't know which way to go, and Selia knew exactly which way she needed to go. The spell didn't hurt, either. It actually made her path through the boxes faster than expected.

Glancing around the small room made from stacked boxes, she knelt beside the Sandman and dropped the magic. He stared at her in disbelief, but fortunately remained silent.

"Stop struggling, Sandman," she barely whispered, a hand on the rope. "Go limp and the ropes will drop."

He rolled his eyes but did as she bid, and the ropes dropped free.

"You just wanted to see if I'd go limp on command, didn't you?" he asked in a voice barely above a whisper.

"Not completely," Selia replied in the same tone. "The spell was designed so the more someone struggled, the tighter the ropes would become. If you stopped wiggling, it wouldn't cut off circulation. The spell also grows stronger from the force of will you expend trying to break it. I couldn't break through both without using most of my magic."

"Okay, fair enough," he replied.

She smiled at him beneath her scarf and stood. Feeling him stiffen, Selia turned around to find a blonde staring at her with soft, baby blue eyes.

The stranger had obviously been beautiful thirty pounds and ten or fifteen years ago. But now her breasts sagged, she was on the chunky side, and her choice of a silky, clinging gold gown did nothing to enhance her complexion or flatter her figure. Her hair, pulled up into an elegant chignon, only enhanced the lines on her face that even the makeup she'd caked on couldn't hide. The dimples in her cheeks deepened as she smirked at Selia and the Sandman.

Selia wrinkled her nose as the faint whiff of rotting flesh and mold tickled her nostrils. She glanced at the Sandman, but he didn't seem to even notice.

I can smell the taint of the spell on you. The words spoken from Selia's headmistress flashed through her thoughts and she suddenly realized what Mistress Anora had meant. Before Selia could even realize what she was doing, she had shoved the Sandman his gear, unsheathed her weapons, and was halfway across the floor twirling her swords before a powerful blast of icy air threw her back against a stack of boxes behind the Sandman.

The sound of three shots echoing across the building pulled Selia out of her daze, and she saw the woman snarling. Selia looked up and was gratified to see the Sandman had pulled the pair of Walther .45 automatic pistols he normally kept in his trench coat and had decided to throw lead at the woman instead of his usual non-fatal approach. It seemed he did know when it was time to break out the big guns, after all.

Selia muttered a phrase and fire flew from her fingertips, countering the spell the woman had thrown at the Sandman. Another shot from the Sandman clipped the woman on her left shoulder and blood began soaking the golden gown. Slapping a hand against her shoulder, the woman turned and darted away. A hand appeared in front of Selia's face, and she grasped the Sandman's wrist, allowing him to pull her up.

"You okay?" he asked. Selia could hear the pain in his breathing.

"I'm fine," she said, snatching up her swords from where they'd fallen. With fury in her eyes, Selia asked maliciously, "Still want to leave witnesses?"

"No," he drawled out. "I feel like killing these assholes."

Selia's eyes narrowed as she rolled her wrists. The Sandman sounded as though he had been pummeled hard and repeatedly during his short stay. His eyes were on their way to becoming true shiners. Taking a moment, she muttered under her breath in Temerian, and a white light swirled around his face. He glanced at her sharply, and she raised her brows.

"Well, I don't want your eyes swelling shut," she murmured as a pair of thugs came barreling towards them even as more came from behind them. "Oh, good! The party has started!" She stepped around until her back was at his.

Realizing she was at a slight disadvantage in the weaponry department, she separated from the Sandman to cut down the first pair of gunmen she saw. She sheathed her swords, picked up the compact machine guns both men had carried, and backed up with an easy, fluid grace. Her thumbs found the fire selector switch on the weapons, and she maneuvered them to the semi-automatic position. She fired as she moved, continuing to carefully place her shots as her back pressed lightly against the Sandman's.

Unlike the gunmen coming into their collective line of fire, the Sandman and Selia had learned how to handle firearms by trained professionals, rather than taking cues from video screens and blowing whole clips at a range just to see how fast the bullet and brass casings would fly. There were a few that actually did some controlled fire, stopping after bursts of five or more rounds and then trying to find cover or a better angle.

Most of them, however, were firing like bullets were cheap and collateral damage was something that only happened in video games. Those gunmen would start firing, and their bodies would begin to pivot up and to the right only seconds later, slaves to the laws of physics dictated by someone firing multiple rounds from high-powered firearms.

Considering that she and the Sandman were constantly on the move and the men didn't really aim, once the first three rounds of each gunman missed, Selia and her partner were safe to take a moment to wait for those bodies to turn. Carefully placed shots went into the exposed sides and chests of the gunmen.

The few that were more seasoned to the realities of fire fights went down last. Two of them actually survived long enough to find adequate cover. Before they could take advantage of the cover and take better aim, the Sandman lobbed two of the small stun grenades he preferred just past the men's cover. The detonations rendered the men unable to do more than clutch at their ringing ears and blinded eyes. They were dispatched into unconsciousness by blows to the head, courtesy of New Campania's crime-fighting duo.

"Thanks for the rescue," the Sandman said to her when the noise and smoke had ceased. "Now we need to see about shutting down that auction. The building is actually open for business, even if it is being watched."

"Do you have something in mind? Selia asked him, her faux blonde eyebrows going up.

"It's time for a little dirty work and improvisation," he replied, a sly twinkle in his eyes.

J. F. Posthumus

Chapter Twenty-Five

Thirty minutes later, Selia was snickering at the sight before her. The Sandman stood with his arms out wide, and asked, "What do you think?" Selia laughed harder. The Sandman was dressed in a generic pair of work coveralls and old, oversized running shoes. He wore a wig that gave him red hair, done up in oversized dreadlocks. Matching facial hair, formed into a goatee and a sparse moustache, adorned his face. He wore the infrared sunglasses and looked like a strung-out wannabe doing a minimum wage stint as a janitor.

"That sounds, like, *perfect* to me," he said as he smiled at her.

Selia gasped for a minute and howled with laughter again: Several front teeth in the Sandman's mouth now sported gold caps.

"Where… where did… where did you-" she gasped.

"I have several theatrical costumers on speed dial. My grandmother was a legend in theater and is still beloved by many in the city's industry. She taught me how to envelope myself into a role, and where to get the best props. Fortunately, one of them also deals in stunt cars. I have a beat-up old Chevy Citation waiting about fifty yards from this building. It's got janitorial supplies jammed into the trunk and back."

"O-okay," Selia tittered. "What can I do?"

"You get to be my unappreciated girlfriend who's dropping me off for work," he said with a gold-tinted grin.

"Ummm… you look like hell, 'sweetheart.' Maybe I should heal you first."

She indicated the multiple cuts and large bruises that were visible where the wig and fake facial hair didn't cover. His lips were split, the skin around his right eye was engorged and purple, and there were small lacerations all over his neck and jawline. She thought there was quite a bit of swelling as well. His face did not look to be shaped the same as it had been when she had seen it partially uncovered and preparing to kiss him. His nose was also shaped differently.

"No, that's for later. Trust me. I can work with this mess." He handed her a pair of sunglasses identical to his own, along with an electronic tablet. Once she had taken them, he continued. "There's an oversized jacket for you to wear, over your suit, in the car. You wear the jacket, zipped to your throat, and the sunglasses. Pull your wig back into a ponytail so the green tips aren't so noticeable. You get to keep the sunglasses."

He produced a hair band from one of the coverall's pockets and handed it to her. She pulled her hair back and tied it up. Putting on the sunglasses, she noticed that everything was brighter but had a green hue to it. The Sandman was multiple colors as a result of his uneven body heat. She nodded to him and looked at the tablet. She saw herself, looking down at the tablet from the Sandman's perspective. A sudden large blob flew into the tablet's view and there was a dull thudding sound from the tablet's speakers. She looked up to see him tapping the front of a nametag pinned to the left side of his chest.

"Mini camera built into the tag," the Sandman explained.

He dropped his right hand down to his side. She glanced at the tablet to see herself once more, decked out in skintight black, wearing sunglasses and holding the tablet.

"You'll have that, and after dropping me off, you'll travel at least two hundred yards away and wait," he said. "You'll see what I see, hear what I hear, and be able to know what I'm doing. If things go south, you can suit up and provide me with backup."

"Don't you mean rescue you, again?" Selia teased.

"Keep that up and I won't rescue *you* next time," he replied. "I will be in there for at least an hour, otherwise suspicions will be raised while it's still possible to make our lives difficult."

She looked closer at the name tag and snickered. "Okay, 'Rex.' Let's get you to work, honey."

Dropping him off ten minutes later, Selia provided the Sandman with the pass card and keys the guard had given her earlier. He removed a miniscule trolley from the Citation's trunk. Once he had retrieved the push broom, dustpan, brush, and mop, the Sandman hollered "Thank ya, baby! See you in a bit!" and let himself in the side entrance. She waved and fired back with "I luuuuv you, baby!" and drove off.

Nervous about what was happening while she got to a safe distance that would go unnoticed by the Family members or anyone else watching the auction house, Selia almost had to sit on her fingers to keep from activating the tablet and calling up the camera feed. She couldn't drive faster because that would draw attention and probably raise suspicions. Then she remembered the earpiece still sitting in her right ear and turned it on.

"Now, easy, boss-man," the Sandman's drawled voice filled her ear drum. "You don't wanna let me do my man's shift, it's cool with me! I just need to call my woman to turn around and come pick me up."

"What I'm saying, sir, is that you aren't the normal janitor," came a second man's voice. This voice was cautious, a little on edge, and very business-like. "I wasn't notified that a substitute was coming tonight."

"Well, ain't it jus' like Mike to not call you people after asking me to cover fer him?" The Sandman replied. "Look, if you wanna follow me around while I sweep up, collect the trash, unclog the shitter, and everything else, I don't care. It's all the same to me. But my man Mike plans on paying me his wage for the night, an' I can sure use the twenty bucks."

"Mike was here about two hours ago-" the other voice began.

"- and he forgot to clean the bathrooms and sweep up the showroom and the hallway," the Sandman finished with his drawing, not-quite-lucid voice. "C'mon, we're in the hallway and you see how dirty it is! What is your problem? You ain't signing the paychecks!"

"No, I'm not," agreed the voice. "And yes, Mike apologized for leaving early, without bothering to explain anything other than muttering 'family problems' when I pushed for reasons why he had to leave, unfinished."

"So instead of causing grief for the higher ups, Mike calls me to come in and finish. He gave me his keys and card to get in. How else would I be in here without trippin' everything off?" The Sandman chided, really throwing himself into the role. "You certainly got here fast once I walked through the door!" There was a pause, and the hyper, not-quite all-there voice got a little calmer and relaxed. "Look, he doesn't want to get written up or fired for having an unfinished day's work, not when there's a major big-shot auction tomorrow. You can understand that, can't ya?"

Satisfied that she had gone far enough, Selia killed the lights on the small compact car. The sunglasses allowed her to see perfectly well in the dark once she had adjusted to the hues visible in the lenses. She drifted as silently as the clunking engine would allow for another two dozen yards before parking. Thankfully, the car's engine idled down and stopped making loud clunking sounds. She left the engine running and fired up the tablet.

The image of a fit, dark skinned security guard came into focus, and she could see his right-hand hovering near a holstered weapon and pepper spray. She wondered briefly where the guard kept his taser.

"So, you're just going to finish up, and then you're out of here," the strong-featured guard's face said.

"Yeah, man, easy-peasy. Hang with me if you wanna," the disembodied voice of the Sandman's current character replied. "Mike said you were a righteous man."

"I'll be monitoring the cameras, which is the biggest part of my job right now," the guard answered. "Stay out of the showroom, though. Mike polished that floor just fine, and the bosses don't want anyone going in there until they return."

"Okay, if you say so. They must have some heavy stuff for sale tomorrow, man. I don't blame 'em for wanting to keep the low-income crew like us out. Clients get mad if they want something and it's not there for them to spend too much money on."

The guard chuckled. "You have a fair point, at that. But Mike wasn't supposed to tell you there's an auction tomorrow. That's against policy."

"Aww, c'mon, man! You be the righteous dude! Mike only told me 'cause he wanted me to understand why it was so important for the work to get finished. Don't ride his ass, man. Don't sell my bro out."

The guard considered. "All right, if you do the work and get out of here within the hour, I'll keep it on the down-low. But remember-" the guard pointed above Selia's sight line, "-I got eyes on you, Rex."

"No worries, man. I won't even light up while I'm here. Just right after. Heh."

The guard smiled, chuckled, and waved the Sandman off.

Selia sighed in relief, just realizing she had been holding her breath. *Silly*, she thought to herself. *The guard wasn't even being threatening.*

For the next forty-five minutes, Selia watched from the Sandman's point of view- or at least, the name tag's point of view- as he pushed a broom around the hallways, stepping into the bathrooms, and doing various other everyday work habits of maintenance workers around the world.

The little extras were what caught her attention, though. After she noticed the first one, she began looking for the next time the Sandman dropped a small, clear bundle the size of a bar of hotel soap into some manner of water reservoir or receptacle. Several toilets, men's' room urinals, the galley's prep sink, and even what looked to be the building's water heater all got one placed into them.

The Sandman didn't speak as he delivered these strange goodies, or even when he was doing some actual clean up. He did keep scatting nonsense lyrics and the camera jiggled often, though. Selia's mind delighted at the image of him in that outrageous costume, shaking his hips, singing, and dancing to music only he could hear… or understand. The guard would be very distracted and put at ease by such absurd behavior.

Finally, the Sandman whispered "Come get me" into Selia's earpiece. She turned the car around, backtracking the way she had come. She turned on the headlights a block later. When she pulled up to the side entrance, the Sandman was standing there with the guard. They were both smoking, although the Sandman's lit cigarette shone out with an odd blue light. The guard was laughing, and the Sandman was talking and smiling.

"Hey, baby! What took you so long?" the Sandman inquired loudly. He slapped the guard on the back. "Remember what I told you, man. The bosses need to get a plumber in here sometime soon. Those pipes are making some weird noises."

The guard agreed that he would and waved at Selia. She waved back as the Sandman put the cleaning supplies in the trunk and back seat. Once that was done, he got into the passenger's seat, buckled up, and waved a final farewell to the guard.

"Where to?" she asked.

"The motorcycle. We're going to leave the Citation, gear, and costumes where it's parked. The shop owners are going to pick it up from there. Then you and I are going to the lair."

"What did you put in the toilets and hot water heater?"

He smiled. "You didn't see me put three of them in the water supply for the sprinkler system, then? Ah well. It's a special compound that reacts very slowly to water. The results are spectacular, though. In four hours, over fifty percent of the pipes in that building are going to burst. The building is going to be unusable as a venue for at least three days."

Chapter Twenty-Six

Selia followed the Sandman back into his lair. Pulling the hair band from the wig, she began removing the pins that kept it in place. She watched him move as though he was finally succumbing to the pain from his severe beating earlier. Dropping the wig and the pins on the coffee table, she grabbed the Sandman and shoved him down onto the sofa.

"Stay," she ordered him, as she slid her trench coat off and tossed it to the side.

A playful "arf" was his reply. She shot him an exasperated expression for all of two seconds before giving in and laughing.

The spell had claimed he was her mate, and she wasn't quite certain how that sat with her. Yeah, she was extremely attracted to him and cared greatly for him, but... her mate? Hell, they hadn't even consummated their budding relationship yet! Shoving the problem to the very recesses of her mind, she tossed her gloves in the same general direction as the coat and knelt on the sofa beside him. She scooted around so she was facing him and gently pulled his mask out of his shirt before slowly pulling it up and over his battered face. Removing it completely, she tossed it onto the coffee table.

Drawing a deep breath, she placed her hands on each side of his face and bowed her head. Softly she spoke, calling forth her magic and allowing it to flow through her and into him. As she had with Soren's injuries, she could feel his wounds being healed.

His bruised bones mended and a few that had been cracked fused back together. Cuts and bruises vanished, along with swelling. The magic ebbed as the spell came to its natural end and she opened her eyes to look into his face.

Her jaw dropped and she sat back, almost falling from the sofa. He was, well, not what she expected. The qualities of his jaw line, mouth and nose were more brutish and Neanderthal-like than she had thought. He still had some handsome features, but she also took a moment to wonder if she had somehow messed up on the spell and given him the magical equivalent of bad plastic surgery.

"Not what you expected, eh? Thinking there's a reason I never really socialized much, are you?" the Sandman suggested with a chuckle.

"I... ah... no, I just..." She was suddenly unable to think of anything that didn't sound disappointed or plainly rude. What was happening here?

"You are impatient. Did Soren ever tell you that?"

He slipped the thumb and forefinger of his right hand into his mouth. His jaw line shifted, and the set of his mouth on one side altered dramatically. Selia almost shrieked. A moment later, he removed a large, bloody bulk from his mouth. It looked like a wax casting for part of a skull. The blood coating made it look like the prop from a horror film. She looked up from it only to be treated to the sight of him pulling a similar object from the left side of his mouth.

Once that was accomplished, he opened his mouth wide, as if stretching the muscles. He tilted his head down and pulled an odd, tweezer-like object from some compartment in his belt. He promptly began digging around in his left nostril with it.

"I mentioned that my maternal grandmother was a legend on the theater scene, remember? She played all the great characters from Shakespeare to every bit of script written until the end of the 1940's," the Sandman remarked. His voice sounded congested, as if he were holding his nose together.

He was now pulling the tweezer-like object back out of his nose. The left nostril was distorting in shape, and she could see something a little larger than his nostril shifting down. Selia briefly wondered if she was going to get queasy or just completely freaked out. A large, waxy mass shaped like a teardrop came free from the nostril, gripped by the device in his fingers. It was more of a mess than the objects he'd withdrawn from his mouth.

"Yep, there's another one in the right nostril. If you want to leave the room, I completely understand," the

Sandman said as he freed the blob from the end of the tool. He then began rooting in his right nostril.

She didn't move but couldn't think of anything to say.

"Still here? Awesome," the Sandman reflected, before continuing. "Long before silicon, latex, plaster of Paris or any of the more well-known movie makeup substances, actors still wanted or needed to alter their appearance for roles. Sometimes they even played monsters."

The second over-sized tear came free with a wet popping sound. The Sandman sighed and rubbed his nose.

"The tricks of the trade were, among other methods, using wax molds to alter the shape of a person's jaw, nose, eyebrows... you get the idea. She also taught me how to appear heavier than what I weighed, as well as thinner. She taught me everything when I was a kid." He dug around in the utility belt and came out with, of all things, a disposable wipe. He began scrubbing his face, especially around his nose and brow as he continued his story.

"She kept all of her supplies and tools of the trade in two large steamer trunks and would not let the city demolish the original theater until she claimed the makeup vanity that had her name on it. When she died, I proved equally stubborn and wouldn't give them any peace until they swore they would keep those objects for me. I used the vanity, and as you can see, I still make use of my grandmother's things."

He rummaged around in the belt compartments again, bringing out a curious article of plastic that had two shallow, circular compartments joined by a strip of plastic. He unscrewed them, revealing tiny pools of clear liquid. Selia was wondering what strange device he had procured, until he brought his fingers to his left eye and removed a contact.

She almost laughed at herself for being so absurd. After he placed that colored contact in one pool of storage solution, he took out the other and did the same. Closing the contact storage case and putting it to the side, he finally looked at her. That is, William Brendan Fredricks looked at Selia.

"Hi, Selia. My friends call me Wil. Nice to finally meet you."

She traced a finger along his face, from the top of his cheek bone to his jaw. Her eyes twinkled as she decided he was even more handsome as himself than any other person he could possibly adopt.

"The pleasure, sir, is all mine," she murmured as she leaned down and kissed him softly. This time, she was willing to let him control the kiss and anything else that might come.

"Ummm... ow?" he said against her lips.

She sat up, confused, and peered at him as a child might observe a talking pillow.

"I don't suppose you've ever actually even been healed with magic, yourself?" he asked by way of explanation.

Selia shook her head. "Uh, no. I've never been injured severe enough to warrant it."

"Okay, I thought not. Let me explain: You know all the discomfort that comes with a scraped knee healing up? The pain of the injury, the itching of the reforming tissue, the soreness of the offended nerves and skin? The day after day until it heals torture?"

"Oh, gods," Selia whispered. "I'm so, so sorry."

"Yes, you heal the wounds, binding tissue and muscle, mending bones, but the body gets the sensations that are usually spread out over hours, days, weeks. All at the same time. It seems it leaves those otherwise healthy places in a new level of sore." He smiled at her. "I'm just glad I didn't get my trusty sidekick caught in my zipper today as well."

Selia's face burned as she blushed and ducked her head. Peeping up at him from beneath her brows, she smiled shyly at him.

"I'm just glad I was able to find you," she murmured, sitting on the sofa beside him.

"So am I," he said, giving her a quick peck on the cheek and then grunting with pain. "And I will be properly grateful when I can once again use my face without feeling like I'm setting my head on fire. How did you do that, by the way? Find me, that is?"

"Oh, uh," Selia glanced away. "I used a spell that allowed me to locate you."

It was attempting to tell him the truth about the spell, but she still wasn't sure if she understood anything about it, or if she should tell him. Let alone how. How did one go about telling someone that according to a spell, he was her mate for life? If it left *her* rattled, someone accustomed to magic and its oddities, how would it leave him?

He peered at her curiously.

"It seems there's more to the explanation than what you're giving me," Wil observed. "But I won't ask. If you decide it's something I need to know, I'm sure you'll tell me in your own good time."

"I... I'm afraid if I try to explain it, you'll either run away, never want to see me again, or think I'm a raving lunatic," Selia admitted, refusing to meet his eyes.

"Okay, the moment just got more awkward. I wasn't fishing for information, Selia," Wil said kindly.

Sighing, she looked up at him. "No, no, you have a right to know, because it concerns you... well, us. Sort of us." Sinking further into herself, she kicked herself mentally for feeling so skittish. It was stupid. Sighing heavily, she scooted to the other side of the sofa, putting a little more room between her and Wil. "The spell I used was one my people often use to find their mate. The focus is always blood. Other than that, I don't know how it works. For me, after the spell was cast, I remembered everything that was special to me about you and it… I… attached your name to the spell."

"Oh," Wil replied, his expression not quite serious. "Well, what's wrong with that?"

Selia looked at him in a mixture of wonder, surprise, and delight. "I… well… I didn't know if you felt the same or would even want to think that way towards me." She paused, tilting her head slightly to the side. "All things considered, I thought you'd be objecting or freaking out at the idea of us being life-mates."

He snorted, and then winced in pain.

"Okay, I'm sorry for laughing, but you understand that you now know more about me than anyone else in my life. Obviously, I'm very comfortable with you, even if I'm not sure why I am, so quickly."

"I understand that now," she replied, softly. "I could say the same about you." She caressed his face gently. "You need something for pain, and I should be getting back to the cabin before Al sends the boys back for my daily check-up. We also need to discuss that necromancer and why she was so interested in you, but not your identity."

"Oh, her. She and Alfi pulled the mask up and took a picture of me," he said casually. At her look of horror, fear, and dismay, he held up his hands. "It's okay, Selia. That's why I put in the wax molds every time the Sandman goes out. In case I get unmasked, people won't actually see what I look like. Are you going to be okay getting back to the bungalow? I can manage the trip." He started to get up.

"You'd better be getting up so you can either go to the bathroom or get into a bed." It was nothing short of a warning. "I can get back to the bungalow on the motorcycle. Alex sort of taught me while Soren was away visiting Temeria one year." She giggled girlishly. "I guess I'll be picking you up tomorrow, won't I?"

They could figure out how to track down the pair later. Selia wasn't anywhere near confident about going up against a necromancer who was obviously older than her, especially when she hadn't been practicing her magic, save for a handful of spells, for the past decade.

Wil stood up and shrugged. "Sounds like a date to me. Hold on." He walked over to a cabinet and pulled out a small flip phone. He tossed it to her.

"It's a direct, untraceable line to me. 'Sandy' is the only name on the phone's contact list. I have a charger if you want it. Otherwise, just keep the phone off unless you need to contact the Sandman."

Great, Selia thought in amusement, *now I'm probably going to want to call him 'Sandy' all the time.*

"Perfect," she said as she studied the phone. She glanced at him, a mischievous smile on her face. "I have a way to contact you, but what happens if I have to get into your secret lair and you're either gone or unconscious? Shall I just pick your locks or simply fritz out your entire security system?"

"Oh. Good point." He turned back to the cabinet, opened a smaller drawer, and withdrew a key. "As long as you're not coming in as Nightshade, use the front door. Here's a key."

She walked over and took it from him. She raised a brow at the simple gift-card type design and the words "your name here" typed on the front. Chuckling, she shook her head at his ingenuity.

"Well, considering it would probably be far better to leave my outfit here, I'll make use of the front door." She paused before asking, "And if I'm coming in as Nightshade?"

He smiled. "Your thumbprint is already saved into the security scanner's database."

"Sneaky," she teased. "Are you going to be okay getting upstairs? Or should I stick around long enough to help tuck you in?"

"I don't plan on sleeping in my bed. After a couple of painkillers, a glass of water and putting away my equipment, this comfy sofa has me for the night," Wil replied.

"Okay," she said slowly. "I'll go get out of this outfit, change into something a little less problematic if they show up before I can undress at the bungalow, and come back down to make sure you're okay before leaving."

"Sounds good," Wil replied, a smile on his face.

Chapter Twenty -Seven

Waking just past noon, yet again, Selia stretched and pondered her choices. She couldn't go anywhere until after dark and the motorcycle was currently hidden by a thick patch of blackberry bushes.

There was that tub though, she thought, and a small smile curved her lips.

Twenty minutes later, she had a tub filled with bubbles that smelled like roses, a glass of wine at one hand and a box of chocolates at her other. She lazily flipped a page of the novel she'd found on the bedside stand, enjoying the hot water and bubbles. Someone had remembered her love for a good mystery, and she was now reading an Agatha Christie whodunit.

She'd barely gotten past the murder when a knock on the door pulled her away from her reading. Sighing, she set the book aside and stepped from the tub. Wrapping a towel around her, she grabbed the wine glass and held it between her fingers as she popped another chocolate into her mouth. Trotting to the door, dripping water on the floor behind her, she took a sip of the red wine before setting the glass down and opening the door. She raised her brows at Alex and Bernie before picking up the glass and taking another sip of wine.

"Again?" she asked, stepping to the side. "What happened this time?"

"Uh, nothing," Alex said; his eyes firmly locked onto hers. "We came by to check in and make sure you were safe and doing well."

"Yeah," added Bernie, who was having difficulty keeping his eyes locked on anything for more than a second. "Boss said to see if you needed anything."

A sly smile pulled at Selia's lips. "Yeah, I could use more freedom. I hate being stuck here all the time." She shrugged and gestured towards the house with the glass of wine. "Feel free to look around if you must. It's just little ol' me here, soaking in the tub, trying to kill time without dying from boredom."

"We'll just check the rooms to see if anyone else is here." Alex assured her. "Quick and easy. Sorry we interrupted your bath."

"Take your time," she drawled out, taking another sip of the wine. "Any news on Alfi? Or how much longer will I be stuck here?"

"Still no sightings." Bernie grunted as he began looking around the living room and kitchenette. He didn't open cabinets but seemed concerned with places a person could hide. "We had the place we thought he'd be staked out, but funny thing: Sometime before dawn, damned near half of the water pipes blew. Place looked like Sea World had exploded inside it."

Selia snickered and Bernie gave her a bright smile that made him look far more boyish and younger than he really was.

"The bosses are still wondering if it's a diversion, or someone tried to take Alfi out and got their timing wrong." Alex offered, as he checked under her bed.

"Yes, I would definitely tuck someone under my bed and not in it," Selia said, watching from the doorway. "That must have been pretty impressive. It sounds more like they didn't want him using that place, if you ask me." She paused and tilted her head to the side, thinking. Alfi had to be somewhere, and he was mixed up with the necromancer, whoever she was. "Where would you go if you wanted to sell something, and you just lost your best option?"

It was a chance to ask, but news of the auction house would be on the news if it was that big. It didn't hurt that Alex and Bernie knew she wasn't a 'dumb blonde'.

"The bosses are trying to figure that out as well." Alex shrugged, while checking the bedroom closet. Selia was glad she had left her Nightshade gear back at Wil's place. "They figure whatever Alfi is trying to sell has to be done in a person-to-person kind of auction. Otherwise, it would have already been sold online or some other silent method. He might be trying to do that now. The hackers are combing the internet for that."

"He's not going to dare put it online," Selia muttered, finally realizing what was going on.

The sorry bastard, and that traitorous bitch, she thought furiously.

The necromancer was working with Alfi. The magic of her island, or rather the mages on her island, was the one thing anyone and everyone would want. No one would believe Alfi's word but having a necromancer on his side would certainly prove anything he said.

Fortunately, Selia knew how to keep her emotions hidden behind a poker face. It was something Soren had taught her the moment her feet had stepped into this strange city so many years ago. She took another sip from her glass, not caring if Alex and Bernie knew she was drinking wine. They'd been the ones to coax her into trying it so many years ago, after all.

"You sound pretty sure about that." Bernie cut in. "How do you figure he wouldn't?"

She gave Bernie an exasperated look. "Remember, he's the idiot who thought he could charm me into his bed by complimenting my *big rack* and *fine ass*. He isn't imaginative and unless he suddenly grew a brain larger than a peanut, he's going to think it has to be kept secret. The internet is anything but secret."

Maybe she knew a little more about Alfi than she had originally thought. Though she doubted a simple locator spell would work if he was mixed up with an undoubtedly powerful necromancer.

"Okay, you got a point." Bernie relented. "How do you figure this auction has to be in person? Because Alex and me, we're still scratching our heads over it. If it's such a valuable commodity, whatever he's selling, why does he have to be in the room? Wouldn't buyers be more interested in the item?"

"Alfi isn't the kind who's going to trust someone else with what he just stole," Selia replied. "If you'd just tried killing me and then went after Soren, would you trust anyone with it? He's a greedy little coward and thinks everyone is like him." She paused long enough to take a sip of wine. "I should know. I was forced to listen to plenty of his delusional rants."

Alex laughed. Bernie gave Selia an approving smile and nod.

"I think you just nailed that little chickenshit's personality," said Bernie. "Score one for the lady."

Selia gave a slight bow, a smile on her lips. "I aim to please."

"Yeah, I bet you do," Bernie said, a little smug. "Any chance I can call your lady friend and ask for details?" He held up his hands and said, "I'm kidding! Gotta pick on ya. Okay, let me check the bathroom while Alex checks the last room, and we're a memory."

Instead of waiting on her reply, Bernie walked over, opened the bathroom door, and peered inside.

"Do you want to check the tub and make sure someone isn't holding their breath under the bubbles?" Selia suggested sarcastically.

"Nah, those rose-scented bubble baths burn the hell out of my eyes and nose," Bernie said reflectively. Selia did not want to know how he knew that tidbit of information. "Nobody can stay underwater with that for long." He continued to look at the tub for a long minute before nodding and closing the door.

Alex came up beside him and the pair walked to the front door.

"Again, sorry we interrupted your bath," Alex apologized. "Hopefully, all this will be done soon, and you won't have this to be bothered with."

"Here's hoping," she agreed. "I much prefer enjoying your company when the threat of my death isn't looming over our heads."

"Yeah, us too," both men said in unison. They closed the door on their way out.

Chuckling, Selia grabbed the phone the Sandman had given her and returned to the bathroom. Dropping the towel beside the tub, she sank back into the hot water and dialed 'Sandy'. Hopefully, he'd be awake, and she could give him something to work on until she arrived later that night.

The call connected after two rings.

"Hello, beautiful," the Sandman's voice purred into her ears.

"Mmmmm... let me tell you what just happened," she said, biting her lower lip, "and then, maybe, I can convince you to keep talking to me in that voice."

Chapter Twenty-Eight

It felt odd using the front door instead of coming up from beneath the house. Using the card key, she entered the townhouse. The door closed and locked with a quiet click as she headed towards Wil's office. She stopped in the doorframe and leaned against it as she smiled at Wil. He hadn't noticed she'd entered, or didn't care, because he was leaning forward at his desk with one hand on the keyboard and the other on the mouse.

"Hey, handsome," Selia said softly, pushing away from the door and walking towards him. Leaning down, she brushed a kiss against his neck. "Find anything interesting?"

For the first time, he wasn't wearing anything to mask his appearance. All things considered, it shouldn't have been surprising, but Selia couldn't help but be delighted at that fact. Impishly, she nuzzled his neck, before nipping his earlobe from behind.

"Alfi has postponed the auction for three days while the mess I made gets cleaned up." He leaned back against her. "That felt great. If you keep it up, I won't be able to tell you the rest, though."

Selia giggled and kissed the top of his head before rolling him and the chair back. Sitting in his lap, she asked, "This better?"

"Depends on what you're trying to improve: my concentration, the amount of distraction I'm dealing with, or how quickly blood will flow to a certain part of my body," he quipped.

He reached around her and clicked the mouse of his laptop.

"It's impossible to try and make a bid for the coordinates using a dummy corporation. Even if I could bid a few billion on the auction, I don't have an identity that is known in the world market or politics. The auction is being attended by heads of state, oil barons and global billionaire corporations. The people are very high profile in the global business and political world. I've Googled every one of the guests that was supposed to be bidding on the chance to plunder your home. Each of them has access to heinous amounts of cash and can be tracked using legitimate sources like Fortune 500, with activities going back years. Alfi wants to be very old school about this. You show up in person, highest bidder wins. A demonstration of the item is supposed to happen. Any thoughts on what that might be?"

"Yeah, the woman is a necromancer. The demonstration will be magical. We'll have to get to Alfi before the auction can happen. He'll have the drive and she probably doesn't know how to get back to the island. If she did, she wouldn't be allying herself with Alfi," Selia explained. She wrapped her arms around his neck, enjoying the closeness. "I could try the basic tracking spell, but I doubt it would work. I tried it with you, and she prevented it somehow. Alex and Bernie don't know anything; either that, or they're keeping it close to their chest."

"So, the witch will be proof of what they're selling. That makes sense," mused Wil. "Let's try the tracking spell first. I'm linked into the Family's search for Alfi. If he uses a credit card or rents a hooker, it'll show up and we'll know."

"Do you have a physical map of the city?" Selia asked suddenly.

She barely remembered a spell she had seen used frequently on Temeria. Unfortunately, she'd only performed it once. Even if it didn't give them Alfi's exact location, it might at least give them the general area, within a three-mile radius.

"If you mean a road map, I have several. Do you want just the streets, or do you want one with the geographic features as well?"

"Streets should be fine," Selia replied. "We often used a spell whenever we were attacked by other Clans. It let the battalion chiefs know about where the armies were, even when a mage shielded their location. It was useful in my land because we knew the geography so well. Maybe it will help us here? If nothing else, it should give us a general idea of where they are."

"Why didn't you use it to find me?" he asked, curious.

Selia shrugged. "I needed an exact location for you. This would give me the block of my target, not the exact building or room."

Wil stared at the monitor for a few moments, considering her reply before giving a shrug of his own. "It's worth a try. Even if it narrows our search down to a few blocks that gives us a much better chance of finding them in time." He smiled at her. "Just all kinds of useful, aren't you? Why are you hanging around with a boring old article writer?"

"You're hot, you're charming, and you saved me?" She said in a questioning tone, her head tilted to the side. "No? How about I have a thing for dangerous men who are compassionate and don't mind a woman who can kick ass, too?"

Laughing, Wil nodded. "Okay, I concede your point!"

"Goodie!" Selia exclaimed before kissing him lightly on his lips and hopping up off his lap. "So… how about that map, handsome?"

Chapter Twenty-Nine

The spell worked well, in their estimation. The spell narrowed the search to a single city block. When Selia made some mention of hoping the spell was accurate and not pointing her towards a shoe store, since she'd only used it once and wasn't entirely certain of the accuracy, Wil waved it off. He gathered their gear, saying it was time to suit up and check the location out. He promised to go shoe shopping with her another time.

Two hours later, they were on the rooftop of a clothing store that had kept a brisk business despite not being downtown and not offering much in the way of inexpensive garments. The block was a city mash-up of apartments, small businesses, and eateries.

It was ten blocks from the beginning of the "official" downtown of New Campania, where shops, banks, four-star restaurants, and the most congested part of the subway system scrambled for space and importance over the rest of the section's more well-known theater, sports, and entertainment companies. Nightshade and the Sandman had kept vigil for over an hour, with little to show for it.

"Maybe I cast the spell wrong-" she began.

"Perhaps you're just impatient, and should be more confident in your abilities," he interrupted.

"This building does sell shoes," she retorted.

Wil gave her a scathing look before turning back to scanning the people moving below, watching the faces and body language of those entering homes, shops, and eateries. What the pedestrians carried out of the shops also was of interest. The Sandman was looking for someone buying food for more than themselves, and not looking to feed a family or a football game party. The cabs and cars might reveal something, so he watched those carefully as well.

"Why do you keep looking at people who are carrying food from the convenience stores or the restaurants?" she asked with genuine interest. "I can understand wondering about people who are shopping at the only grocery store on this block. If someone comes out with a lot of microwave food and they look like they usually dine in four- or five-star locations; that would be obvious."

"Alfi is, at his core, a spoiled brat," the Sandman explained. "He's not out getting attention and he's not at his comfortable home. He doesn't even get the worshipful affection of his mistress. Alfi is going to be hating that and getting worse the longer it lasts. He likely planned on being rich and plotting which airport to depart the country from by now. The deal's put off. He has to stay low for much longer than expected. Follow so far?"

Nightshade nodded, bidding him to continue.

"So, he's going to want as much attention and finery as he can get to quell not getting what he wants, when he expected it." The Sandman continued as he scanned the people and vehicles. "He's used to a certain level of comfort, a lot of luxuries, and the man loves good Italian food. And of course, attention from a woman, especially one he can be a little rough with. That will make him feel powerful again."

"So, we're looking for beautiful women who charge by the hour, big screen TVs for rent being delivered, large deliveries of booze and possibly Italian food all going to the same location?" she proposed.

"Something like that, yes," he agreed with a chuckle.

Nightshade was beginning to lose confidence in their ability to find any leads at this location. People were blurring in her mind into a large ant colony, moving about, picking up this and that, all in a hurry. If you weren't one of the ants, however, it all seemed pretty pointless, and certainly no help in the investigation.

"I just spotted Raman 'The Finger' Tarducia and his favorite pal going into the Italian eatery," the Sandman said, interrupting her hazy thoughts.

Tarducia, nicknamed 'The Finger' for having an itchy trigger finger and who would rather shoot anyone than be bothered for anything, was Alfi's primary enforcer. He looked like a high school football coach gone to pot and pissed about it. He also had a bad comb-over that could not be missed or imitated.

The other constant about Tarducia was his choice of partner: A skinny, twitchy man of the same approximate age, mid-fifties, with thinning blonde hair, bulging eyes, and a "hy-yuk" style of laughing that should have been lost at puberty. The man was nicknamed 'The Pill' because he left a bitter taste in anyone's mouth- except Tarducia, it seemed - and because everything he claimed was difficult to swallow. He loved to ramble on about the people he killed, the women he'd had, and the fortunes he'd spent. The Pill also preferred shooting people to dealing with them.

She shook her head and asked, "The real Italian eatery, or the national chain sub shop with cardboard crust pizza?" She paused, and then half-joked, "Oh, now I'm hungry."

"Now I know what to get for lunch tomorrow. Got a favorite dish from there?" he teased.

She pulled out the small binoculars that he had given her before they left the lair from the utility belt similar to his own, also a gift. He apologized for the lack of goodies, promising to fill the compartments after she decided what she wanted to be equipped with.

"I'll tell you later. They went in..." She adjusted the focus on the small lenses and found the two men inside the eatery. "They're at the counter and joking with Sal's sous chef."

"They placed a large order," the Sandman added. "Since they stood at the counter, sous chef Johnny has been cracking the whip over the rest of the kitchen staff's head. I've counted seven dishes being prepped since they first talked to Johnny. No one else has walked in to place an order since they arrived."

"Did you see where they came from?" she asked.

"No. We wait until they leave and follow. If they get into a car, we'll tag and follow it." He sat back a little. "Do you want to change positions? I can see into the shop window without the need of binoculars. Now that I know where to keep my eyes, it won't matter if I move."

"No, I'm fine." She smiled. "I'm getting used to the gadgets and these infrared sunglasses. Always fun to have cool toys."

"Just remember that the stun grenades have a five-second fuse," warned the Sandman. "It may seem like a short wait, but if you miscalculate? Well, it can be bad."

"Five seconds, huh?" she mused. "Where did you learn all this?"

It probably wasn't the most opportune time to ask him such a question, but it sort of just popped out.

"School of hard knocks, ringing ears, and temporary blindness. Also, a minor in 'how to get shot by making foolish combat mistakes' when I first started," he replied.

"Care to share?"

"About a month after I first started going out, I wound up in a storage facility with a dealer who was shooting at me," he confessed. "I threw the grenade, landing it exactly where I wanted it to be. It didn't go off."

"Instead of realizing that only two seconds had passed, I stepped out to get closer to my target. Because he was still in position, he shot me in the stomach. Then the grenade went off, blinding and deafening us both." The Sandman grunted. "Since he was right beside the blast, he was disoriented longer than I was. But I had to drag myself away to hide. He got away after he came to."

Selia knew about gut-wounds. She suspected, though, spears were a lot more forgiving than bullets that shattered, but not by much.

"You were lucky," she murmured. "How badly were you hurt?"

"Oh, not that bad, but it was only the second time I'd been shot. Kevlar stops most handgun bullets, but the impact isn't dampened down that much. I imagine getting mule-kicked in the stomach is about as pleasant as that felt."

She snorted. Of course he'd been wearing Kevlar. Maybe eventually she'd get used to that article of clothing, especially since she was currently wearing a low-cut Kevlar top herself.

"I'm glad it wasn't that bad," she said.

"Thanks." He paused and glanced at her briefly as he said, "Which reminds me. If you continue to wear that outfit, you'd better hope you don't run into any gunwomen. They'll shoot you in the cleavage just out of breast envy."

Selia snickered. "Yeah, well, it's beneficial towards the gun*men*." Glancing over, she added with a wink, "And torturing you."

"That it is," he agreed.

Still looking through the binoculars, she watched the Finger and the Pill receive three large bags and start for the front entrance of Sal's.

"They're coming out," she said at the same moment as the Sandman. She glanced over at him, and she suspected he was smiling under his mask as widely as she was under hers.

The two men exited the establishment and turned right. As she went to stow away her binoculars in one of the belt's compartments, the Sandman was already on the move. She caught up with him as they moved to the adjacent roof.

The Finger and the Pill walked up the steps of the second set of apartments. As Nightshade looked to the Sandman to ask him about how they were going to figure out which apartment the pair was going into, she noticed he had brought a new piece of equipment.

It looked like something between a small paintball gun and tranquilizer gun. The Sandman sighted down the barrel and squeezed the trigger. There was a quick "thump" of compressed air being released. The Finger yelped out and spun around on Pill.

Pill was ahead of him, opening the door. Finger looked around, still holding the bags of Italian cuisine. Pill spoke to him, and the Finger replied, but their voices were lost in the distance and neighborhood noise. Finger turned away from Pill, talking to him over his shoulder. Pill looked at the back of Finger's expensive suit, smiled cruelly and said something. Finger spun around and said something to Pill. Pill nodded.

"Fucking kids!" Finger shouted loud enough to be heard on the rooftop. He looked back and forth down the street, seeming to be looking for a culprit. Pill said something, the leering, cruel smile even wider on his narrow face. Finger's face went red, and he turned to the man. Pushing past Pill, Finger shouted "Asshole!" which provoked Pill into laughing merrily. The pair disappeared into the building and the door was shut.

Nightshade looked at the Sandman.

"You're wondering what I did," he said without looking at her. He was holstering the odd device with his right hand and reaching into a belt compartment with his left. "I shot him with a paintball filled with transparent, mildly radioactive fluid. It looks like a wet spot after it hits. So now Finger looks like he had a bit of trouble with his bowels. It would look like his bladder, but if I shot him in the front, there's no way he wouldn't drop all that food."

His left hand came up with a small device. He turned it on, and the screen flashed with a small arrow pointing towards the apartment complex. "And now we can track him, or at least his pants, to whatever apartment they're at."

It took five minutes to leave the roof they were on, scale the first building in the complex attached to the apartments where their intended prey was located and make their way to the proper roof. The Sandman and Nightshade slowly descended the fire escape.

He had the small tracking device out, and they followed its prompts until they reached the third floor, when it told them they needed to go left. At the second window, the Sandman nodded, and put the device away. Using a small metal tool, he unlocked the window, and they slipped inside.

Finding themselves in the bathroom, the duo pulled out their silent weapons. Selia had her swords but chose to arm herself with steel batons that matched the

Sandman's. The infrared lenses they now both wore did not show any significant heat sources nearby, so they eased the door open and moved into the hallway.

A single person came into the hallway as they emerged. A young woman, possibly in her early twenties, though barely out of high school. She wore a silk shirt and micro skirt. Both looked to have been hastily put on. The black heels she wore were scuffed and had dried droplets of fluid on them. She walked with her head down, her gate unsteady. As she wobbled toward them, seeming to be either intoxicated or sore, or both, the Sandman came forward and around her. His arms snaked around her neck and mouth as he began moving her toward the bathroom. In the ten seconds it took him to bring her to the door, which Nightshade opened, the young woman had lost consciousness. The Sandman took care to lay the woman down gently on the tile floor of the bathroom, and locked the bathroom door, leaving her safely inside.

The duo moved down the hallway in the direction the woman had come from. They spotted a male lying casually in one bedroom, apparently naked beneath the covers, his eyes closed as he smoked a cigarette. Nightshade came up on him swiftly, clubbing him across the temple with the baton in her right hand. He slumped, slack-jawed in the bed. She picked up the lit cigarette from his now-unresponsive fingers and put it in the ashtray that was on the nightstand. The man wasn't Alfi, nor was he the Finger or Pill. Searching her memory, she recognized him as Alfi's driver, whose name she didn't know. Looking at the Sandman, she shook her head at him. He nodded and indicated that they move further down the hallway.

They passed another bedroom, which was empty. The end of the hallway opened into what must have been the living room. The sound of a television playing some violent movie could be heard, and below that, the use of forks and knives. At least one person was in there.

The Sandman gestured to the other end of the hall, where a kitchen area and one more door could be seen. They hadn't checked that end yet. He used hand gestures to indicate he would check them out, and she should remain here, in case whoever was in the living room decided to take a trip down the hall while the Sandman was investigating.

She nodded and pressed her body to the wall so she could watch him as he investigated.

It didn't take the Sandman more than two minutes to come back and indicate there was no one in the kitchen or behind the last door. Nodding her understanding, she hefted her batons and they stepped into the living room.

The living room was bigger than the bedrooms and furnished with a wrap-around couch and a glass coffee table. The television was at least sixty-two inches and apparently equipped for 3D viewing. Finger and the Pill sat comfortably on the couch, eating Italian food from the large assortment spread out on the glass table. Both wore 3D glasses, of the variety that cost at least a hundred dollars each. They weren't immediately aware of their intruders. They were preoccupied with whatever movie was playing and the explosions that sounded from the speakers. The volume was turned up all the way.

Glancing at the Sandman, Nightshade noticed his mask stretching around the mouth in what was probably a smile. He knelt, slamming the baton in his left hand against the floor. It collapsed efficiently; the sound masked by the movie playing out some widespread destruction. The Sandman rose, switching the batons in his hands. The right hand now held the closed baton, making it just under twelve inches in length. He pulled his arm back, paused, and threw it at the couch.

The baton pinwheeled through the air and smashed into Finger's head, dead-center and right above his ears. The man grunted and sagged on the couch. The fork and plate dropped from his hands, spilling ravioli and garlic bread onto his pants and the carpeted floor. Pill didn't notice.

Trying not to giggle, Nightshade looked at the Sandman. He gestured, gentlemanly, for her to take out Pill. She thought about how she would do it, and then acted.

Moving with stealthy ease, Nightshade got right up beside the Pill. She sat next to him on the couch. When Pill looked over to see what the unexplained settling in the couch was, she smashed his left knee with her baton. He squawked in pain and tried to go for something inside his jacket. Nightshade pivoted off the couch, spun, and brought her other baton around in a fast arc. The baton smashed into the area of jacket where Pill's hand had gone. There was a satisfying crunch, and Pill shuddered before vomiting his dinner all over his lap.

The Sandman was beside her in an instant, grabbing Pill by his unsoiled lapel and pulling him off the couch. The man tried to stand and bring his undamaged hand around to choke or grapple Nightshade. The Sandman promptly smashed Pill's uninjured knee. Pill collapsed, gurgling as he tried to gasp. The Sandman dragged him from the room, down the hall and released him when they arrived in the kitchen.

"So, now that you've been on the receiving end of your own methods, do you feel some sympathy for all the kneecaps you've broken?" the Sandman asked the Pill. "How about those people with broken or missing fingers?"

"Go fuck yourself," Pill gasped out.

"Now, that's just rude. You still have one functioning hand, after all," the Sandman remarked jovially. "You want to keep that? I'm curious what kind of workman's compensation Alfi's going to offer you."

"Pity he isn't here, you could ask him yourself before he kills you," retorted Pill.

"Yes, it's a shame he isn't here, because now you have to tell me," replied the Sandman. He pushed his foot down on one of Pill's injured knees. "Where is Alfi at? In this building?"

"Not telling you anything, mama's boy," Pill said with a groan.

"Maybe you think I won't kill you," the Sandman reflected. "Perhaps you figure dying would be the easiest way out of the pain. But I'm not even close to being finished with you. You see, I watched a lot of spy movies, and I loved that TV show with the linear time frame."

The Sandman stepped back and started pulling knives and other kitchen utensils out of drawers, considering them. "You know the one. The good guy is a sweet and loving parent and good to his wife, but get him in a room with a terrorist and he goes psycho? I always thought he went too easy."

"You aren't impressing me with this shit," Pill said defiantly. "You sound more like that wimpy captain on the my least favorite *Star Trek* show."

"See, now that you've insulted Archer, I'm gonna have to make you suffer more," the Sandman declared, holding up an ice pick in one hand and a large corkscrew in the other. "If you meant the reboot movie, you suffer even more. Chris Pine rocked the Kirk role, you Philistine."

"Oh, the hell with this!" Nightshade roared.

Pill looked startled and looked at her, as if he hadn't even realized she'd been there. She grabbed the ice pick from the Sandman as Pill tried to sit up and swing at her with his usable hand.

She promptly impaled the pick through his palm. She then nailed the hand to the floor.

Rising, Nightshade kicked Pill's legs apart, striking each injured knee with the tip of one boot. Pill yelped in pain. She knelt between his legs and pulled the glove off her right hand. Holding it palm up over his crotch, she asked him a question.

"How do you like your balls, Pill?" Fire ignited in her open palm. Blue flames danced six inches above her fingers. Pill's eyes, already bug-like, looked ready to burst from his skull. "Original recipe or extra crispy?"

"He's staying in the loft apartment two buildings over! Top floor!" Pill screeched. "He's got the rest of his crew with him, and sometimes that scary bitch! We take breaks from guard duty in this apartment! Anything else you want to know?"

"I think I'll shrivel your balls anyway because I don't like you," Nightshade declared casually.

"Hey! No! He's got the flash drive on him! No copies were made! He's paranoid about it! I'm cooperating! I'm cooperating!"

The Sandman coughed, and Nightshade suspected it was to cover an impulse to laugh. However, she nodded as if he had given her a signal and extinguished the flame. She got up and walked over to the fridge. Opening it, she found her favorite brand of bottled water in addition to numerous bottles of wine and twelve packs of beer. She pulled an unopened water bottle, turned away from Pill's sight, and pulled the scarf down before taking a long, satisfying drink.

"Geezus, man! Why did you have to bring her into your business? She's worse than you've ever been!" Pill said to the Sandman.

"Oh, didn't you know?" the Sandman asked. "I'm *her* sidekick. She brought me into this business. Got tired of me playing nice. I'm kinda being evaluated right now."

Replacing her scarf, she capped the water and turned back around.

"Yes, and you're going to have to do much, much better to satisfy me, Sandman," she announced loftily. "I suppose you have objections to burning everything in this apartment to prevent them from ratting us out? Causing a much-needed distraction towards Alfi and the crew in the loft?"

Shrugging, the Sandman replied, "Well, the hooker in the bathroom didn't do anything to warrant death."

"No, but she probably did business with all three of the douchebags in this apartment. She'd probably welcome death."

The Sandman coughed again. "A fair point. Can we spare them to avoid inadvertently killing any of the other tenants in the complex, or damaging their property?"

Nightshade rolled her eyes for dramatic effect and sighed. She was enjoying this "good cop, bad cop" routine far, far too much. But she couldn't help it. She glared at Pill, sweating, shaking, and bleeding on the floor.

"Damned liberals." She spat and exited the kitchen.

Chapter Thirty

Somehow, Alfi and his henchmen knew Nightshade and the Sandman were coming. The apartment was likely bugged, and they hadn't done a sweep before getting their intel. The duo was outside the window of the only seemingly empty room of the loft. Before they entered, the Sandman adjusted the range of the infrared glasses, sensing something amiss.

"We can't leave the power levels this high. The batteries will be dead in about five minutes," he explained.

It only took a few seconds to see his instincts were accurate: The crouching figures of several people, positioned strategically, were now visible to them both via the infrared lenses. The outlines of the walls and furniture the people were squatting behind gave the duo the layout of the loft and their targets' positions.

"Think we can take care of them in five minutes?" Nightshade asked.

"I think we'd be better off memorizing where they are, and work from there," the Sandman suggested. "Otherwise, should it take longer than five minutes, we're wearing sunglasses in the dark, against hostile forces."

Nightshade didn't consider it for more than a second. "Okay, I've got their positions memorized. Power the glasses down, and we go from there."

They took thirty seconds to formulate their battle plan. The Sandman then lowered the infrared settings to conserve power and let them have the advantage they were used to with the lenses. He planted three small explosives on the windows, and they moved back a safe distance.

The front windows shattered when the explosives were triggered. At the same moment, Nightshade used one of the Sandman's devices to unlock and open the window to the unoccupied bathroom. Unlike the previous incursion, only Nightshade entered that way. The Sandman went through the exploded windows, drawing fire.

The plan was for the Sandman to enter the apartment where the occupants expected the assault: He would throw stun grenades and then press the attack with his .45s. They both agreed there was little need for prisoners. She would come out after she heard a fourth stun grenade go off. From her position, she and the Sandman would catch the enemy in crossfire.

The first two grenades went off before she came through the window. Nightshade was expecting the percussive thump of them exploding, so her progress through the window was not impeded. The heavy roar of the Sandman's .45s came next, followed by the loud, racketing sound of machine gun fire, along with smaller explosions that came from other caliber handguns. Nightshade pulled out the new weapons given to her, a pair of Smith and Wesson M&P .45 handguns and waited.

The third grenade went off, and Nightshade checked her side arms before replacing one to free up a hand to open the bathroom door. She placed her hand on the doorknob, wishing she was already a part of the action. More rounds from various guns went off, including the Sandman's .45s. There was a yelp, followed by a spray of automatic gunfire. Bullets pierced the wall above Nightshade's head.

Holding her position, Nightshade waited for the fourth grenade to go off. She took a moment to reach out with her senses and try to detect the necromancer. The smell of her black magic was around, but not strong. Nightshade guessed that she was either here and hadn't used her magic recently or had left.

There were curses, sporadic gunfire, followed by the fourth stun grenade going off. Nightshade turned the knob and bolted out into the hall. Keeping low, she glanced down the hallway opposite of the firefight, to see the two gunmen holding their positions away from the rest. She dropped them both with two shots from the M&P in her hand even as she pulled the other from its holster. Pivoting, Nightshade sighted her weapons on the three remaining gunmen and opened fire. She cut them down in seconds and grew even more attached to her newest gifts from the Sandman in the process.

As the Sandman came into sight from the end of the hallway, Nightshade lowered her weapons and looked at the two dozen fallen men. The last one she had shot, the one standing behind all the rest, had been Alfi. She allowed herself a satisfied smile. It lasted for one second.

The smell hit her first. Before she could react, a cold hand gripped her throat. Her body convulsed from the spell the necromancer cast.

Electricity poured into Nightshade's body, causing her fingers to tighten. Both guns discharged. Then the electricity stopped, and coldness spread throughout her. The guns dropped from her useless hands, and she began to shake. The necromancer held Nightshade in front of her, using her as a shield.

"Quite clever, vigilante." The woman's honey-sweet voice came from over Nightshade's shoulder. "You certainly caught these fools off-guard. Not that doing so is a difficult task." She laughed briefly. "Nice to see a man that uses his brain a little more than most."

"Alfi's dead, and that means your auction is off," the Sandman said in his deadliest voice. "I doubt a woman of your talents cares much about that. You wouldn't put all your bets on that idiot. You have greater plans. Ones reaching farther than selling out Temeria."

"Oh, and he's flattering as well!" The necromancer laughed. "No wonder you like him, dear. He's darling. Is he any good as a lover?"

Nightshade couldn't move, let alone speak. She felt the woman's breath against the nape of her neck and ear.

"My, my, our little Selia has no comment," the necromancer scolded in the same honey-sweet tone. "Sounds like you aren't measuring up, Sandman, but then, what man does? So few, so very few, which is why we Temerian women know the benefit of our own gender."

The Sandman remained as he had been: Standing, with his guns at either side. His mask and sunglasses hiding any expression he might have worn. Selia briefly wondered how this bitch knew her name.

"If you're trying to seduce me, you might want to project images of Selia with another attractive woman, instead of you."

Oh, shit, Selia thought, *this is not going to go well.*

Power swirled around her. She felt the dark energy growing in the woman holding her, being released into the air. The stench was so strong that Selia felt she would vomit, if her body were her own again. Right now, she did not feel like Nightshade, who was powerful, sure, and deadly. At this moment, she felt like the wallflower again: unable to do anything but be a part of the scenery.

The power was coalescing into a spell. The infrared lenses that Selia was wearing gave an unusual perspective of the energy as it swirled and roped into new form, branching off and touching all of the bodies on the floor. The Sandman had his guns up, obviously trying to get a clear shot at the necromancer's head.

"Ah, the hell with this," the Sandman grumbled. He dropped the barrels of both guns and fired one round from each.

The effect on the spell was immediate. The energy intensified and then was gone. The necromancer hissed in pain and called him a bastard in Temerian.

She drew in a deep breath and shouted. "Not good enough, Sandman! You're going to be busy dying, so I'm going to have some fun with the lovely Selia!" Selia felt the woman's teeth bite gently on her earlobe and pull. "Girl talk!" The necromancer squealed and began pulling Selia down the hallway.

The Sandman was trying to get another shot at the necromancer. Selia noticed with dismay that he was oblivious to the reanimated bodies slowly rising from the floor. She tried to scream a warning, but her voice was as unresponsive as her body. Then, she was pulled out of the hallway and could see him no longer.

Chapter Thirty-One

Selia's vision swam, and her stomach lurched. She felt as though she was blacking out. Her eyes started to focus as she felt herself falling.

Her back was against the gravel that made up the floor of the roof.

I must have passed out, she reasoned, *I can't remember how we got to the roof.*

She looked up into the sky. She could hear gunshots, sirens, groaning and on the street below, people shrieking.

It might have been her imagination, but she thought she heard the Sandman distantly yelling, *"Zombies? Are you kidding me?"*

"So, my delightful little treat, are you ready to take your place?" The necromancer reached down and pulled the scarf off Selia's face. "Such a pretty face," the woman chided, "Shouldn't be kept hidden." She paused. "Don't worry, I won't be posting your face on the Internet."

"Who are you?" Selia asked, finally able to talk. Her body was slowly, far too slowly in her opinion, starting to respond to her.

"Oh, I suppose I should introduce myself." The necromancer gave a put-upon sigh, as though Selia should have known who she was already. "I'm Moreisa, darling, and if you're wondering about your 'place', it will be at my side." Another pause, and then she leaned forward almost conspiratorially. "Well, at my feet would be more accurate."

No, thank you, Selia thought. *Only someone with a fetish for necrophilia would want to bed you. Or a mortal who can't smell the retched stench of rotting flesh pouring from you. Not someone from our homeland who could guess about why you aren't living there, and the forbidden arts you're using to spy on or reanimate other beings.*

The stench was more than enough to cause her stomach to flip and Selia felt as though it wanted to expel everything she'd eaten. She wiggled her toes in her boots and smiled inwardly. Her strength was finally returning. Closing her eyes, she gave the impression of slumping back against the gravel of the roof. Taking a moment, she thought of the Sandman and concern for him fueled her recovery. Or maybe it was magic. It was hard to tell.

She opened her eyes and struggled to a sitting position. She leaned to her side, bent over as though she were having difficulty breathing. Looking up, Moreisa was studying her hips and muttering under her breath about men and their stupidity.

"You're a necromancer," Selia gasped, the pain in her voice not an act. "What do you want me for?"

"Unlike men, I do not plan to be alone at the top. Nor do I need to be," Moreisa replied. "We are alike, in many ways. We both escaped the tyranny and small-mindedness of Temeria when we were young. The Art is strong in both of us. We can have men at our beck and call."

Just keep talking, Selia thought. She tensed her back and legs and was gratified that they did not cramp. Her body would be ready for combat soon.

"You need guidance to properly use the Art and all its glorious forms. I will teach you. I will teach you... many things. Strength and passion and how they can entwine between two women, in all aspects. How to use men, to make them do what we wish, while never truly giving them our bodies."

"Never had much difficulty in being a tease," Selia retorted.

"Oh, that is the most juvenile of womanly arts," mocked Moreisa. "I am talking of the supreme art of the woman: taking all the pleasures you can from a man, making him think he owns you, even as you completely own him. Or have you begun to do that with the Sandman? We will find better, more attentive males for your use, and training. Your stubbornness and wit are part of why I haven't just killed you. They show some steel in your spine."

"Thanks!" Selia replied, and leaped at Moreisa, pulling her left sword from its sheath.

Moreisa gestured, and Selia was caught in midair, suspended by a holding spell. The necromancer plucked the sword from her hands and admired it.

"The Japanese know craftsmanship so much better than many countries, including our own. I, like you, prefer their swords to any other in the world or history." Moreisa examined the blade and placed it down on the gravel. "I have a better set, myself. One of the many benefits of having true power and wealth. Of course, one can never have enough of either."

"Unlike you, I did not come to this city with a wealthy escort who pampered me. Nor did I become weak, as you have," Moreisa said in a chiding tone. "I stowed away on a ship. Before I arrived here, I had been with every member of the crew, and I owned them all. They would do anything, even fight over me, to have my favor."

She gestured again, and Selia's body pivoted until she was kneeling at Moreisa's feet.

"That is where I prefer my subjects. You would have learned to appreciate my generosity." Moreisa viciously kicked Selia in the stomach. "You would have known worship second only to me. I could have purged your weakness from you. I would have taught you my knowledge of truth: Necromancy is the key to ruling. Necromancy and the power of Magic. The power of life and death. I studied the tomes as I seduced and used more and more wealthy and powerful people. Each one teaching me the ways that ordinary humans gain control over others. Coupled with my magic, I have built my empire. The selling of Temeria would have been a coup on multiple scales. But I will find another way to have my homeland finance my final ascension to complete power."

She kicked Selia again, harder this time.

"I selected you to be at my side, and you fail to see how inevitable my rule shall be, how complete my victory. Your poor decision to not join me can haunt you in Hell, where I will-"

The gunshot was deafening.

Moreisa bellowed in pain and outrage. Her right hand went to her backside. There was another shot, and Selia saw the bullet exit Moreisa's torso just below her collarbone. As she fell, the Sandman came into sight behind her. He held a compact Walther .380 in both hands. It was his holdout gun. The one he kept in one of his boots. She could see the .45s in their holsters. He must have run out of ammo.

"Really? *Monologuing?*" the Sandman all but yelled at the fallen necromancer. "Do you *not* know how that works out for the villain?"

Selia collapsed, released from the spell. Her stomach felt like a burning knot in the middle of her body, but she picked up her sword and stood. She looked down at Moreisa.

"That's arterial bleeding from the chest wound," Selia observed. "You have, maybe, two major spells left in you before you are too far gone to heal. Only one, if you cast against more than a single person. Surrender, or one of us will kill you."

"I'm for shooting her more while she thinks it over," the Sandman added.

"Another time," Moreisa gasped, and she was surrounded by a golden light.

Selia moved forward to strike, but the woman disappeared. Not a nanosecond later, three shots slammed against the gravel where she had been. Selia glanced back at the Sandman, whose gun was issuing a stream of smoke, and was now empty. He reached into his left boot and brought out a spare clip.

Reloading the small automatic, he explained, "I thought she had gone invisible. Didn't want her to get away."

"That was a teleportation spell," Selia gasped as her chest tightened, an after effect of the necromantic spells. She swiftly replaced her scarf. "She's probably less than a hundred yards away right now and will need to use the last of her magic to heal herself. Otherwise, she'll die."

The Sandman nodded. "We won't be able to look for her. The police have entered the buildings and are going floor to floor. We've gotta get out of here. Across the rooftops until we're off the block, and even then, if you can manage it, we may need your magical cover. I'm too spent to trust my ability to sneak past four dozen 'on high alert' cops. On the bright side, if she's anywhere in the buildings, she'll have to explain the four bullet wounds." The Sandman paused, eyeing Selia closely. "Alfi wasn't one of the zombies. I didn't get a chance to search him for the drive."

As if on cue, a reanimated Alfi lurched over the fire escape ladder and spilled onto the roof. He shambled to a standing position before approaching them. His right hand was open and clawed, his left still held an oversized .50 caliber handgun.

"Guess he was a little slower than the rest," observed the Sandman as he took aim.

"Don't bother," Nightshade said, stepping past him and beheading the reanimated gangster in a single stroke. She knelt, rummaging through the corpse's pockets. Nightshade found the flash drive in his inside jacket pocket.

"There we go," she announced, holding it up. "Now, I just need one more thing."

When they arrived at the rented bungalow a little over an hour later, the Sandman came into the bungalow with her. He pulled off his mask, breathing heavily. He placed the plastic bag, containing that 'one more thing', in the fridge.

"Can I ask you something?" Selia asked as she removed her outfit.

"Of course," he replied.

"You said she, the necromancer, has four bullet wounds. You got her just below the collarbone. The two shots in the loft..."

"I grazed her on both hips. It was the only visible part of her around you," he answered.

"When you got to the roof, you shot her in the ass, didn't you?"

"I was woozy, gun hand was unsteady," Wil said as he pulled off his mask. "So, I aimed for the largest target I had."

Selia laughed, despite how much it made her body hurt.

Chapter Thirty-Two

Selia woke the next day and groaned as she rolled over onto her back. Everything up until last night had been like a workout. Last night had been a true battle that left her aching. Considering she had come out of it unscathed, except for the bruises suffered at Moreisa's feet and spells, Selia was willing to place the full blame of her aching body on the necromancer.

Stretching carefully, she yawned and pried her eyes open, blinking in the sunlight that managed to sneak into her bedroom. Rolling into a sitting position, Selia slowly stood and shuffled into the bathroom, grabbing the two cell phones as she left the bedroom. No way was she going to take the chance of not answering a call from Wil, Soren, or Al.

Turning on the hot water, she sat on the side of the tub and watched as the steam filled the room. She still needed to contact Lucien and inform him that Alfi was dead and she had the drive, but at the moment, her body felt as though the muscles hadn't been used for days, or even weeks.

Lowering herself into the tub, the jets pulsed against her worn body, and she sighed. Lucien could wait. In fact, everything could wait until after her body relaxed and the aches were massaged away by the hot water and jets. As the water neared the top of the tub, she turned it off, allowing the jets to continue their soothing pulsing against her body.

Over an hour later, the water was room temperature when she decided to leave the comfort of the pulsing jets to get dressed. One more day meant one more visit from the brothers and she had no desire to let them see her bruised and battered. It would raise too many questions. Questions she had no desire to answer.

Grabbing a t-shirt, lightweight sweater, and a pair of silk-like pants, she padded into the kitchen and opened the freezer. A tub of Ben & Jerry's Peanut Butter Cup ice cream, her favorite ever, sat next to a box of Klondike bars and another container of off-brand chocolate and vanilla swirl ice cream. Grabbing the Ben & Jerry's and a spoon, she plopped down on the sofa and clicked on the TV. Flipping through the channels, she settled on some cartoons and began digging into the ice cream.

Maybe not the healthiest meal, but she'd earned the right to it. Besides, she had no doubt that she'd be working off the calories in the coming days as she hit the gym, either at the Sandman's lair or the one she frequented that wasn't used by any of the Family, except her.

The day dragged by and Selia started to think she was either going to be granted a reprieve from the boys or get caught by not being there when they showed up past dark. She was proven wrong when the clock blinked seven o'clock and someone knocked on the door.

"Door's open, come on in." She glanced up as the pair came into the room. "You two are going to be so bored after all this."

"Nah, we'll just come knock on your apartment door," Bernie joked as he and Alex stepped inside.

Selia snickered. "Yeah, well, I can't promise I'll be home or alone."

"Oh?" Alex asked, giving Bernie a smack on the head before he could say anything.

"I'm twenty-six, guys," she explained in an overly-patient tone. "I think I'm allowed to have a social life. I also plan on visiting Soren more often." She turned back to the TV, waving them off. "Search, peek, enjoy."

"Uh, good point. I'm sure Soren will enjoy that," Alex said.

"How come the sudden change?" Bernie asked, checking all the usual places in the kitchen and living room. At least he ducked while passing between her and the TV.

Selia shrugged and scooped up more ice cream, trying to ignore her still stiff-and-sore body. "Coming close to death for the first time tends to give someone a new perspective on life. I'd like to at least think that I have a chance of finding someone to have a family with."

A certain pair of eyes flashed in front of her, and she hid a smile behind a spoonful of Ben & Jerry's. Bernie headed towards the spare bedroom as Alex went to hers.

"I can't see you having a problem with finding a guy," Alex called, his voice slightly muffled.

"Yeah, there are plenty of men who would want to be with you," Bernie agreed. Selia suspected he was choosing his words very carefully.

She finished chewing, swallowed, and replied, "For a couple dates, sure, but for long-term?"

Again, she thought of Wil and the heated attraction between them. She tried to keep from thinking of him as her guaranteed mate but couldn't quite keep from it.

"Ah, come on, Lia," Bernie said, stopping just outside the bathroom door. "Anyone would be lucky to have you. Not just for a night, but a lifetime."

"That's the sweetest thing you've ever said to me," Selia said, smiling at him. Bernie flushed and ducked into the bathroom.

"Don't get used to it," Alex said dryly, coming out of her bedroom. "It's a rarity when his mind isn't stuck in the gutter."

Selia laughed. "I probably don't help much, huh?"

"Not hardly," Alex muttered, glancing towards his brother. He looked back to her. "How are you holding up? You look tired."

I look like something the cat dragged in, she amended silently.

"I'm really missing my own comfy bed," Selia said honestly. "I guess the Chinese didn't sit too well with me last night. Guess it was a bad batch or something. It doesn't help that I don't sleep good if I'm not in my own bed." She paused and added, "Have any suggestions?"

Alex and Bernie looked at each other. Alex had an expression of mingled enticement and indecisiveness while Bernie was trying to figure out if he wanted to reply or hang himself.

"I'm never going to be able to look at you the same after this," Alex grumbled.

"Oh, finally realizing I'm a woman and not some wild child that Soren pulled from the jungle, or an island of savages?" Selia joked innocently.

"I am not going to answer that," Alex countered, grinning. "We don't think it'll be too much longer before you can go home."

"I hope you're right," Selia said, digging into her ice cream again. "Though, the downside will be no more fun visits from you two trying to find non-existent lovers. I'm going to miss these visits."

Alex and Bernie chuckled.

"See ya around, Lia," Bernie said.

"Take care of yourself," Alex added as the two left.

One more night and then she'd be free. Though, she wouldn't be surprised if Al put a tail on her for a while after this was over. At least until he was convinced she wasn't Nightshade or a threat to the Family, or even him personally.

Her body still ached from the beating she took from Moreisa, and she knew she'd have to return to studying her tomes. Magic would have to be bested by magic and somehow Selia had to figure out how to defeat a necromancer who was older and far more skilled than her. Selia doubted that even had she kept up her magical lessons and knowledge, she still wouldn't have the ability to defeat someone with more years of training under their belt. Not to mention the decades of malicious cunning and cruelty Moreisa had nurtured.

Perhaps Papa will have an idea, she thought as she got up and put the half-eaten container of ice cream back in the freezer.

Grabbing a fleece blanket from her closet, Selia returned to the living room and curled up on the sofa. Yawning, she pulled the fleece around her and smiled as the cartoons played. It was still a few hours until the Sandman would show up, so she slowly let sleep overcome her.

Chapter Thirty-Three

Selia woke up to a hand caressing her cheeks, brushing the hair from her face. Giving a soft sigh of pleasure, she slowly opened her eyes and smiled up at the Sandman. His mask was off, but he still had his usual disguise using the wax molds. His eyes were warm but filled with concern.

"How are you feeling?" he asked as she leaned into his touch.

"Sore," she replied truthfully. "My body feels as though it were run over by a couple dozen horses. Whatever Moreisa used was harsher than anything else I've been dealt."

Wil raised his brows. "What else have you been dealt?"

That wasn't a short list, she thought, but decided to give him the briefest rundown.

"A couple broken bones and I've been bruised pretty badly from falls. I took a few forms of martial arts and have been banged up pretty good from those." She shrugged and grimaced from the stiffness returning to her muscles. "The spell she used is one meant to disable a victim, allowing the caster to torture the person before dealing a swift death, if the prisoner is lucky. There are written reports of how many times the prisoner is immobilized by a necromancer, only to have the necromancer take her time killing them. Slowly, with extreme pain, with the prisoner fully aware of what's happening." She grimaced, adding, "Think about being tasered at the highest power possible and then have your core temperature dropped to where you're almost in danger of hypothermia."

Wil's face twisted in sympathy and anger. "Do you still believe what your headmistress told you?"

"I don't know," Selia replied truthfully. "I could smell the death on her, but Moreisa isn't a happy-go-lucky pacifist. She's a cruel, malicious bitch who doesn't care how she gets what she wants, or who is hurt in the process. She also uses the hard-core necromantic spells and death magic."

She snuggled closer to Wil, who was sitting on the edge of the sofa. Selia had never coupled with another woman. Not because she hadn't received plenty of offers, quite the opposite. She'd received plenty on Temeria and even more in New Campania, but her eyes had always been on the males.

On Temeria, she hadn't had any lovers. Though she'd enjoyed the flirtations and foreplay of many males, none had been serious. In her homeland, it had been normal for women to wait until they had completed their studies to enjoy the company of another woman. When the land is ruled by women, enjoying a night with a male was more to ease the woman's sexual desires or procreate than to enter into a meaningful relationship. The queen's

Ladies in Waiting attended to her every whim and desire. Both inside and outside the bedroom. Very few women on Temeria used men as more than a device to conceive daughters, let alone saw them as anything other than a very lowly servant.

In the city, Selia had enjoyed a night with a lover here and there when her desires had grown too strong for her to ignore, but she had, again, never taken a woman as a lover. The chance of being caught and drawing attention to herself by breaking one of the Church's rules hadn't seemed the brightest idea. Not when it meant causing trouble for not only her, but Soren as well.

But none of her previous lovers had touched her the same way Wil did. From the moment he had entered the scene, she had felt an immediate attraction to him, even after discovering he was the city's masked vigilante hated by the Families.

Wil chuckled and pulled her gently into his lap, breaking her train of thought. She curled around him as he slid back onto the sofa, resting her head against his shoulder, enjoying the warmth and closeness. Soren more or less approved, so that was all that mattered. The rest of the Family, Al in particular, could just deal with her choice in a mate.

"It isn't over yet, though," she sighed, turning her thoughts to their current situation. "I still have to meet up with Lucien and return the drive."

"You're still going to do that?" Wil asked, running a hand through her hair and down her back.

It felt so good. She didn't want him to stop, but she nodded anyway. "It's for the greater good." He snorted. Selia sighed and tipped her head back so she could look up at him. "The balance must be kept, Wil. There is a reason Lucien wants that drive and if Alfi betrayed my Family, what's to say Ignacio didn't betray Lucien? Plus, I need to show Lucien that he can trust me."

"Why?" Wil asked, though it wasn't said in disgust or annoyance, or even in a challenge. It was pure curiosity.

Selia smiled. "If Moreisa is bent on carnage and destruction, which I suspect she is, she'll want to bring this city down around us all. That means going after both ruling syndicates, if not all the syndicates. Since I'm the only other Temerian here, I have to put myself in a position where Lucien will call me. Or, if I need to enter his territory to take her out, he won't feel the need to start a full-blown war with Al, and subsequently, Soren."

"You, dear lady, are devious," Wil said, kissing her forehead. "When did you become so knowledgeable in subterfuge?"

"I had a good instructor," she replied, smiling at him. "He's pretty handsome, too, and likes to kick ass in this sexy, black outfit."

"Uh huh, right," Wil replied, brushing a kiss across her lips. "You learned it from your people, didn't you?"

"Some," she admitted. "Though you helped remind me of what I forgot and taught me things I didn't know."

"You better go get dressed, if you want to be free of this gilded cage," Wil said after a long pause, his eyes burning with desire.

Selia sighed and unwrapped herself from Wil. With a smile, she said, "Only because I want to be able to be with you without having to worry about my two appointed guard dogs interrupting our fun."

Fifteen minutes later she was standing in the living room wearing a pair of black leather pants that hugged her legs and hips. A black silk vest hugged the rest of her, and Selia had left the top-most buttons undone, so the swell of her breasts was visible. Her hair was pulled back and pinned up, ready for her Nightshade wig. She already wore her holster and one of her shiny new M&Ps.

"We can go from here to wherever Lucien plans on meeting me," she said. "I can't show up to his meeting as Nightshade. Did you bring my trench?"

Wil nodded and tossed it to her; it had been sitting behind him on the sofa the whole time, unnoticed by her. She slipped it on. From a pocket she pulled out a long, wide, and fairly thick scarf and began wrapping it snugly around her head and face. Once done, she pulled the bottom portion down from her mouth and grabbed her phone, punching in Lucien's number. He answered on the third ring.

"Hello, Lucien," she said as a way of greeting.

"Selia, a delight to hear your lovely voice," Lucien replied. The soft sound of orchestral music could be heard in the background. "I presume you are calling about our agreement."

"Indeed I am," Selia replied, swatting Wil as he snickered softly. "Say, we meet tonight? Same place as last time?"

"I would love nothing more than the pleasure of your company, little belladonna." Lucien replied in his cloyingly sweet voice.

The man never stops! Selia thought, her nose wrinkling in disgust. *It's as though he's trying to seduce me over the phone. Ick! He's old enough to be my father!*

She managed to keep her distaste from her voice as she replied, "You say such sweet things. What time, then?"

"Unfortunately, I have business and pleasure to attend to tonight that cannot be put off." Lucien sighed, and he almost sounded sorrowful. "Can we make it tomorrow afternoon? Say, at one o'clock? I can have lunch provided."

"Sounds perfect," she said with as much pleasantness as she could stomach. "I will see you then."

Turning to Wil, Selia began pulling off her outfit and gave him a thoroughly wicked and mischievous grin. "I think I've earned a night out, don't you? How about meeting me at the Blu Light?"

Chapter Thirty-Four

Selia pulled into a parking space at the Blu Light and glanced in the rearview mirror. She'd spotted the pair following her, which was to be expected. Not that she was going to allow the brothers to interrupt her fun. Tonight, she was going to go and enjoy herself, rules be damned.

She'd busted her ass for the past several days, wearing herself out avenging Soren and removing the pest that was Alfi. Her entire body ached, and she wanted a night of fun that didn't involve anyone shooting at her. Wil would show up soon, and though she wasn't certain what his disguise would be, she had no doubt she'd recognize him. Of course, the question would be who would see whom first.

Considering she was wearing a red metallic dress with a black mesh overlay and tiny straps that hugged every curve, she doubted he would have any problem finding her. The outfit was complete with a pair of black stiletto heels that added a couple extra inches to her height.

It wouldn't be a challenge for the guard dog brothers to find her, since she hadn't bothered with a disguise of any sort. After all, it wasn't like she was in any danger. Alfi was dead and the necromancer was gods-knew-where; not that anyone other than Wil and she knew that little fact. As for anything else, Al's top enforcers were going to be watching her every move. If trouble arose, they'd step in.

She stepped from the car, her little purse hanging from her wrist. Inside was a tube of lipstick, her phone, and wallet with the ID Al had given her along with a couple hundred dollars. If she used anything else, Alex and Bernie would probably get suspicious.

Striding to the door, she gave the bouncer a bright smile and flashed her ID and a twenty. The guard took the cover charge, barely glanced at the ID, and waved her in, a smug smile on his face. Selia wove her way through the crowd and slid onto a bar stool, where she turned her attention to the mirror against the bar's wall and waited for Alex and Bernie.

The moment the pair entered she made her way to the dance floor where a rock song played. Letting her body sway and move with the music, she laughed as others danced close to her. Swirling around, she stepped out of reaching hands, a teasing smile on her lips. As she danced, she watched for her guardians and saw that Bernie and Alex had split up.

Bernie paced the perimeter of the dance floor, shoulders hunched and glowering like an angry bear. Alex, meanwhile, was making himself at home at one of the tables that faced the dance floor on the other side.

Such sweet fellows, she thought. *Here to make sure little ol' me isn't harmed.*

The song ended and another slower beat started. Selia slipped from the dance floor and headed back to the bar taking the edge closest to Bernie, just to annoy him. Sliding onto a bar stool, she waved to the bartender and ordered a soda.

"Can I buy the lady a drink?" a voice said from beside her and she looked up to find a burly blonde leering down at her. His breath smelled like he'd had one too many drinks already and he had stains around his armpits.

Selia offered a polite smile. "No thanks." She slid a ten across to the bartender who accepted it with a smile and nod. "Not interested."

"Why the hell not?" the man demanded in a surly tone.

Selia felt Bernie tensing up to jump the drunkard. She decided bloodshed would spoil the rest of her evening.

"I'm waiting on my date. I got here early." She shrugged. "Thanks for the offer, though."

"Oh," the man said, and he paused as if considering her words, or at least trying to get his sodden brain to process them. "Well, if you decide you want to trade up, I'll be around."

She smiled politely and turned away from him. She knew when he finally wandered off because Bernie relaxed.

"You got a date?" Bernie asked, as he sat down next to her on a bar stool.

Selia glanced over at Bernie, a smile on her lips. "Nope, but he doesn't need to know that."

"I wouldn't have let that idiot lay a paw on you, ya know," Bernie said, almost defensively.

"I know," Selia replied. "But I'd rather you not get bounced for starting a fight when I could just brush him off. I'd feel terribly guilty if Alex was the only one being tortured." She paused and took a sip of her drink. "I'm surprised you aren't dragging me out of here. Didn't you call Uncle Al and tell him that I'm disobeying direct orders by coming here?"

"He's surprised you waited this long to disobey orders." Bernie confided. "You might be a quiet one most of the time, but that doesn't make you boring or a recluse."

Selia chuckled. "Hey, I try to be the dutiful daughter to Soren!" She glanced up at the mirror, wondering if Wil had arrived and she hadn't realized it. "I promise to behave while I enjoy myself tonight, and I won't take anyone home with me, either."

"That really wouldn't be a problem," Bernie assured her. "As long as it isn't someone from the opposition. Maybe your friend from the shower will be here tonight?"

It was all Selia could do to not choke on her soda. "Um, I didn't call her." She couldn't stop the smile from pulling at her lips though. "Besides, I already got chastised from

Al about that 'transgression'. I really don't want to anger him further." She paused and turned to Bernie, something clicking into place. "Wait a minute... what do you mean that wouldn't be a problem? I didn't think I was allowed to have anyone over."

"No one that wasn't approved of," Bernie replied with a shrug. "If Alex and me are here, we can intervene if you try to take someone we don't trust back to the bungalow."

Selia rolled her eyes and turned away from Bernie. "Great. I now have to have my would-be-lovers screened by you two. I think I'll wait until this is over before taking anyone home with me." She gave Bernie a sidelong look. "With my luck, you two would have any guy who wanted to take me home running for another continent after two questions."

"Lia," Bernie groaned, putting his hand to his heart. "You wound me, sweetheart."

"Oh, so it'd be more like from 'hello'?" she teased. "Gotcha."

It felt good, laughing and joking with Bernie. The fun jesting reminded her of more normal times when they'd hung out frequently. She sipped her soda, silently acknowledging how much she'd missed their camaraderie.

Finally, she broke the silence, asking, "So, why were you and Alex sweeping the place? Did Uncle Al think I had found some hot thing from the other side?"

"Just being cautious," Bernie said, and took a pull from a longneck beer. "He doesn't know who might come after you, and it never hurts to check up on people. Most people didn't see Alfi turning traitor."

"There's only one way I would turn traitor," Selia said softly. The heavy pounding of the music kept anyone from overhearing them. "That would be if someone murdered Soren, which I can't see happening. I have no reason to want to betray the people who gave me a home."

She swirled her straw around her glass. If they knew she'd fallen head-over-heels in love with the Sandman, they'd claim she was a traitor. The problem with that was, she hadn't moved against anyone in the Family, except Alfi. Would that change? She didn't know, but she did know Nightshade wouldn't go near Soren and neither would the Sandman.

"Hello," a soft-spoken male voice said, and her heart skipped a beat while her skin warmed.

She turned and found Wil standing between her and Bernie. He wore an electric blue shirt unbuttoned almost to his navel. Tight black jeans were adorned with a spiked belt. He had a gold ring in his right nostril, and five more in his right ear. His wig was a straight black affair, touching his collar and covering his ears. Bangs stopped severely at his eyebrows. She didn't take notice of what kind of footwear he wore.

"Would you like to dance?" he asked.

"Sure," she said with a smile, and looked at Bernie. "Would you keep an eye on my drink, for me?"

Bernie rolled his eyes, nodded, and took a sip of his beer.

"Actually, I was asking your hot honey bear of a friend to dance," Wil said, his voice completely convincing in its bored delivery.

Bernie spewed beer all over the bar.

Selia burst out laughing. "Oh, my gods," she managed to gasp. "I didn't know you could turn so many shades of red, Bernie!"

"Gah, um..." Bernie seemed to be gagging on words. He wiped his mouth with the cuff of his jacket. He seemed to be gathering steam as he turned on Wil and said, "Hey, man, you need to-"

"Ohhh, I get it," Wil interrupted with the same bored tone. "You only dig other bears. I get it. It's cool." He glanced at Selia.

"Okay, you'll do, then."

Selia giggled and let her eyes roam over Wil. She'd seen nearly every inch of him already, but damn, the man was handsome.

She grinned and gave a shrug. "Well, at least that means I'll be safe from groping hands."

Sliding a hand around his waist as she moved around him, she snagged a finger in a belt loop and led him onto the dance floor. Pressing up against him, she swayed with the music. There was barely more than a hair's breadth between them. Her eyes twinkled as she slid her hands over his bare skin, enjoying the muscles that rippled beneath her palms.

"You are evil, sir," she whispered into his ear. The colored lights flashed and blinked around them. As they danced, she waited until the pulsing lights put her in the shadows and she nipped his collar bone. "Maybe I should ask Bernie if I can take you home with me."

"That would be *awesome*." He dragged out the last word, making it last for several seconds, in the same bored tone. But he dropped a wink at her.

They continued to dance, and she was surprised to discover that he was completely uninhibited. He ground against her, shook his hips, let his arms flow about him as if he were moving in water, and was, in a word, outrageous.

"Want to make Bernie even more miserable?" he asked in his true voice.

"Oh, yes!" Selia said, laughing, as she pressed up against him. "I'm more than willing to torture him!" She giggled. "So, what's your name, handsome?"

"Brad. Now turn around and put that shapely butt out," he instructed.

She did, shaking her hips and dancing as if to invite him. Selia felt his hips slam against her bottom in time with the drums of the song. A playful slap struck against her right hip, and she turned around.

"Brad" was staring right at Bernie while licking his lips. He continued to jackhammer at her backside and slap her bottom on every other down beat in the music.

Bernie looked like he was going to soil himself, throw up, or both.

Selia smiled and shook her head in mock ecstasy to avoid laughing. She stole another glance at Bernie, just in time to see Alex tap him on the shoulder. Bernie flinched as though shot, bringing up a fist. Alex looked at him reproachfully.

It was too much. She spun around, grabbed Wil, and turned him so his back was to the brothers. Once out of their line of sight, she burst out laughing, barely able to stay on her feet. Wil smiled at her, but he just kept on dancing.

"And I thought *I* enjoyed making Bernie miserable," Selia finally said, her laughter ebbing. "Pity you can't do the same to Alex."

"Alex would handle it better. He isn't questioning his sexuality," Wil replied, knowingly.

"Part of why I like him so much," Selia agreed. She kissed Wil's cheek then bobbed her brows. "Want to meet Alex? Or would you prefer to wait until... later?"

"No, no. We've successfully created your 'safe' environment for the night." Wil chuckled. "No need to push it. I'll 'meet' him another time." He paused and then chuckled again. "You know, I've met them both eight separate times."

"Really?" she asked, intrigued. "When did you meet them?" She paused, tilting her head to the side. "Does that mean you've seen me before?"

"How do you think I've pooled so much knowledge about the Families, the dealers, and everything else?" Wil asked. "I do a lot of surveillance; and in the beginning it was all done without any cameras. I never do surveillance as myself, and only about a fourth of it has been done as... your favorite fellow. As for you? Yes, I've seen you before we met on the fire escape. But met you?" He paused, thinking. "You thanked me for opening the door for you at the Lascari office building, twice. No... three times."

Selia giggled and leaned against Wil as the songs changed and the music slowed.

"You know, you could come home with me tonight," she murmured in his ear.

"I could, but I'm betting you ate all the Ben and Jerry's today," he scolded her. "You meanie."

"There's some left-" she started to reply, stopping in mid-sentence. She lifted her head and stopped moving. "Wait... you put the Ben & Jerry's in the freezer? But... when?" Her brows furrowed and she eyed him suspiciously. "How did you know I was eating it today?"

He leaned into her ear and purred, "Man of mystery. Get used to it." Then he kissed her earlobe.

She gave a soft moan of pleasure and pressed closer against him, moving in time with the music again. "Keep that up and I'll be dragging you back with me." She pressed herself against his pelvis as she rocked her hips. Nuzzling his neck, she whispered, "I have something to confess."

He nodded against her, encouraging.

"I might have the magic, but you're the one who's enchanted me," she whispered, nibbling at his earlobe beneath his wig. "I've fallen in love with you."

There was the slightest pause in his dancing. She felt it, but doubted Alex and Bernie could have noticed it, even if they were staring.

"I feel the same way about you," he breathed back. "But to be fair, you barely know me."

Selia laughed softly, her breath warm against his skin; she could feel him shiver from the pleasure. "I know enough and what I don't know already, I'm willing to learn." She chuckled, and then nipped his earlobe. "I don't think my heart cares how little or how much I know you."

"The erection in my pants doesn't care that I am portraying a very gay man, either" Wil rejoined. "But you and I both know that once the excitement and adrenaline wears down, say on the trip to anywhere but here, the exhaustion, damage, and Ben and Jerry's are going to catch up to you. I told you before: I want you in the best way, and with no distractions."

Selia groaned and pouted. A part of her felt as though she were being pushed away. At the same time, she couldn't blame him for his choice.

"But I wanna feel you more," she grumbled, dropping her chin onto his shoulder.

"That's fine. Feel away," he said, and she could feel him smiling. "I can't let you get far from me until certain parts calm down, after all. That will probably take a while."

She snickered softly. "Well, I could take care of it for you, but you won't let me."

"Are you *always* this pouty when you don't get your way?" he said with mock exasperation.

"Only with you," she countered, giggling. Taking a step away, she twirled around, her dark brown hair swirling around her face.

He pulled her back against him, and she felt that part of him that hadn't calmed down at all. He suddenly pulled out his phone and held it out away from them.

"Smile!" he said.

She gave him a warm, sultry smile. A smile meant only for him. He pressed his cheek up against hers and snapped the picture.

"Okay, back to you being the one that'll do since I can't have Bernie. We have fun dancing, or we have a drink, or I'm going to ruin these pants," Wil confessed.

"How about a drink?" Selia suggested. "I'll be less tempted to seduce you that way."

"That's fine with me."

Selia led him to the bar, away from Bernie and Alex. She smiled at the pair and pulled Wil down beside her. They sat together, talking softly about normal, everyday life. From music to movies, to discussing their favorite TV shows. It was relaxing and felt more normal than anything else had in the past several days. Over an hour later, Selia's purse rang. Or rather, the phone in her purse rang. Surprised, she pulled it out, and upon seeing the name, groaned.

"Hello, Uncle," she said, not bothering to hide her annoyance.

Wil looked at her, curious. She shrugged and mouthed the words 'Big Al'.

"I think it would be best if you call it a night." Al's voice was calm and cool.

"But it's just barely after midnight," Selia grumbled. "I'm being good, too!"

"The point is that you need to get some rest, and so do my gentlemen." Al's voice did not waver. "Also, the later you are out, the more opportunity there is for... unfortunate things to occur."

Selia's eyes narrowed. She wasn't certain if that was a threat or a warning.

"Fine," she sighed, relenting. "I'll be a good little girl and go home. I'll even go home alone. This time."

"You have always been a reasonable woman," Al said. There was a trace of something -- perhaps smugness, maybe satisfaction -- in his voice. "Feel free to go out tomorrow night if you want. The brothers will be available to maintain your safety."

"Thanks," she replied, dryly. "Have a good night, dear uncle." She hung up before he could reply.

"Guess that's it for my night out," she grumbled. "I can't tell if he was making a threat towards me or if he was truly worried about a possible danger."

"Hard to tell with his type," Wil mused. "Do I need to sneak you out in the early afternoon for your meeting?"

"Afraid so, handsome," Selia replied. "I'm allowed out, but only with the brothers over there as my guardians."

"Okay. I will be in my usual spot in the woods. In the meantime..." He took her right hand and kissed it. "Sweet dreams."

Selia gave a sigh of longing. "You, too, handsome."

She kissed his cheek, stood, and headed back to where Bernie and Alex were sitting. Stopping between the pair, she draped her arms over their shoulders and leaned down between them.

"Uncle Al called and said I've been naughty by staying out past my bedtime. He said I need to go home. Thought I should let you boys know and see who wants to escort me to my car."

Both men rose to their feet. A smile on her lips, she walked out, arm in arm, with the two enforcers.

J. F. Posthumus

Chapter Thirty-Five

For once, Selia woke before noon. Her body was no longer aching or sore and she felt refreshed. More like her usual self.

Fixing herself an omelet of bacon, eggs, and cheese, she ate alone, unlike the last time when Wil had fixed her breakfast. She discovered a selection of teas and made herself a cup of Earl Grey to complete her meal.

A quick shower later, she stood in her lingerie trying to figure out what she should wear to her meeting with Lucien. She grabbed her phone and making certain it was the one for 'Sandy', dialed his number.

"Can you bring me something to wear?" she asked, shoving mini-dresses and skimpy skirts to the side. There was nothing in the closet she could wear to a luncheon with Lucien.

"Is it for your lunch with Lucien, or something else?" Wil asked her, sounding curious.

"For Lucien," she grumbled. "Though, I wouldn't object to wearing something you'd like to see me in... or rather, take off of me."

"Right, so business suit for lunch, French maid outfit for later."

"Je suis impatient de vous servir plus tard," Selia replied in a sultry voice. She hadn't learned French for

nothing and offering to service him hadn't been a slip of the tongue.

"Okay. You have succeeded in distracting me from all else," Wil breathed. "Wow. Are you fluent in French, or just at seductive lines?"

"Oh, I'm fairly fluent," Selia replied, laughter in her voice. "Not as good as a native, but I'm better than the average tourist or visitor." She paused as she studied the contents of her lingerie drawer. "Of course, the real question is if you'll have that French Maid outfit for me so I can speak more French."

"You'd be amazed how fast I'm typing in my credit card number on the lingerie boutique website," he countered, sounding hurried.

Selia giggled again. "Awww, does that mean you won't have it by tonight?"

"If it's going to go on your body, I refuse to buy anything but the best. The best isn't in New Campania," he stated. "Well maybe it is, but I'm not looking all over the city when I can order it and overnight it for less than shops around here would charge for it."

Selia laughed. "Fine, you can take me out of the pantsuit later, then."

"Better if you take it off," Wil said. "That way it'll still be usable afterwards."

"Okay," Selia replied thoughtfully, pulling out a sheer lacy bra. "I'll just do a striptease for you."

Wil groaned.

"See you in a few hours," Selia said sweetly.

Around noon, Selia sauntered into the woods. She somehow could sense Wil as he approached on his motorcycle. The trees and bushes concealed her from prying eyes, and she took her time getting to where Wil typically parked. Walking over, she grabbed the helmet she used and slid on behind him. Whispering softly, she vanished from the sight of anyone who might be watching.

Hugging him tightly, she waited until he parked in the city before releasing the spell.

She looked around and asked, "Where are we?"

"This shop has your suit. The car I'm parked behind is the rental I got for you to use," Wil explained. He was wearing motocross gear, and when he took off his helmet, he had spiked blonde hair with a matching goatee and mustache. "You drive that to the graveyard. I'll be about three blocks away, but able to keep track of you." He handed her the small earpiece she wore with her Nightshade outfit.

She put the earpiece in with a smile. Instead of kissing his cheek, she pressed her mouth against his, nibbling at his lower lip. He kissed her back, pulling her against him. When they finally parted, she was breathless.

"Wow, I should have worn my Fandral disguise sooner," he quipped.

"He didn't have spiky blond hair," she countered with a grin.

"Hey, it wasn't spiky before I put on the helmet." Wil objected. "It was lovely and feathered."

Selia giggled and gave him another, briefer, kiss. "I think I like it better spiky." Sighing, she added, "I'd better go before I'm late for my meeting. I want this over with so I can take you home with me."

"Sounds good," he said with a nod. "I'll be nearby."

Selia returned the nod and vanished into the shop. Fifteen minutes later, she was in a figure-flattering black pantsuit with a white blouse. A pearl necklace wrapped around her neck. A black and white checkered scarf was wrapped snugly around her hair and a pair of wide-rimmed sunglasses hid her eyes and most of her features.

Twenty minutes after leaving the shop, she parked at the chosen meeting place. Stepping from the car, she headed towards the two sedans and the limo parked between them. In the daylight, Lucien's hair shone with rich, dark brown highlights. She didn't like the feeling of being out in the open, but there was little to be done about it. This time he wore a warm charcoal gray suit, crisp ivory shirt, and a black tie that wasn't a clip-on. Pulling off her sunglasses, she strode towards the small army of guards and the don.

"You do know I'm supposed to be safely tucked away from everything, right? That if I'm seen with you, it's my life that's going to be cut very short," Selia said by way of a greeting once she was close to Lucien.

"I am aware." Lucien said lazily. "Nor is a graveyard the proper locale to have lunch with a beautiful woman." As if on cue -it probably was- the door of the limo opened, and he gestured for her to enter it.

Giving Lucien a polite smile, Selia stepped into the limo, taking the seat near the opposite side of the vehicle. Fortunately, the dark, tinted windows would prevent anyone from seeing her.

"Just out of curiosity," Selia asked, leaning casually against the window, "Why did you ask to meet me in the middle of the day?"

"To see if you would do it, actually," Lucien replied in a smug voice.

The conniving bastard, Selia fumed silently. *Perhaps I should have refused and insisted on meeting at night, instead.* She did not, however, allow her irritation at him to show on her face. If she had nothing else to thank Soren for, she could definitely thank him for teaching her the importance of an expert poker face.

"Ah, and so I prove my mettle by risking being seen in broad daylight meeting my Family's enemy in a neutral territory after I've been ordered to stay tucked away by my don." Selia's polite, cool, matter-of-fact tone never wavered. She might hate the games the Families played, but that didn't mean she didn't know how to play them.

"Audacity, courage, and more than a little thick-minded behavior are, after all, cornerstones of your homeland," countered Lucien.

"They also aren't characteristics encouraged or approved of in women in my Family," Selia said, not bothering to hide her amusement. "I have a suspicion it isn't unique to just one faction."

"Nor in women around the world," amended Lucien.

"Oh, I have discovered it isn't unique to just my homeland." Selia raised her brows. "But am I to believe you approve of such attributes in women?"

"Believe what you wish. You are free to discover what I like in a woman whenever you desire."

A good thing she wasn't drinking anything, Selia thought, otherwise it would have been spewed across the limo.

"An intriguing offer, Lucien, but one that will have to remain for another time," Selia said smoothly. *Like, say, never.*

She leaned down and picked up the black leather duffle bag she'd brought with her and slid it across the seat to Lucien.

"A gift," she said with a mischievous twinkle in her eyes. "I'm fairly certain no other woman has given you anything quite as unique before now."

"You'd be surprised what women have given me." His reply was casual but sinister as he took possession of the bag. Lucien unzipped it, peered inside, and smiled.

"Ah, another reason I enjoy my dealings with Temerians," he said as he zipped the bag closed. "Your people have a splendid grasp of how to finalize a deal."

Selia laughed softly as she pulled the drive from a pocket on her jacket.

"Your drive, as promised," she said as she held it out in the palm of her hand. "It's the only one Alfi had in his possession."

Opening a section of the shelf next to his seat, Lucien retrieved a small netbook and powered it on. He took the drive from her as it booted. There was silence as they waited for the computer to finish its startup routine. Once that was completed, Lucien plugged in the flash drive and checked the contents. He nodded with satisfaction once more.

"You have completed your end of our agreement, and with style." Lucien complimented Selia with a level, and she supposed, suggestive gaze. She simply nodded her thanks and waited.

Lucien placed the drive in his inner jacket pocket and closed the tablet. Smiling, he brought a smartphone from another pocket. His index finger stabbed at the screen a few times, and then he held out the phone. He had put it on speakerphone, and Selia could hear the phone ringing. She glanced at the screen and noticed there was a candid shot of Al on the display, with the words "The Adversary" beneath the image.

Selia suppressed a laugh, but she didn't hide her smile. She could only imagine what was on Al's phone.

The line connected and Al's voice came through clearly. He did not sound angry; only focused and business-like. "Yes?"

"I am calling you as a courtesy," Lucien responded in an identical manner. Selia thought briefly of slapping him upside the head and yelling at both of them to stop acting like puffed up peacocks.

"Accepted," replied Al. "What occasion affords me this courtesy?"

"You should know that your traitor, Alfi, has been dealt with by my people." Lucien winked at Selia. "They have also recovered the information stolen from one of my business interests, and it is now in my possession. I consider the matter to be closed on all accounts."

There was a long pause.

"I see," Al responded, finally. "That is quite gracious of you. May I inquire as to the nature of your peaceful overture?"

"A common enemy was responsible for the situation," Lucien said. "I have knowledge that people from your organization were making attempts to accomplish what my people have done. Had your people succeeded, I have little doubt that you would have seen that I was notified, and the data returned."

There was more silence. Lucien took the time to point at the picture of Al and roll his eyes, mouthing "He is so slow, sometimes" toward Selia.

"You are certain that Alfi will no longer be a concern?" Al finally interjected. "Which common enemy is responsible?"

"I have witnessed Alfi's remains. Would you like me to send you a photo?" Lucien was close to teasing Al. Instead of pushing Al further, Lucien addressed the man's second question. "This is someone new, Lascari. A new foe that has only their own interests in mind and their interests run contrary to yours and mine. It is not, however, anyone who wears a mask."

Selia stiffened slightly at the reference to her and the Sandman. She hoped Lucien didn't notice.

"Very well." Al's voice was a bit more relaxed. "If you would care to coordinate against this foe, I would recommend we meet. Otherwise, we shall work against this adversary from our own corners."

"I would welcome a pooling of resources in this matter," Lucien replied quickly. "Is your man, Soren, recovered from his injuries?"

"He should be soon. Would you like to meet with him first? He does have a knack for these kinds of dealings."

"I would prefer him for the initial meetings in this matter. I have another person in mind for the official liaison in this operation, but that is for another time. In the meantime, have Soren contact me when he is able."

"Very well," Al responded, and hung up.

"You see?" Lucien said, waving the phone. "He is slow, except to anger and suspicion, but enough of my misgivings. Are you satisfied that I have upheld my end of our agreement?"

"Very satisfied," Selia replied graciously. "You're an honorable man, Lucien. I appreciate what you've done." She paused before asking, "A common enemy. You're aware of who Alfi allied himself with, aren't you?"

"Not entirely. I am aware that Alfi was not acting in the interests of his own people, and he was not being funded by anyone in my Family. Nor is he savvy enough, either as a businessman or as keeper of his own checking account, to organize and execute what was intended to happen with the flash drive." Lucien leveled his gaze at her. "Therefore, the only logical conclusion is that another party was involved, and one that has knowledge of Temeria."

"You're entirely correct, but that is my problem now. In fact, you would probably sleep better not knowing," Selia said dryly. "I only wish I could say the same."

"If you wish to keep knowledge to yourself, I understand." Lucien replied soberly. "But I will eventually find out."

"Perhaps, and if you do, I'll gladly offer my assistance should you request it," Selia replied smoothly. Weapons wouldn't win this fight and she wanted to see Moreisa dead. "As enjoyable as your companionship is," Selia continued, "I really must return to my safehouse before anyone realizes I've snuck out unsupervised."

"Ah, is that what they have done with you?" Lucien laughed. "They hid away their mightiest warrior even as their strongest mind mends his body. Ironic and sad. But, yes, you are free to go."

He rapped against the window nearest him, and the door was opened a second later. One of Lucien's goons was holding it open, looking around as he did so.

"You can chide Al about it later. He might even listen to you," Selia replied, laughter in her voice. Lucien stepped out, allowing her to climb out of the limo. She offered him her hand. "Thank you again, Lucien. I hope the next time we see each other, it won't be as enemies."

"I hope not. It would be a most unfortunate turn of events," Lucien said. He did not imply who would come up the worst for such a situation. He kissed the offered hand. "Be well, beautiful belladonna, and be safe."

Selia smiled and nodded once before turning and sliding her sunglasses back onto her face.

"Please tell me you have some hand sanitizer somewhere," she murmured, once she was out of their hearing range. Her answer was a deep chuckle that filled her eardrum. Sliding into the driver's seat, she started the car and muttered darkly, "He didn't kiss *your* hand." Another laugh, this one louder and she smiled. "Meet you back at the store, handsome. Then you can take me home."

Chapter Thirty-Six

Much to Selia's disappointment, Wil dropped her off at the bungalow, gave her a long, knee-weakening kiss, and bid her good night. She had changed back into her previous outfit, leaving the pantsuit with Wil. Trudging back to the bungalow, she changed into a pair of silk pajamas. It wasn't like she'd be going out tonight. Wil had work, actual work rather than Sandman-type work, to do and she didn't want to press her luck with Al. By the time the sun was setting, she'd finished up the Ben & Jerry's and had burned herself out on surfing the net.

Fortunately, a knock on the door saved her from more indecisive boredom.

"Come on in, guys," she called as she rummaged through the shelves.

The door opened and she glanced down from her precarious perch on the edge of the counter to find Alex and Bernie walking in and staring up at her. Oddly enough, both were wearing dressy clothes and ties, perfect for a night out.

"Any ideas where the popcorn would be?" she asked.

"It's on the shelf above the microwave, actually," Alex answered.

"Ah," Selia replied, walking across the counter, and opening the cabinet door. Grabbing the family pack box, she tossed it to Bernie. With an impish grin, she asked Alex, "Shall I just hop down or are you going to be a gentleman and give me a hand?"

Alex came over and helped her down. He looked around after doing so and asked, "Got plans tonight?"

"Nope," she replied. "I was actually hoping you guys would keep me company tonight."

"Oh, okay," Alex said, obvious surprise in his voice and manner. "What did you have in mind? Popcorn and a movie?"

Her eyes twinkled as she grinned at him. "Maybe a couple pizzas or take out?" She paused, a look of concern crossing her face. "That isn't going to cause a problem with Al, is it? I mean, we used to hang out..."

"It shouldn't." Alex said with a shrug. "Part of the reason we got assigned to you is because we used to hang out. Al knew we wouldn't want you getting into danger or getting hurt. I can call him and verify it's okay, though."

"How long has it been since we've enjoyed a movie night?" Selia asked, leaning against the counter. "If you think you should call Al, I won't object." She dropped a wink as she added, "I might object if he says you can't keep me company, though."

"I'll be sure to mention that," Alex said with a smile. He took out his phone and hit the speed dial for his boss.

Selia looked at Bernie. "So, since I'm inviting you guys to play babysitter again, does that mean you still have to check the place out?"

"Is there some reason you don't want us to check the place out?" Bernie interjected, sounding suspicious.

Selia rolled her eyes. "If I had someone here, do you really think I'd be asking you to watch a movie and enjoy take out or a pizza with me?" She looked over at Alex imploringly. "Is he always this paranoid?"

"Hasn't he always been?" countered Alex as he covered the speaker on his cell. "He just likes to make sure the job gets done. Let him do the check, and then we can enjoy the evening." He went back to his discussion with Al.

Taking the popcorn box from Bernie, she gave him a shove towards the bedrooms. "Fine, fine, go and get your job done. I'll stay here with the intelligent one."

Bernie grunted and made his way to the bedroom just as Alex finished his call and put away his phone.

"We're green-lit for the evening," Alex announced, a boyish smile on his face. "Al said this will be his least stressful evening in a while as a result."

Selia squealed in the same girlish tone she'd used every time Soren had left the pair as her babysitters. Bouncing, she jumped into Alex's arms and gave him a hug.

"So, what's Bernie going to go pick up for us tonight? Chinese? Pizza? Italian?" she asked, a bright smile on her face.

"You mentioned pizza earlier, but you know me, I can eat anything," Alex said, chuckling. He nodded toward the bedroom where Bernie was searching. "We can always wait and see what 'Grumpy' would prefer."

"Sounds like a plan," Selia replied with a smile. "At least you aren't thinking I've got someone else here. It sounds like Al doesn't think I do, either."

"Why would you have someone else here, unless you were having some fun?" Alex said dismissively. "We've already interrupted that once, and if you were going to do that every night, we'd be wondering about you."

"Good point," she replied, leaning against the counter. "This is probably one of your easiest assignments ever, huh?"

"Certainly one of the most pleasant ones in a while," Alex confirmed.

Noticing Bernie's return, she smiled innocently. "Did you check under my bed? I thought I heard a few monsters growling under there last night."

"The place is clean, as far as real concerns go," Bernie answered.

She raised her brows. "Found a few cobwebs, did you? I'm definitely going to need a teddy bear to fend off the monsters and spiders, then. Maybe you could pick me up one while you're out getting dinner?"

"Oh, please. A teddy bear?" complained Bernie. "Ain't it bad enough I end up being the errand boy whenever something is needed? Now I gotta pick up toys?"

Turning to Alex, she gave him a sad, pouty expression and said in a decidedly unhappy tone, "Alex, Bernie's being mean to me." It took everything she had to keep the pout from turning into laughter. "He won't get me a teddy bear to fight away the monsters under my bed."

"Oh my god, are you really going to do this?" Bernie all but shouted. "Are you really going to pull that 'you're my favorite, he's the meanie' shit again? We didn't get enough of that when you were sixteen? Seventeen? Twenty-one, twenty-two, twenty-three years old?"

"She pulled it last year when you accidentally broke her iPad and wouldn't replace it," Alex chimed in with an impish smile. "Meanie."

"Dammit!" Bernie roared, throwing his hands into the air.

"You shouldn't be so mean to me," Selia said slyly as she grabbed Alex's arm and draped it around her shoulders. "As I have heard you say often, dearest Bernie: payback is a bitch."

Bernie just stared coldly, his hands on his hips.

"You want me to get pizza, don't you?" Bernie breathed through clenched teeth. "You want me to get that stuff with the white sauce, and the ham and the pineapple, or the mushroom and spinach. *That's not real pizza!"* He bellowed the last four words. "Pizza is tomato sauce, cheese and pepperoni. Or sausage. Or both." He ranted. "What the hell happened to the world? Geezus!"

"I was thinking maybe bacon and onion." Alex threw in with a smirk.

"Well, that's not so bad, and at least it's- *Dammit!* I *am* going to get pizza, aren't I?" Bernie loosened his tie, and he went on, his face red. "Fine, fine, fine, fine! I will go out, and I will buy a pizza for my asshole brother who everyone thinks is nice, one for the princess, and one for the only sensible one in this crowd!" He went to the front door, flung it open, and declared "And I'll get a damn teddy bear!" before storming out.

"Wait for it," Alex whispered, still smirking.

Selia and Alex turned to the front door. They waited for ten seconds. Bernie came through the door, his expression sour, his anger replaced with a tired acceptance.

"What do you want on your pizza, Lia?" he grudgingly asked.

An hour later, Selia sat between Bernie and Alex on the sofa opposite the door, munching on a slice of ham, bacon, and onion pizza. Bernie sat on one side of her, gnawing on a slice of pepperoni pizza, more or less content. Alex was on her other side, enjoying a slice of the same pizza Selia had. A very expensive, dark brown fuzzy teddy bear, with cashmere-like fur, sat in her lap. She had no clue where in the hell Bernie had found the adorable toy that was dressed like a knight in shining armor. It *had* won him a few brownie points and a big hug, though.

"So," Selia asked, handling the TV remote deftly as she surfed through the 'on demand' movie options. "What are we in the mood to watch?"

"Nothing violent," both men chimed in, mimicking Selia's voice when she was seventeen years old.

Giggling, she nibbled at the cheese on her pizza, turned slightly on the sofa and leaned back against Alex's side. "Fine, how about a really bad horror film we can mock endlessly?"

There was a glance between the two men, and they nodded.

"Fine by us," Bernie declared.

Selia pushed a button on the remote and *Night of the Killer Shrews* began loading. She snuggled against Alex, getting comfortable, and finished devouring her slice of pizza. Wiping her fingers on a napkin, she smiled contentedly. It was nice having the brothers here, eating pizza and watching a movie.

It felt like old times. Considering she'd come close to dying without anyone knowing, being surrounded by two people she considered near and dear was pretty damned comforting. Not that she could possibly tell them she'd nearly died, but she could definitely enjoy their companionship now and in the future. It was amazing how a near-death experience could really put things, and people, into perspective.

Alex patted her on the top of the head, and she sighed in contentment. Bernie then caressed her knee.

"It's not going to be *that* kind of a night, Bernie, so don't be getting any ideas," Selia said, her voice dropping a few degrees. "Be a good boy and move your hand before I break your fingers."

Bernie snatched his hand away. Selia felt Alex slide his arm around her, but she waited a moment. She was rewarded a moment later with the sound of Alex slapping Bernie upside the head before retracting his arm back to its original position.

Giggling, she nestled against Alex. Grabbing his left arm, she pulled it around her. Now, between his arm and shoulder, she had a comfy little pillow. Bernie had a petulant expression on his face and was stuffing his mouth with pizza again.

Yep, it was just like when she was a teen, again: Bernie trying to hit on her and Alex being the heavy.

"You always had a crush on Alex," Bernie grumbled.

Heat crept up Selia's cheeks. It wasn't a lie. She had crushed hard on Alex from pretty much the moment she'd met him. Handsome, kind, and caring, he'd treated her as a person. He hadn't seen her as a burden or annoying task, but as someone who needed help adjusting to a strange new world. His protectiveness of her only added to his charm.

"Jealous?" Selia teased Bernie. "You should try being a gentleman, Bernie. It might get you further than your usual high school mannerisms do."

She tilted her head so she could glance up at Alex, curious as to how he felt on the subject. Maybe if things had been different, she'd have fallen harder for him than she had, but Alex had not once reciprocated and eventually her puppy love had turned into strong affection.

Things hadn't been different, and all things considered, she was glad for that fact. Alex would never have allowed her to step out and do what she had done. It wasn't in his nature. Nope, she was very satisfied with Wil and how things had turned out.

"She is just appreciative of someone who treats her like a human being, and doesn't think every comfortable gesture is an invitation," Alex said without looking at her. His eyes were fixed to the screen. The movie had started.

The narrator began, and upon hearing the words 'The most dangerous animals' Alex chimed in with, "...are in Vegas."

"-are the shrew," the narrator continued.

All three of them shouted at the screen, "A *shrew?*"

As the narrator went on about the movie's reason for the shrew being vicious and so forth, Bernie added, sarcastically, "Yeah, just go with us on that!"

The three of them looked at each other, laughed at happy memories, and settled in to mock the rest of the feature in good humor.

Chapter Thirty-Seven

Selia woke up to the phone ringing, still cuddling the teddy bear Bernie had given her. Not that she'd ever admit to that to anyone other than Wil or Soren. She reached over and grabbed the phone.

"Hello?" she asked, still sleepy.

It had been a late night of watching bad horror flicks and keeping a running commentary about them. There had been popcorn, pizza, candy, and lots of drinks. If she had to stay at the bungalow longer, there would have to be a restocking of snacks, beverages, and someone would have to bring in a home gym.

"Good morning, beautiful," Wil's voice filled her ears.

"Good morning," Selia replied, as she stretched beneath the covers. "I like hearing your voice first thing in the morning."

"Good to hear yours too, but it's the afternoon," Wil said with a laugh in his voice.

"Huh?" She looked at the phone. "Oh, it is, isn't it? It's going to be hell getting back into a normal sleeping pattern after this."

"I have faith in your ability to recover, yes, even from this," he teased.

Giggling, she rubbed her eyes. "You meanie," she said with a laugh. "I missed you last night."

"Missed you, too. I hope you had more fun than I did," Wil said. "After writing a week's worth of articles, I mended the costumes and cleaned all the gear."

"I feel guilty, now," she said, a smile on her face. "I stayed up late with Bernie and Alex watching really bad horror flicks and mocking them."

"Oh, that is very unfair," Wil said flatly. "You riffed on bad films and didn't involve me? You, dear lady, have some apologizing to do."

Selia laughed. She replied in a soft, silky voice, "I'll make it up to you later, I promise."

"That has yet to be proven, she-of-the-bosoms-I-could-drown-in. Better have back-up plans," he retorted playfully.

"You're the one who keeps saying I can't bring you home with me," Selia countered, trying to not laugh. "How about this for a 'back-up plan': dinner, on me, at a place of your choosing?"

"Oh, good. I hear Wendy's has put my favorite bacon and Swiss burger back on the menu; for a limited time only."

"Wendy's? Really?" Selia asked. She wasn't sure if he was serious or pulling her leg. "Of all the places I could take you, you want a fast-food joint?"

Wil just laughed.

"You smartass," she replied, laughing. "Good thing I'm nuts about you."

"I'll remember that when we're in the drive-thru and you're complaining," he replied easily. Shifting conversational gears, he amended, "You can take me to a favorite restaurant of yours."

"I should pick one of the five-star black-tie only restaurants," she teased. Then, thoughtfully, she added, "Actually, I wouldn't mind taking my mate to one of those places as himself. I'd love the chance of taking a suit off you."

"Still on the 'mate' theory, eh? Gee, no pressure on me." Selia could hear his smile behind the sarcasm. "I think I've got a tuxedo or three tucked around here somewhere. My favorite one is baby blue with big 70s style lapels. Sound good?"

"I will kill you," Selia countered. "Unless you want me taking you shopping at one of the exclusive men's boutiques in the city, you'll wear something else."

"Fine, be difficult." Wil joked. "I'll wear the one an actor borrowed from me to attend the Oscars. You can't complain about that one."

"Sure I can," she said, enjoying their playful bantering. "I'm a woman. I can complain about anything."

"I'll amend my statement. You can complain but I won't listen," he retorted dryly.

"I'm sure you'll look absolutely dashing."

"So do I get to dictate what you'll be wearing on this hypothetical dinner date?"

"Sure," Selia replied. "It's only fair."

"Oh, good. You'll regret ever crossing me, then," he said with just enough challenge to pique her interest.

"Oh, really?" She asked. "Going to dress me up in something skimpy? Or are you going to aim for old and frumpy?"

"Such a limited imagination you must think I have," Wil said with a sigh. "When I'm done, people will be asking you for autographs, swearing they met one of the top pop divas. But I promise your outfit won't give you a risk of contracting Mad Cow Disease or worse."

Selia burst out into laughter and continued laughing until her eyes watered.

"Oh, gods," she managed to gasp. "Okay, no black-tie affairs unless you want to go to them."

"Victory is mine!" Wil declared with a British accent added to his voice.

"Does that mean you won't come to any of the parties I have to attend?" Selia asked, disappointment in her voice.

His voice became very serious and concerned. "No, not at all, Selia. I'll attend any party you want, when I'm able to. I thought we were having fun, here."

"We were," Selia replied, smiling again. "I was just afraid you wouldn't want to come because you didn't like wearing tuxes."

"Oh, I despise wearing tuxes, but that wouldn't keep me away," he assured her.

"I'm glad," she said softly, snuggling down into her pillow. She glanced at the teddy bear beside her and laughed softly. "You know, I really should warn you about Alex. Of all the Family members, he's the only one who could prove to be a, um, problem."

"Okay, explain to me what problem he could cause," Wil requested immediately.

"He's the only one in the Family, aside from Soren, who keeps a really close eye on me." She paused, trying to find the right words to explain it. "Let me try to explain. I, um, sort of crushed hard on him when I first arrived in New Campania. He has since been something of a protector; he gives me space and lets me date, but he keeps a really close watch on me."

"Oh, that's all?" Wil sounded relieved. "I thought you meant he was a threat of some kind. The only threat to my... um... 'secret identity' is me becoming complacent and sloppy. Or if he becomes an enemy to you."

"Awww, that's sweet," Selia said, feeling giddy. "Alex does what he's told by Al and Soren, but he's always given me warnings about stuff when he could. He told me he'd been sent to kill me after that first photo popped up online. That isn't typical protocol, I assure you." She shrugged despite the fact Wil couldn't see it. "If anyone was to figure out I'm dating the same person who is wearing multiple disguises, it would be Alex. Though, I doubt he'd tell anyone. Unless he's under orders, he has always come to me about anything I do that's suspicious."

It was, after all, how she'd ended up on her first hunting trip with him and Bernie.

"Then there should be little problem, or nothing we can't handle," Wil assured her.

"I'll trust you in that," Selia replied. "What are your plans for tonight?"

"From what I can tell, things are peaceful on both sides of the Mafioso." Wil's voice became slower and deeper, as if the Sandman was creeping into his voice. It made her toes want to curl, and not in fear. "The smaller concerns have been laying low for the past few days. Seems the idea of two vigilantes in the city, one of them a woman on permanent PMS, has them being cautious. I hear a certain patient is ready for release this evening, however. I might go make sure he gets home safely."

"Soren's going home today?" Selia asked quietly, trying to keep from screaming in joy and excitement. "Damn the rules. If I don't get released from this prison, I'll go to Soren *without* Al's permission." Her mind latched onto his comment about her alter ego, and she laughed. "Permanent PMS, huh? Well, it should make the nightlife a little quieter for a while, what with the threat of a blood-thirsty woman on the loose."

"Blood-thirsty woman with sharp swords and guns, no less," added Wil. "Although you don't want to know how many hits you have on YouTube right now. Best if you don't read the comments, either, since you seem to blush easily."

Selia giggled. "Guess a woman with weapons, who knows how to use them, is rather attractive, huh?"

"I find it interesting that you skipped over what exactly was on YouTube." Wil chuckled. Before she could answer, he added, "Want to know what the website about your bosom is called?"

"What?" she screeched, sitting up in the bed. "I figured it was just the rave! What the hell is on the internet, anyway? Please don't tell me something from the last fight got online..."

"Oh, someone had a really nice camera in the crowd instead of just a smartphone," he explained. "I'm betting it was the tall guy dressed up like the ex-delivery boy in my favorite cult musical. Anyway, he got your whole exchange with the dealers and pushers. From the instant you pick up my batons. The video is in startling HD quality. You look fabulous, by the way. The website is called, I wish I were kidding, 'Nightshade's Knockers: A study of perfection.' It's got fifty thousand followers already."

"You are making that up!" Selia nearly screamed in mortification. "If not the website, then certainly the number!"

"Nope. I can take a picture of the homepage and the subscriber counter and send it to your phone, if you like!"

"Oh, gods," Selia groaned and dropped back to the bed. It was so very tempting to hide *under* the bed. "Thank the gods no one knows it's me." She paused and laughed. "Though, it's a pity we can't cash in on merchandising rights."

There was a very still silence on the other end of the line. As if someone didn't want to say something... or give something away.

"Wil," she said, drawing his name out.

"Um, yes?" he asked, a little too innocently.

"Spill it, handsome," she demanded, not quite ridding her voice of all her amusement.

"Well, I told you I had a diverse portfolio. I bet I didn't mention that I own stock in most of the companies that the Sandman's gear comes from." There was an audible cough. "And a lot of local costume shops. I might have suggested the managers stock up on skintight pleather catsuits and blonde wigs, along with scarves. I have a number of lawyers, you know..." He sounded almost childlike, as if trying to get out of something bad. "I kinda, sorta had your likeness and name trademarked."

Selia laughed again, harder this time. "You've been a rather busy fellow, haven't you?" She giggled again, staring up at the ceiling, a bright smile on her face. "Sounds like you're using my alter ego to take the heat off a certain other fellow."

"Oh, I actually had my little friend's image taken care of right before he started stalking the night," Wil said, his voice approaching normal. "Last thing I needed as a vigilante was for someone to make me a web phenomenon, someone else trademark my image, and then have a standing court order to pay them money if I planned to keep using the costume they 'owned.' It didn't happen with the Sandman- I managed to keep a low enough profile. Nightshade, however; well, the costume stores have already sold out of those catsuits and wigs. I hear trench coats are flying off the shelves."

There was another cough.

"The lawyers for the Nightshade trademark are already fielding calls and offers, as well as looking for potential image violations. I even hear there's some minor interest in the Sandman." He cleared his throat.

"You already had the ball rolling on the Nightshade costume the moment I told you about it, didn't you?" Selia accused him, though her tone was playful. "My dear man, you are simply remarkable."

"I'm just glad I didn't make the mistake of trademarking Nightshade under a different dummy business," Wil breathed. "Otherwise, my own lawyers would be trying to sue each other right now. I'd go broke in a few months with all that billing."

Selia laughed. "That could've proven rather amusing, though." She picked the teddy bear up and moved its little arm, as though she were making it slash with the sword. "You know, I'd love to have a plush Sandman toy to snuggle with when I can't have you."

"Wow! That's a great marketing idea." He sounded serious. "I'll have some made up. But you get to choose what the final market design gets to be."

Rolling her eyes, Selia smacked herself on the head with the toy. "Goodie. We can sell them as sets," she said dryly.

"Oh, yeah. Gotta make the Nightshade plushy. Girls will scoop that up." Excitement crept into Wil's voice. "Jeez, I need to make more calls, then."

"I'm going to hang up now," Selia said. "I'll just sleep with my nice, new, fuzzy teddy bear."

"Uh oh. I went overboard, didn't I?" Wil sighed. "Sorry. Sometimes I get caught up in all that mess. Did Alex get you a teddy bear?"

"Nope, I guilt-tripped Bernie into it," Selia said smugly. "He was mean, so I made him get me a teddy bear as payback. This one is dressed up as a knight in shining armor, complete with sword to fight the monsters under my bed."

Wil laughed. "That's brilliant. But if Bernie got it for you, I'd check it for a spycam, just to be safe."

"Alex did that for me," Selia replied with a laugh. "He trusts Bernie even less than I do where I'm concerned. A fear of Soren, I think. Of course, the fact that their brothers, means Alex will try to keep Bernie out of trouble, when he can."

"All right. Well, shall we catch up later? Let me know if you need to sneak out to be with Soren when he's released around six o'clock?"

"I'll let you know, but if I'm hoping that if Soren is getting out today, that means I'll be released today, too," Selia assured him. In almost a whisper, she added, "I love you."

She held her breath, almost afraid of what his reply would be.

"You know what?" Wil whispered back. "I love you, too."

Chapter Thirty-Eight

Practically bouncing off the walls with the possibility that she would be freed, Selia took a quick shower and began rooting around in her closet for something to wear. Settling on a black velvety mini-skirt and blood-red blouse, she pulled on a pair of black leather knee-high boots to complete the outfit. Gathering everything she'd brought together, she piled it onto the single chair in her bedroom before returning to the living room.

The phone Wil had given her was in her purse and the pair from Al and Soren were sitting on the kitchen table next to her shiny new laptop that was packed away into its briefcase. The briefcase currently had the leftover cash Al gave her and it finally dawned on her: Wil still had her old laptop and the duffle bag. At least Al wasn't aware Soren had brought her the duffle bag and the phones. Her own phone was turned off and in the bottom of the purse she'd taken when she'd visited Al in his penthouse.

Though only an hour had passed before the brothers arrived, it felt like a whole day to Selia. Wanting nothing more than to be released was a sensation that people might think they understand, like as the last hour of school passes, or the final minutes of a hard shift at work slowly ticks away, but it isn't the same. Not knowing when you will be free, but only that it will happen sometime, drags the time and grates against a person's soul.

When she heard a car pulling up, Selia bit her tongue to keep from screaming in elation. She waited, hearing the car doors close, first one then a second, and began bouncing with hope and excitement. Knuckles rapped against the door, and she nearly toppled over her own feet when she dashed for the door.

Opening the door, she blinked against the sunlight and verified that Alex and Bernie were standing there, smiling. It wasn't her mind playing a mean trick, hallucinating over a pair of missionaries coming to tell her the good news about Christ, or worse, the police. It was the brothers.

"Looks like somebody's ready to get the hell outta here," observed Bernie.

"Can I?" Selia almost squeaked. "Am I free to go home?"

"We are duly authorized to escort you back to the garage where your vehicle awaits." Alex declared proudly. "From there, you are free to go home, or wherever you want, kiddo."

She tackled both men in a wide-armed embrace. She laughed, her body still all but vibrating. The brothers hugged her back, and Bernie didn't even try to sneak an inappropriate caress or squeeze. Later, as she doubled checked to make sure she had everything, she reflected that her left breast was pressed so hard against Bernie that he could probably feel her heartbeat

The brothers helped her pack the luggage and gear into the rental car and instructed her to follow. She was a little awkward behind the wheel, having spent almost no time in the rental's luxury. Al had gotten a rental with cruise control, GPS, an mp3 and DVD player, as well as satellite radio. She found a station that suited her mood and followed the brothers for the forty-five minutes it took to arrive at the garage owned by Soren, where her car was kept.

Fifteen minutes away from the garage, the hot tea she'd had with her breakfast decided to invade her bladder. Selia flashed her headlights at the brothers and pulled into the parking lot of a large convenience store. When she had first come to this city, this had once been home to a half dozen gas pumps and a small building with a register, lukewarm drinks, bored clerks, and cigarettes.

Not having much time to spare, Selia parked at the far side of the lot. That entrance was closest to the bathrooms. She dashed in and took care of the troubling pressure provided by the tea finishing its grand tour of her digestive system.

On the way out, Selia walked rapidly out the same entrance, and glanced down to fish out the rental key from her pocket. Something, or someone, sucker punched the area just behind her right ear. Large black spots obscured her vision. Her body felt like she was sinking in water. Hands clamped around her throat. Selia's fingers tried to get underneath the grip cutting off her ability to breathe.

"We aren't done, my delicious little treat," said Moreisa's hissing voice in Selia's ear. "Do you want to suffer for ages, or shall we just end it now? I want you to beg for your preference."

Her head was pounding, every beat of her quickening pulse thrummed in her neck against the rough palms and fingers the kept pressing harder. Selia tried to gather her calm, then her anger, anything to summon enough energy to fight back, and she was failing...failing...

...falling...

Somewhere above her, Selia thought she heard the sound of something being struck and voices yelling. The claws that were choking the life out of her fell away abruptly. Air rushed into her lungs, clarity coming far quicker than Selia could believe. It was like... a spell being broken.

"Da fuck do you think ya lookin' at?" Bernie's voice, at its roughest, and angriest, was roaring somewhere nearby. His accent was cranked up as well. "Yeah, keep pointing that gizmo at me! You gonna film me putting two in this bitch's head if she so much as twitches! See if I give a fuck!"

"We appreciate your concern, but our friend was attacked," Alex's stiff but calmer voice was coming from a closer position. "Authorities have been notified. They will take care of this."

"Did you film her getting attacked? Nah? Then what good is pointing that piece of shit over here now?" Bernie challenged.

Selia opened her eyes in time to see him snatch something out of a very young man's hand just before smashing it to the ground. His right hand held his .44 caliber snub nose revolver. His left hand snaked into his jacket pocket, returned with a handful of hundred-dollar bills. He threw this wad at the young man. The kid almost didn't react fast enough to catch the money. His eyes were still wide as he hurried to leave.

"That's right! Get outta here! Have a nice goddamn day, you hear?" Bernie yelled after the retreating would-be filmographer.

"You okay, Lia?" Alex knelt next to her; one had offered to aid her getting up.

She then realized she was on her knees. Everything caught up to her in a rush, and she leapt to her feet. Her equilibrium objected to the sudden movement. As she wobbled, Alex grabbed her elbow and moved in to keep her standing.

"Whoa, easy. Not so fast," he said. "Why the hell did that bag lady jump you?"

"She-" Selia began, looking around for Moreisa. The crumbled body was four feet away, blocking the entrance Selia had come out from. Selia took two long steps, ignored the unsteady way her body moved, until she could glower down at the damn witch.

It wasn't Moreisa. Didn't look a thing like her, in fact. Alex had called this person a bag lady, and Selia could see why. She was desperately thin, looked to be in her mid-nineties just by the wrinkles and lines throughout her face. Mismatched, ill-fitting filthy clothing. A smell that would curl the nose of even a hardened alcoholic wafted from the poor woman's body. Her eyes were clouded but open.

It didn't matter. She was dead. The blood from the three-inch gash above her eyebrows was barely trickling down into her temples and hairline. Selia glanced over at Bernie.

Specifically, the muzzle of Bernie's gun. She saw wetness around the front sight and the front of the barrel. The sound Selia had heard, she deduced, right before the choking had ended, was Bernie pistol whipping this person. That's what had opened the gash on her forehead.

"I have no idea why this sad being jumped me," Selia finally replied. "But thankfully you two were here."

"You good to go? Can you drive?" Bernie was up beside her, his voice low and concerned.

"Yeah, I'm good."

"Cool, 'cause nice guy over here actually did call the Fuzz, and they don't want us anywhere around when they arrive," Bernie finished.

She nodded and they quickly made their getaway.

At the garage, the brothers transplanted her stuff to her vehicle, took the keys to the rental, and said they'd take care of everything. Selia hugged them individually, got into her car, and then drove home. While she traveled, the thought she had kept from the brothers, and would later neglect to mention to Soren or Wil, flowered in her mind.

The poor old woman who attacked me didn't die when Bernie hit her. He just broke the reanimation by head trauma.

She'd been dead for at least a day before she came after me. And Moreisa had spoken through her, to me.

No, they definitely were not done.

An hour later, she unlocked the door to her townhouse in Upper Midtown. The doorman of the complex, a handsome fellow named Jose, was behind her with all her stuff. She walked in and breathed a heavy sigh of unexpected relief.

The place was spotless and hadn't been tossed or trashed. All of her furniture was where she had left it. Her television stood in the same place. Her collection of porcelain dolls was untouched, lining the wall-mounted shelf that had been installed beside her large china press where she kept her dishes, silverware, and a few precious keepsakes. The "C" shaped leather couch faced the TV and state of the art entertainment center, along with her favorite console system. The glass coffee table gleamed.

Selia nodded at her living room and invited Jose to bring in her things and put them next to the door.

"Good to be home, eh, Selia?" Jose observed.

She had insisted all the staff call her by her first name. Selia disliked formality, especially where they all existed together to make some semblance of a home. Jose had become something of a friend. He never treated her with any less respect, and she responded in kind.

"It is, Jose. Could you thank the cleaning staff for keeping my home so well kept while I was gone?" She smiled at him. "Thanks for bringing up my things." She fished out a fifty-dollar bill and pressed it into the lapel pocket of his uniform.

"Anytime, Selia." Jose smiled, while patting his pocket. "And not just because you tip like you mean it." He gave her a wink and closed the door.

Selia ignored her baggage for the moment and checked on her kitchen. The stainless-steel stove, range and fridge shone under the lights, and her counter was clean enough to eat off. Her pantry and shelves were stocked with fresh food and staples, as was her fridge. She popped open an ice-cold can of Coke and sipped at it. Wondering who she had to thank for the newly stocked kitchen, she checked her bathroom, outside patio, and finally her bedroom.

Every area looked like it was ready for a photo shoot in an advertisement. Her bed had fresh sheets. New sheets, in fact, since she had never owned black silk sheets in her life. She put the Coke on the bedside cabinet and stretched out on the bed. The sheets felt amazing.

Someone was going to be getting a very big amount of thanks, Selia thought. If any of this had been due to Wil, and she hoped it was, he would be getting thanks until one of them couldn't walk.

One of her phones was ringing. She reluctantly got off the bed and moved into the living room. When she realized the ringtone indicated that Wil was calling her, she hurried.

Grabbing the phone and swiping her finger across the screen, she playfully said, "Hello?"

"Hello, beautiful. Care to meet me at the hospital?"

Chapter Thirty-Nine

It took Selia twenty minutes to get to the hospital, and most of that was arguing with traffic. Parking her car and all but skipping with joy, Selia made her way to the front. Her eyes danced with delight at the knowledge she was finally free, and Soren was being released to go home. She studied the handful of people standing outside until her gaze lighted upon a fit male nurse in scrubs. Wil once again had that odd, blue-tipped cigarette and was chatting with a couple other staff members. One woman, a pretty brunette who barely came to his shoulder, looked suspiciously like a doctor.

She slowed her steps until she was close to them and beneath the shoulder-length wavy brown hair, she recognized his brown eyes. Of course, the fluttering in her stomach would have told her who he was if nothing else did.

"Miss Lascari," the 'nurse' addressed her with a smile. He tucked the black cigarette into his scrubs pocket and approached her. His voice was flavored with a thick city accent. "I suppose you wanna get your dad outta here?"

"I do, indeed," Selia replied, a bright smile on her face. "I'm sure he's chomping at the bit to get out, too."

"Oh, yeah. Talked about little else since the doc cleared him to go." He chuckled. "Had to take a break and get away from it, personally. But you're here, so let's get the cranky bastard gone."

Selia laughed. "Yeah, that sounds like Papa. Never has liked appearing weak in front of anyone."

"Weak? Are you kidding? The docs are still trying to figure out how he's healed so well... and arguing about who can take the credit."

There were many things that sucked majorly about having to pretend she and Wil didn't know each other; one was they couldn't have a normal conversation. She had to be careful what she said, and what she did. Eventually, though, they wouldn't have to hide their attraction, and she was thoroughly looking forward to that day.

"Guess he had a guardian angel," she replied, keeping her gaze locked on Wil. So, maybe she'd used a bit too much magic when she'd healed him, but it wasn't like she could have left him in so much pain! She wasn't cruel, after all.

Entering through the ER, Wil led her to the nearest elevator and made sure they were alone when the doors closed.

"You look fantastic," he said in his true voice.

"Thanks," she breathed. "You look pretty amazing, yourself." She giggled. "Do you know how much I want to kiss you right now?"

"We've got 28.4 seconds. Show me."

Smiling, her eyes twinkling with mischief, she gently pulled him to her and pressed her lips against his, her tongue running over his before she deepened the kiss. Pressing up against him, she held the collar of his shirt tightly in her hands. As the sensation of the elevator came to an end, she broke the kiss and took a swift step back, a Cheshire cat grin on her face.

"*Okay.* You really wanted to kiss me," he breathed, composing himself as the elevator doors opened.

Turning to the left, they bypassed the nurses' station. Another few moments and they were outside his room.

"You go on. I'll grab him a wheelchair to refuse," Wil said with a smile.

Selia took a breath and stepped into the room. Soren was looking out the window, dressed in one of his best suits. He stood without a cane or other assistance.

"I can't tell you how glad I am to see you up and looking like your handsome, dashing self again," Selia said after the door closed behind her.

Soren turned and looked her over before smiling. "I could say the same of you, Selia." He nodded outside. "I've been worried about your state of health since you started spending your nights with him."

"I, um, that is…" Selia floundered for words. "What do you mean? I haven't been spending my nights with him. I've been spending my nights keeping my vow to you." She crossed to Soren and gave him a hug. "I've missed you, Papa."

"So, the rumors I've been hearing from the staff around here," Soren said evenly. "Of a woman vigilante fighting along-side or better than the Sandman aren't just tall tales."

Selia dropped her head against Soren's chest and shook it. "No, Papa, they aren't tall tales," she said with a heavy sigh. She lifted her head until she met his eyes. "I'm fairly certain you aren't going to like what I'm going to tell you."

"I'm fairly certain you're right," Soren said sternly. But then he smiled and rubbed her back. "But, you're safe, and whole, and those are the things I am concerned with the most."

"Um, well," Selia said, looking away from him. "There's been a little bit of a complication between us, that is, him and me." She cringed as she whispered, "I, um, we're... let's just go with I love him."

"Do you, now?" His voice wasn't angry or expressing much surprise. There was a weary sadness to his voice, tinged with what, she hoped, could be happiness.

"Yes," she replied, almost cautiously. "He's sort of my mate?" Tilting her head to the side, she peered at him curiously. "You're not angry?"

"I've seen love, my dear child, and I've experienced it. I know what it looks like." He shrugged. "Not liking what I see is a part of existence. As for being angry? No, I'm not. I didn't want you to marry into the Family. I am just concerned about your safety and happiness. One thing before we go on. Please tell me he doesn't really look like that nurse disguise."

Laughing, Selia shook her head. "Oh, no, he definitely does not." She sighed contentedly and leaned against Soren's chest. "So much has changed, Papa. There's so much I have to tell you. You were right, you know, about there being another player. She isn't dead, and she's a Temerian necromancer."

Soren stroked her back and leaned against her. "Tell me what happened." He kissed her forehead.

"I'll give you the short version, for now." She gave him a recap of everything that had happened, before turning back to the subject of her and Wil. "He got caught and I had to cast a spell to find him. It was a spell to locate a life-mate. The spell worked, and it took me to him."

Selia paused and took a moment to enjoy feeling perfectly comfortable and at home in Soren's arms. Soren, meanwhile, was rubbing her back as though she were his birth daughter and had done it from her childhood. It felt comforting and natural. Something she'd been missing her entire life.

"That isn't all of it," Soren said, breaking into her thoughts.

"The necromancer, Moreisa, and Alfi had caught him. We got away, taking out pretty much everyone in the warehouse. When we finally figured out where Alfi and Moreisa were hiding out, I ended up being caught by her." Selia leaned away from Soren and stared into his eyes. "I... I don't know if I have the knowledge in magic to defeat her, Papa. If it hadn't been for the Sandman, she would have killed me."

"So, he saved you," Soren mused. "Why didn't he kill the woman?"

"He tried, but she teleported out before either of us could," she explained, a tad grumpy. "There was also the fact he had to fight his way out of a room full of reanimated corpses before he could get to the roof where she had taken me." Selia giggled. "I should probably also tell you that it wasn't another woman I was with that one night. I shoved him into the shower to keep from being caught. I've never been so glad that Alex and Bernie don't know about my magical skills."

Soren burst out laughing. It took him several moments to compose himself, and he leaned on her as he did. "Were you two in the middle of... anything?" he finally gasped.

Selia's mouth dropped open even as she felt her face burn. "No!" She exclaimed. "We haven't done *anything*!" A scowl formed as she grumbled, "Not that I haven't tried. But, no, he refuses to do anything just yet, despite all my best attempts at the contrary. Damn it."

"My, my. What reason has he given for refusing your advances?" Soren asked, genuinely interested.

Crossing her arms, she glowered out the window, almost petulant. "He wants me to be at my fittest, doesn't want anything to interrupt us..." She trailed off, still annoyed. "The one time I'm trying to jump a guy at every turn, and he refuses! What the hell is wrong with him?"

"He doesn't want to disappoint you," explained Soren. "He wants to eliminate as many chances as possible to make the experience the best he can."

She gave a sigh and turned back to Soren. "Have any suggestions?" It felt right asking him for advice. She guessed this was what it felt like to have a father who loved her.

"Stop going out at night to break teenagers' hearts and businessmen's faces," he said with only a little exasperation. "Give yourself, and him, a chance to have an evening free of distraction. If he doesn't step up to the plate, then he's either too intimidated by you... or he has a small cannoli."

She certainly couldn't say he had a 'small cannoli', not after seeing him in his white briefs. A girlish grin pulled at her lips as she ducked her head.

"Um, do you think we could throw a masquerade party?" Selia asked, changing the topic, as a thought occurred to her. "I'm sure we can come up with a good reason for it, if Al asks."

"Sure. I don't need a reason. I just got out of the hospital. Where do you want to have it?" he asked.

"Somewhere he won't feel threatened by the Families," Selia replied without thinking. Realizing what she'd said, she blushed. "This is going to be an interesting relationship, isn't it?"

"Most of the good ones are," Soren quipped. "Now, go get your man. We need to speak."

"Okay," Selia replied, almost uncertainly. She poked her head out into the hall and found Wil standing beside the door, leaning against the wall. "Um, he wants to talk to you."

Wil came in and stood before Soren. He stood in a way that was respectful but unyielding. The phrase "immovable object, meet irresistible force" blinked through Selia's mind. The men faced each other for a long moment.

"You understand," Soren began, "that if you are responsible for any harm coming to her, you are going to lose both kneecaps? That's going to just be the warm-up?"

"Oh, I do," Wil said immediately. "I am also aware that if I do something to harm her, she's going to beat you to my kneecaps... and the rest of me."

Soren held for a moment before laughing aloud. He put his hand out to Wil. "You have my blessing... provisionally."

"I understand the provisions, and accept them," Wil said, taking Soren's hand and shaking it. "You have, no doubt, noticed that I only intervene on Family business that involves breaking the law? Violence, drugs, that sort of thing?"

"Among other things," Soren corrected. "You, I trust, have been aware that my personal business dealings have been aimed at more legitimate business practices?"

"I am. All business money is blood money in some ways," Wil observed. "We may just get along."

"Yes, we just might," agreed Soren.

Epilogue

The Sandman ended his patrol early that night. The peace on the streets, uneasy and temporary as it no doubt was, was still in effect. He came in through the lair's entrance, entering the sub-basement and securing the door once he was inside.

The motion-sensitive cameras were equipped in every room of the lair and townhouse he used as his personal home, tracked every movement he made, every step he took. That wasn't why he had installed them, of course. The purpose was to make sure that if anyone entered, there was a record of what happened.

Wil's routine in the morning was to exercise, eat breakfast, and check the recordings. He hardly ever had a reason to keep them, so they were deleted every night. Even the files of when Selia had been there had been deleted, out of respect.

After securing the sub-basement, he removed his equipment and placed them in their proper racks, shelves, hidden compartments, and so forth. His uniform came off next. He put it onto the mannequin that helped the uniform keep its shape when he wasn't wearing it. Every careful, considerate motion was viewable on the laptop computer in his office and the desktop he kept in the lair. He had them linked to each other so he could retrieve or delete files between both systems.

Sitting at his grandmother's vanity, he removed that evening's choice of wax moldings and other prosthetic appliances that concealed his true appearance. He did not notice that his laptop was not in its usual place, because he did not look at his desk before he exited the lair for his bedroom in the adjoining townhouse, wearing only his underwear.

He opened the bedroom door and was taken completely by surprise. He did not anticipate that his lair and home had been invaded, and that his own security measures were being used against him.

Selia raised her gaze from the laptop screen, a sly, sultry smile on her lips. Stretched out beneath his covers, the sheets pulled up to her chin, only her arms were visible. She set the laptop on the nightstand next to the bed.

"I have to admit, I didn't expect you to take quite so long undressing and putting everything away."

"It's a methodical process for me," Wil admitted. "So, why have you invaded my humble abode?"

"Oh, I thought I'd come over and torture you when I know something *can* happen," Selia said, almost nonchalantly. "Since I'm at my best and there won't be any distractions."

"Oh, are you, now?" Wil said. The corners of his lips twitched as he kept a smile from appearing.

Tossing the covers to the side, she revealed she wore nothing more than a hungry, sultry smile.

"One way to find out," she challenged him.

Smiling broadly, Wil 'the Sandman' Fredericks, entered the bedroom and closed the door behind him.

The End